I0733695

SIDANELA

A Story of Family

BY

DAVID LONG

Published by Christmas Lake Press 2023

www.christmaslakecreative.com

Copyright © 2023 by David Long

ISBN: 978-1-960865-00-7

All rights reserved. No part of this publication may be reproduced, stored in a retrieval system, or transmitted in any form, or by any means, electronic, mechanical, photocopying, recording, or otherwise without the prior permission in writing of the copyright holder, nor be otherwise circulated in any form or binding or cover other than in which it is published without a similar condition being imposed on the subsequent publisher.

Interior layout by Daiana Marchesi

Dedication

To *those* who push me to be a better human, even as *they* push my buttons.

Acknowledgments

This book would not have been possible without inspiration from those who have lived, loved, and died in ways that stir the soul to spill forth its contents.

Table of Contents

Chapter One

Three Sisters

Secrets are strange and wily creatures, binding together unstable groups while tearing apart the individuals who bear them. Red Willow carried a secret that weighed heavily on her shoulders, as if she were toting a black bear cub on her back. She desperately wanted to be free of the burden but simultaneously dreaded that freedom, knowing it would cause her entire world to crumble. Memories of "the horrible event"—the only words she could find to describe it—seeped into her mind, the way darkness slips in to overtake daylight, creating a mental fog that made it hard for her to focus. She wished she had only dreamed it. But she had to find a way to press through and ground herself. It was spring, and there was critical work to be done. Her family was relying on her to help keep them fed. So, her secret, and the agonizing choice of whether to share it or bear it, would have to wait.

Red Willow and her family were part of the Pee Dee tribe, a close-knit group of some five hundred villagers. The tribe was over two hundred years old. She lived on the outskirts of the Town Creek ceremonial center—in what is now known as North Carolina—with her mother, Gray Dove, and her brother, Running Wolf. The Vikings were the only Europeans who had ever set foot on Red Willow's continent, and the enormous wave of European immigration was still over three centuries away.

A large temple, where the priests conducted worship and the council made essential decisions of the tribe, dominated Town Creek. The temple sat high upon a mound, and the people could only gain access by climbing a tall set of stairs—as if they were walking straight to the heavens. The temple's base was a large and open court, where the tribe would gather for their seasonal and ritual ceremonies. A spiked barrier bordered the court on one side, a river touched it on another. Together, these two boundaries provided vital security against neighboring hostiles, chief among them the fierce Tuscarora.

The political situation of the village was surprisingly complex, given the relatively small population. There were four distinct clans within the larger tribe: the bear, the deer, the wolf, and the beaver. Red Willow and her family were members of the bear clan. Each group lived in separate enclaves surrounding the ceremonial center, and each elected its own leaders. The leaders of the four clans met together as a council regularly to discuss matters of importance to the tribe.

Though Red Willow was only seventeen, she was mature beyond her years and even beyond her tribe's wisest elders. Since the death of her father, her family had experienced many hardships, forcing her to take on adult responsibilities. Her father's absence also required her to do things not customary for women. She hunted as well as, or even better than, all the men. But despite being highly skilled at this typically masculine pursuit, she maintained a robust feminine nature. She had long, jet-black hair tied into a single braid that hung to one side and brown eyes that revealed a depth in her soul that seemed to stretch to infinity.

One of Red Willow's primary responsibilities was maintaining her family's garden, and she used the traditional Pee Dee method referred to as the "three sisters." The three sisters of the plot were corn, bean, and squash—planted together in a mutually beneficial way to create an abundant harvest. The sustenance the plants provided for each other reminded Red Willow of the strength her tiny family of three took from their closeness. The first seed to be planted was sister corn. Her job in the garden family was to provide a tall and solid support system for the beans to climb when they started to grow, much like her mother's stability aided the growth of Red Willow and her brother. Red Willow's first task was to shape several planting hills and plant four corn seeds in the center of each mound. She set out to get this done early one morning and worked tirelessly throughout the day, sending thoughts of the horrible event to the far reaches of her mind. She wished she could pull these thoughts out, like weeds, but by now they had deep roots. The best she could do was snap off the tops and hope they wouldn't return too soon.

After completing her planting, Red Willow returned to her family home for dinner. The one-room mud hut was nothing special, but it was everything they needed. The hut was a simple structure composed of a wooden pole frame with four sides braced together with smaller wooden branches. A hardened layer of thick clay and straw covered the frame, providing a solid wall structure. Lashed wooden poles, sheathed with a layer of thatched straw, supplied the roof and gave protection from the elements. An opening in the top's center ventilated the central fire pit they used for cooking and let light in during the day. A single uncovered doorway served as both entrance and exit.

Skye, the family wolf-dog, greeted Red Willow as she walked in. A stocky, athletic creature with a ginger-colored coat of short, smooth hair, he had tall, pointy ears and a long, narrow snout, constantly monitoring sounds and smells. But Skye's most striking feature was his oversized set of paws. These gigantic pads were like an anchor, connecting him solidly to the earth and making him the perfect animal for carrying large loads. When Red Willow breached the doorway, Skye leaped into her arms and pressed his paws onto her chest in excitement. She gave him a neck scratch, then gently placed him back on the ground.

"He missed you today," Gray Dove said to Red Willow, chuckling at the sight of the upright animal on her daughter's chest. "I think he's upset that you didn't take him with you."

"It's not like I was out hunting. I was working in the garden, and Skye would've slowed me down." Red Willow plopped her exhausted body down in her deerskin hammock.

"Don't tell me that," Gray Dove gestured towards Skye. "Tell him. He's the one who's upset."

Red Willow rolled her eyes before asking her mother what was for dinner. Gray Dove set out a bowl of stew and a corn cake on the braided bark mat that served as their table. Red Willow pulled herself slowly out of her hammock and shuffled over for dinner. It was a small meal and one that she had eaten hundreds of times before, but she was still grateful to the Great Spirit for her sustenance.

"Where is Running Wolf?" Red Willow asked, between sips of her stew.

"You just missed him." Gray Dove looked out of the doorway into the distance. "He came in to get something to eat then left as fast as he came."

Red Willow noticed that Running Wolf had been spending more time away from the family than usual, and she wondered if he was intentionally avoiding them to ease his guilt surrounding the horrible event. Even though Running Wolf was the source of her inner distress, Red Willow still felt sorry for him. It was early in the evening, and she was fatigued from her long day's labor, so she retired to her hammock, tucked into one corner of the hut, and lowered her reed curtain from the ceiling to give herself some privacy. She tossed and turned for a bit as she tried to make herself comfortable before falling quickly to sleep.

A few restless hours later she awakened with thoughts arriving and buzzing around in her head like so many irritating gnats. It was useless to swat them away, so she let them come. *How can I let him get away with what he did? Maybe what he did was the right thing to do, and I should just keep my mouth shut.*

The scales of justice are often unbalanced, and the heavy side of the scale felt as if it was dropping directly on Red Willow's soul. From her father, Hunting Bear, she had absorbed a strong sense of right and wrong. Hunting Bear spent a few years of his life as a member of the tribal council during the formative years of her childhood and earned a reputation as a no-nonsense arbiter of justice. In Hunting Bear's eyes, what was right was right and what was wrong was wrong, no matter who committed the crime or why. Of course, it's easy to have a black and white notion of justice when you don't have a close personal relationship with the offender. But Hunting Bear never had to deal with a situation like the one his daughter now faced. How can you keep a black and white sense of justice when your brother is the perpetrator? And when the offense is . . . Red Willow saw the horrible event happening over and over again. Her father's justice offered her no good answers—none she could live with—and no middle ground. For Red Willow, the situation was as gray as the sky on a cloudy autumn day.

Red Willow rocked herself back to sleep for a few more restless hours before the morning sun signaled a new dawn and a new set of responsibilities. The fire needed rekindling; her mother couldn't cook breakfast without it.

"Could you please rekindle the fire, my little ayoli?" Gray Dove asked.

"You know I am not little anymore." Red Willow rolled her eyes.

Glancing lovingly at her daughter, Gray Dove replied, "While it is true that you are no longer a little one in this great big world, you will always be my child."

Red Willow rekindled the fire and began to help her mother. She went to the shelf hollowed out in the wall, grabbed a clay pot full of hickory nuts, placed several handfuls in the small clay saucer used for cooking, and roasted them over the fire.

"Let me guess," Red Willow said as she chomped down on the hickory nuts, "my udo is gone again."

"Yes, he is. Why do you ask?" Gray Dove held her daughter's gaze.

"Don't you think he has been gone a lot lately?"

Gray Dove had either not noticed or, more likely, was dismissing her son's frequent and increasingly long absences. Red Willow, however, was keenly aware that her brother was doing everything he could to steer clear of the family, and though she wished she didn't, she knew exactly why.

� ✼ ✼

Running Wolf had lived his life in fear since the horrible event. He knew the consequences if anyone learned the truth. He was almost certain no one had been around to witness his crime, but he couldn't rule out some random tribe member lurking in the forest when it had happened. After all, what better place for spying than the densely packed forest that could be nearly as dark as the night sky, even on the sunniest of days? But Running Wolf had to dampen his fear to face the challenges of his everyday life. Besides, he reassured himself, if anyone had witnessed his crime, they would have come forward by now to confront him.

Running Wolf was two years younger than his sister but significantly more immature. He had grown up physically with a muscular build for his age, but he was emotionally stunted. His father's death had impacted him quite differently than Red Willow, and the lack of a male role model had left him in a perpetually childlike state unbefitting a young man of his age. He acted impulsively and made poor decisions, leaving his family to clean up his messes. Despite his flaws, his mother and his sister still loved him.

"It was not a blessed morning on the river this morning. I only managed to spear a single redfish." Running Wolf walked through the doorway with his head hung low.

"Any morning with any amount of fish is a blessed morning." Gray Dove took the fish from Running Wolf and headed toward her small food preparation area. "Come sit down and warm yourself by the fire, my brave atsutsa."

Running Wolf sat down with his family but found it difficult to relax. To suppress his guilt and fear since the horrible event, he was constantly trying to keep his mind and body occupied. The wild strawberries had begun to appear, providing him the opportunity to do some foraging. He also considered collecting firewood during his potential expedition. These thoughts provided a temporary distraction, but his feelings refused to stay under the surface, and he knew he needed to find a better way to deal with them.

Running Wolf had heard his friends speak of a ceremonial substance that could take him to the spiritual plane, where he might find an answer, but there were potentially dangerous side effects. Several of its takers had gone temporarily mad. The prospect of accessing the spiritual plane was enticing for Running Wolf, as he might be able to find the relief he was seeking, but was it worth the risk of losing his mind? He had been smoking his mother's tobacco pipe relentlessly to calm himself, but the effects were short-lived. He knew he needed something . . . permanent. After scarfing down a large handful of the roasted hickory nuts, he got out of his seat to leave.

"Must you go so soon, my brave atsutsa?" After speaking with Red Willow, Gray Dove was now conscious of Running Wolf's consistent absences.

"Yes, Etsi. As always, there is work to be done." He hurried towards the doorway.

"Red Willow, why don't you go with your udo and help him?" Gray Dove said. "I'm sure he could use an extra pair of hands."

Red Willow and Running Wolf looked at each other with annoyed faces, as neither one was too keen on spending the day together.

"I'd rather not." Red Willow curled up her nose in disgust.

"Well then, I guess you can stay here with me and weave baskets all day," Gray Dove replied as she arched her eyebrow and glanced at Red Willow.

Gray Dove knew that Red Willow loathed basket weaving more than anything in the world. It was Red Willow's worst skillset and a task full of pure struggle. Red Willow would rather walk across hot coals than weave baskets.

"Fine, I'll go with him," Red Willow replied, her teeth gritted.

Running Wolf and Red Willow set off foraging, leaving Gray Dove by herself. She sat down in her braided bark bed with her tobacco pipe and took an abnormally long inhale. Gray Dove had seen her share of turmoil and often wondered how to make sense of it. She was 36 years old, but her hair was already graying, and the bags under her eyes were puffy, giving her the look of someone at least ten years older. Despite her haggard face, she maintained her sense of dignity.

Gray Dove had not always been so full of stress and so tired looking. She had fond memories of her younger days when her husband, Hunting Bear, was still in her life. When she was seventeen, her parents had forced an arranged marriage between Gray Dove and Hunting Bear. The fact they did not know each other until the day of the wedding ceremony made for an amusingly awkward beginning to their relationship, but Hunting Bear had a kind and patient way about him that put Gray Dove at ease. They quickly fell in love, and she eventually bore him two children.

Those were the happiest days of Gray Dove's life, raising her little children alongside her loving spouse. She fondly remembered the family gathering around the fire to listen to Hunting Bear tell stories about his hunting adventures and brave feats he had witnessed in battle. Hunting Bear loved to tell stories almost as much as the children loved to listen. He was an enthusiastic and animated narrator, and the colorful tales enraptured his son and daughter. Gray Dove remembered even more fondly what took place after the children were asleep. All these years later, those memories of nighttime adult fun were enough to send shivers down Gray Dove's spine.

Hunting Bear loved both his children, but his bond with Red Willow was special. Ordinarily, in the Pee Dee tribe, girls were not taught the skills of hunting and fishing, but from a young age, Red Willow begged her father to instruct her. Hunting Bear agreed to train her, but only when her brother, too, was old enough to learn. Hunting Bear was keenly aware of the shame Running Wolf might have felt if his father instructed his sister before him. When Red Willow was eleven and Running Wolf was nine, they were both old enough to begin their lessons.

The best way for young Pee Dee braves to learn was through experience, so Hunting Bear took his children into the woods to hunt for small game in the first phase of their training. He tried to teach them the art of throwing a stick to bring down rabbits and squirrels. Red Willow was a fast learner, quickly mastering this discipline, while Running Wolf struggled and could not match his sister's proficiency. Red Willow's hunting skills impressed her father. One night during their training, when Running Wolf was fast asleep, Hunting Bear shook his daughter awake. She rolled over and rubbed her eyes to see her father's beaming face.

"I'm sorry to wake you, ayoli. I have something I want to give you while your udo is asleep." He reached behind his back and pulled out his prized throwing stick.

Red Willow placed her hand gently on her chest. "For me?"

"You've earned it," Hunting Bear smiled, handing the stick to his daughter. "Now get some sleep. We've got a long day, starting at sunlight."

Hunting Bear tousled Red Willow's hair. She took the stick and cradled it in her arms, a smile beaming from ear to ear. It would not be easy to get back to sleep, as the pride-derived adrenaline rushed through her body.

Tragically, that would be the last tender memory she and her father shared. The following year, when she was twelve and her brother was ten, Tuscarora raiders kidnaped some young Pee Dee men. The kidnappings sent shockwaves through the tribe and terrified young Running Wolf, who spent the next several moons unable to sleep for fear of being abducted. Sensing his son's anxiety, Hunting Bear promised Running Wolf he would right the wrong of the evil Tuscarora.

Hunting Bear and some of the other fathers organized a revenge party to kill the Tuscarora raiders and retrieve the kidnapped children. They were successful in their mission but at significant cost. The group returned with the missing children and everyone, including Hunting Bear's family, came to welcome the heroes back. But there was no hero's welcome for Hunting Bear, as Tuscarora warriors had killed him in the skirmish. As the men carried in Hunting Bear's lifeless body, the sight of it took Gray Dove to her knees. Running Wolf clung tightly to his mother as she went to the ground and sobbed. Young Red Willow took off like a lightning bolt into the surrounding woods, unable to cope with what she had just witnessed.

Hunting Bear's death devastated Gray Dove and the family. Red Willow looked inward for solace and found little, while Running Wolf lapsed into a state of aimlessness, and Gray Dove did her best to keep everyone's head above water. They desperately needed help, and that help came in the form of Eternal Blossom, Gray Dove's younger sister. Eternal Blossom prepared meals, took care of the children when Gray Dove could not handle them, and spent many nights at Gray Dove's hut. Gray Dove and the children appreciated her efforts, but her husband Howling Coyote did not. She and Howling Coyote were newly married, and he resented the fact that his wife was giving so much attention to her sister rather than to him. Howling Coyote already had a reputation within the tribe of being a smoldering fire, and his resentment fanned the flames of his anger.

It took Gray Dove many moon cycles to recover from her grief with the consistent help of her sister, entirely too much time in the mind of Howling Coyote. His resentment boiled into a bubbling cauldron of rage. One night, he approached Gray Dove to express his displeasure. He found her alone in her hut, cleaning her clay cooking pots.

Howling Coyote barged into the house with an intense and troubled countenance, interrupting Gray Dove. "Your agilvgi is neglecting her duties at home to be here with you all the time, and it is not right."

Gray Dove ignored him and continued tending to her chores. "That sounds like an issue between the two of you. Why bring it to me?"

Howling Coyote raised his hands in frustration and placed them on the back of his head. "She does not listen to me, but she does listen to you. So, I need *you* to tell her to spend more time at home with me."

Gray Dove took a step back from the visibly frustrated Howling Coyote. "My agilvgi is a grown woman. The only one she needs to listen to is the Great Spirit. Why do you bring these problems to me?"

Howling Coyote stepped towards the retreating Gray Dove. "You speak very disrespectfully for a woman with no uyehi; you should do what a man asks."

"I don't do what is expected. I do what is right." Gray Dove tensed her body in fear.

Howling Coyote grabbed Gray Dove by the back of her hair and looked her square in the face. Staring deeply into his eyes, she saw a wave of intense anger that frightened her to the core. He sensed her fear, and the power he realized he had over her excited him most awfully. He smacked her across the lip, causing a small drop of blood to appear. The exertion of his power sent a rush of adrenaline through Howling Coyote's body, and in that instant, the adrenaline created an unholy addiction.

"You must learn manners, agilvgi," Howling Coyote said with a menacing scowl. He pushed Gray Dove to the ground and turned to walk away.

The abuse from Howling Coyote towards Gray Dove continued off and on for the next few years. She prayed for it to stop, but the Great Spirit did not answer. She prevented herself from seeking help out of an irrational fear of what might happen to her or her children if she disclosed the abuse. It was a dark time for Gray Dove and her family.

These memories, both the good and the bad, combined to shape Gray Dove into the haggard and stressed woman she was that day as she sat in her bed, smoking her pipe. She struggled to find the meaning in all her joys and sorrows, hoping someday it might make sense.

After her smoke, Gray Dove began her morning tasks. Her chores had become more time-consuming lately, and she found herself more easily fatigued. It frustrated her not to be as energetic and strong as she thought she should be for a woman her age, and she wondered how bad it would get for her if her decline continued.

It was time for Gray Dove to make a new water jug to replace the old one, which was starting to show signs of cracking. She grabbed a lump of clay and rolled it out into several long thin ropes, then flattened another lump out like a pancake. Ever so delicately, she coiled the ropes around in a circular motion on top of the base, stacking them row by row on top of each other until she reached the desired height. Once she had piled all the clay coils, Gray Dove pulled out her pottery paddle and swung it against the sides of the jug to meld the stacked ropes together into one continuous surface.

Gray Dove was exhausted by the process, much more than usual, and perplexed by her intense fatigue but satisfied by her efforts. It was a skill she had learned from her grandmother and hoped to pass on to Red Willow one day soon. The physical exertion of the grabbing and the pounding provided an emotional release that she severely needed. She set the jug out to dry in the sun and returned to the house to rest before the children returned. As she sat down, she heard a voice from behind.

"Sister, may the children and I join you for lunch?" Eternal Blossom asked, with a soft voice that revealed a desperate need for help.

"Welcome agilvgi." Gray Dove walked over to greet her sister and the children. "You know that anything you need, I will give."

Eternal Blossom sighed and bowed in shame that her situation had reduced her to begging for help. "I hate to be a burden."

Gray Dove placed her hand on Eternal Blossom's shoulder. "Do not consider yourself a burden. I have been in the same situation as you are now. You were there for me, and now I am here for you."

Eternal Blossom was ten years younger than her sister, but she looked more like twenty years her junior. She had long, dark brown hair that fanned down gently to caress her buttocks. Her eyes were greenish-brown and nearly translucent, signifying a profound openness to the world. But her most distinctive feature was her melodious voice. So gentle and soothing was its sound that everyone who knew her said she could put even the angriest of bears to sleep.

The sisters' mother had died during childbirth, making Gray Dove the only mother Eternal Blossom ever knew. Gray Dove was there when Eternal Blossom took her first steps, there when Eternal Blossom learned how to speak, and there when Eternal Blossom matured into womanhood. Gray Dove was her sister's mentor in every sense of the word.

Gray Dove invited Eternal Blossom and her children into the hut to share a meal of hickory nuts and cornmeal. They all ate and were satisfied. Then she took her nieces and nephews outside to play while Eternal Blossom laid down to rest.

Chapter Two

Foragers

Red Willow and Running Wolf's foraging foray was a great success. Wild strawberries were plentiful as was kindling for the fire. Moreover, the two had managed to keep their distance from each other the entire time, speaking not a word between them.

As Red Willow was foraging for her portion of the produce, she heard a rustling in the underbrush twenty yards ahead. Reaching for her father's hickory rabbit stick she had dubbed "the truth," she poised herself in a crouched position, sensing a potential kill. Then she kissed the stick and asked for her father's guidance. About thirty seconds later, a family of four rabbits emerged from the bushes. Red Willow grabbed the staff and hurled it, knocking one of the rabbits down as the others scurried away.

Red Willow approached the fallen animal with mixed feelings, as was always the case after a successful kill. Arriving at the rabbit carcass, she said a brief prayer to the Great Spirit, both of thanks and regret. After finishing her prayer, she grabbed her knife and slit the rabbit's throat from ear to ear, completing her kill. Red Willow hated that she had to take another creature's life but loved being able to provide for her family. It was a stark reminder to her that the giving of life to one creature often meant the taking of life from another. She rejoined Running Wolf to show him her prize.

"Look at what I got, udo." She held up the carcass by its feet and dangled it in front of Running Wolf's face. "We will eat well tonight."

Running Wolf looked at the rabbit then back at Red Willow. He was proud of his sister, but he would never let her know it. She was better at hunting and never missed an opportunity to remind him. Complimenting her would only give her a more giant head than she already had. He could only give her a brief "that's good" before changing the subject to the great harvest of wild strawberries he had collected.

Red Willow peered down into Running Wolf's satchel half-filled with strawberries. She was unimpressed but did not want to hurt her little brother's feelings. "Those are . . . nice. They will make a good addition to this juicy rabbit that I got for us."

Red Willow and Running Wolf began their journey home with their supplies, walking through a densely packed pine forest. The trees gave off a sweet and refreshing smell, and inhaling their odor cleared the mind. The only drawback was dodging the sharp, prickly cones littering the forest floor. The Pee Dee wore moccasins that served their general purpose, but they were almost useless if you crunched directly onto one of the needle-sharp cones.

Whether it was the mental clarity brought on by the pine smell or the concentration it took to dodge all the pinecones, Red Willow and Running Wolf managed to make it halfway home without saying a word, the ever-growing silence giving Red Willow too much time to think. The images from the horrible event flickered in and out of her consciousness, interfering with her ability to recognize the flow of time. The episode had happened only a few moon cycles ago, but to her it felt like it was happening in the present time.

On that morning Red Willow had decided to follow Running Wolf and their uncle, Howling Coyote, down to the river. They were off together on a fishing excursion, highly unusual for the pair, which aroused Red Willow's suspicions. As her brother and uncle set off, Red Willow stealthily departed behind them, trailing far enough away that they would not notice her presence.

Howling Coyote and Running Wolf found a suitable spot alongside the river and stopped to begin preparing their fishing gear. Red Willow halted in the distance and set up her spy nest in a nearby stand of bushes. Settling in to observe the scene unfolding in front of her, she saw Running Wolf get out his spear and hurl it into the river unsuccessfully a few times. Howling Coyote mocked his young nephew for his failures, while mending one of their broken fish traps. Discouraged, Running Wolf tossed his spear onto the riverbank and got out one of the traps that worked. Howling Coyote took his time fixing the net, while Running Wolf patiently waited and watched the river.

After thirty minutes, Red Willow began to grow bored with her mission and was ready to head home. Just then, Howling Coyote and

Running Wolf began a heated conversation. Red Willow could not hear their words, only their muffled voices. She wanted to get closer but was afraid she would be seen.

As she slowly maneuvered herself into a better position to hear, she saw her uncle turn his back to her brother to set one of their fish traps. In a flash, Running Wolf grabbed a rock from the riverbank and lifted it above his head. Then, in what seemed like slow motion, Running Wolf slammed the stone down with full force onto the back of Howling Coyote's skull. Blood from the impact spattered back onto Running Wolf's menacing face, and Howling Coyote collapsed into the river. Even from a distance, Red Willow was sure her uncle was dead. Even so, she watched with horror as Running Wolf jumped onto their uncle's body and held his head under the water for two minutes to ensure he finished the job.

Red Willow's head began to spin, and her heart thumped as if it would pop out of her chest. She tried to convince herself that what she had just witnessed was not real but looking back at Howling Coyote's bloody corpse lying face down in the river convinced her she hadn't imagined it. She stared in shock as her brother washed his own bloody face with river water and repositioned Howling Coyote's body next to one of the sharp rocks poking out of the riverbed to make the murder look like an accident, not a crime.

Red Willow tried desperately to process what she had witnessed. How could her brother do this? Commit murder, and then lie to cover it up! This was not the brother she knew. If only she had not followed them down to the river that day! She could have grieved her uncle's accidental death and been none the wiser. Instead, the horrible experience was now seared into her spirit forever as if she were tattooed with the trauma.

The implications for not just her but her entire family were staggering. If anyone found out what happened, Running Wolf would be subject to retributive justice—in the form of execution. Everything their mother had sacrificed for their close-knit brood of three would be torn asunder in a flash. A sinking feeling developed in the pit of her stomach, a feeling that would prove impossible to shake.

✖ ✖ ✖

Snapping back into the present moment and finding herself in the piney woods with her brother, Red Willow suddenly grabbed Running Wolf by the arm and yanked him close. "I saw what you did to our agidutsi with my own two eyes. How could you do it, udo? You know what will happen if anyone finds out!"

Running Wolf was caught off guard by his sister's sudden outburst. It took him a moment to realize what she was saying, but it stopped him dead in his tracks when he did. A sudden wind swept in and rustled the needles in the trees overhead.

"You know that our agidutsi fell and drowned in the river," Running Wolf replied, stiffening his body into a defensive posture.

"I know that is your story, udo," Red Willow pointed her finger sharply at her brother, "but I also know the truth. I was a witness. And now I am faced with the most agonizing decision of my life. Do I inform the tribe of your murderous ways or let a murder go unpunished because I want to protect you?" Red Willow pushed her finger deeply into Running Wolf's chest. "Do you understand the situation *you* put me in?"

Running Wolf knew that his secret was out. And of all the people that could have witnessed the murder, it had to be his sister! Her words bounced around in his brain like a jumping squirrel high on black tea. "The situation *I* put *her* in? Aargh!" It was crystal clear what she was referring to, the looming specter of what would happen at the Green Corn Ceremony if anyone found out. The only question was would she be willing to keep their secret and protect him or reveal it—and in doing so sentence him to death? The choice was clear cut in his mind, but he knew his sister's commitment to justice might keep her on the fence. He was her brother, but he was also a murderer, and it would be hard to blame her if she chose justice. The guilt weighed heavily on his heart, but his anger subsumed everything else. He balled up his fists tightly. "I had had enough of him! I could not stand his presence anymore. And . . . and he deserved to die!"

Saying those words aloud transported Running Wolf's spirit back to the painful memories of his adolescence from a few Green Corn cycles ago, including a particularly vivid memory of the first time he saw Howling Coyote hit his mother.

✖✖✖

The pre-teen Running Wolf awoke one night to the sound of a heated argument between Gray Dove and Howling Coyote. They had fought before, but something sounded different. He rolled over in his hammock just in time to see Howling Coyote raise his fist and smack Gray Dove across the cheek. His body clenched in fear, Running Wolf wanted to help his mother, but he found himself unable to move a muscle. Gasping for breath and suppressing his tears, he struggled to reposition himself, arms draped over his face in an attempt to pretend he hadn't seen anything. When he woke the following day, he hoped it had all been a dream, but then he saw his mother's swollen lip and realized the violence was real and he had failed to protect her. Ashamed, he vowed the next time he saw Howling Coyote hit his mother, he would stop it once and for all.

A few nights later, Running Wolf's chance to be the hero arrived. Asleep in his hammock, he was once again aroused by raised voices. Instead of waiting for something to happen, Running Wolf took the initiative and confronted Howling Coyote. He ran over and positioned his gangly pubescent body between the quarreling adults. Staring up slowly at the menacing presence of his uncle, he timidly yelled for Howling Coyote to leave. Howling Coyote mocked his young nephew's futile attempt to intervene and threw him to the ground. Gray Dove shoved Howling Coyote out of the way and rushed to her son's side, shouting, "Leave! Leave at once!"

Howling Coyote stomped across the room and leaned down close to where Gray Dove and Running Wolf lay. "I will go," he pointed menacingly at the boy, "but the next time this one stands in my way will be the last time he does anything on this earth."

Howling Coyote lumbered out of the hut, grumbling angrily the entire way. Gray Dove and Running Wolf were left slumped together on the floor, clinging tightly to each other for support. Tears welled up in the exhausted mother's eyes as she rocked her baby boy back and forth. Running Wolf's breath raced through his upper chest, terrified as he was by Howling Coyote's death threat. But once he gained control of his breathing a strange feeling developed in the young boy. It was a feeling that he had not experienced before and could be best described as pride, if he knew the word to describe it. He'd stood up to a bully and protected his mother, and he knew his father would have approved had he been witness to it. The feeling soothed his nerves and helped him get back to sleep, despite the previous hour's madness.

Running Wolf awoke early the next morning to begin his next fishing foray. Surprisingly, he found his mother already awake and stoking the fire. This was not part of their normal routine, and her presence left the young boy perplexed. "Did you sleep well?" she asked with her back turned to the boy.

"As good as I could, I guess," Running Wolf replied as he cleared his throat.

Gray Dove slumped her shoulders and sighed. "I didn't sleep at all."

Running Wolf swallowed the deep lump that developed in his throat when he realized how much pain his mother was still in. He gingerly walked over to her and hesitantly placed his hand on her shoulder. He had no idea how to provide the comfort she needed, but he was doing his best under the circumstances.

Gray Dove grabbed Running Wolf's hand. "I need you to tell you something," she said as she turned to look up at the boy. Running Wolf's anxiety began to dissipate as he anticipated that his mother was about to thank him for coming to her rescue last night. "I want you to promise me that no matter what you hear or see, do not try to step in to help when Howling Coyote is here."

Running Wolf's heart sank. "But he is hurting you!"

"I know it is hard for you to understand, usdi," Gray Dove sighed deeply. "Just promise me."

Running Wolf's eyes darted around the room briefly before he gave a half-hearted nod. Gray Dove's sentiment left him feeling confused and powerless. Wasn't he supposed to protect her? That feeling of powerlessness and shame reared its ugly head every subsequent time he heard Howling Coyote and his mother arguing, and every time he closed his eyes and covered his ears to avoid seeing and hearing what came next.

As the months turned into years, Running Wolf decided he had had enough of being powerless. His body was growing in leaps and bounds, leading to increased confidence in his physical prowess. Plans for revenge swirled in his volatile adolescent brain, all while he slowly regained his uncle's trust in order to betray him. Those plans led him to that fateful day at the river, where his revenge manifested itself in the most heinous way possible.

✖✖✖

"He deserved what he got," Running Wolf practically spit, pointing his finger at Red Willow. "And," he continued, "no one will ever find out, will they?" The look he gave Red Willow was at once fearful and threatening.

"You know, brother, that our father believed a crime was a crime, no matter who perpetrated it or why. What do you think he would say if he were here?" Red Willow placed her hands on her hips in an accusatory posture. "Because I think he would call you a criminal, as difficult as that might be for you to understand."

"You know, sister, I think he would understand that I was just trying to protect my family," Running Wolf replied through gritted teeth. "And he would have a much easier time forgiving me than you seem to be able to."

Red Willow began pacing back and forth. "One thing I must know, udo, did the other villagers completely believe your story about our agidutsi falling into the river accidentally?"

"Yes," Running Wolf nodded. "To be honest, when I told everyone back in the village that Howling Coyote had died, there was not a lot of questioning. You know his reputation within the tribe as a scoundrel.

I think many people were indifferent towards his death, no matter the circumstances. You are the only one who knows the real truth, and," he fixed his gaze on her, "you must keep it that way."

"But what makes you think you have the right to take a life like that and not have to face any consequences?" Red Willow questioned.

"We take lives all the time. Just think about the dead rabbit you have in your pouch. Didn't you take its life?" Running Wolf shot back as he pointed to the rabbit carcass.

"I took this animal's life knowing that it would sustain our family," Red Willow shook her head. "You should know the difference."

"Ah, but I did the same with our agidutsi," Running Wolf replied smugly, knowing he'd made a sound point. "I took his life knowing that it would sustain *our* family. I could not let him continue to abuse our etsi and get away with it."

Deep in her heart Red Willow understood why Running Wolf had murdered their uncle. She empathized with him so much that she often wished that she would've been the one to take Howling Coyote out, or even that they had done it together, which in a way, they had. But that empathy clashed with the strong notion of absolute right and wrong that defined her conscience. Red Willow could not comprehend how she would be able to both protect her brother and satisfy the tribal demand for justice. For her, it felt like being inside a pitch-dark cave with no food and a hungry bear outside waiting to attack. She could either starve to death or get eaten by the hungry bear. There were no good options.

"I do not know what to do, udo." Red Willow hunched her shoulders, exhausted from the intense conversation and the insoluble predicament. "I am thoroughly confused. My head feels like it is constantly underwater. I want to keep your secret and protect you, but I know that the laws of our tribe require that justice be done."

"What is confusing to you?" Running Wolf asked in a higher-pitched voice. "Just don't tell anyone."

"You know the law of the tribe, and you know what should be done," Red Willow shook her finger at him.

"The law did not protect our etsi," Running Wolf scoffed. "So what good is the law? And why should we follow it?"

"The law is there for a reason." Red Willow was now speaking with calm and clarity. "It maintains the harmony within the tribe and ties us all together in the Great Spirit. It is not something you just ignore when it suits you, even if you feel it is flawed. I have a decision to make before the Green Corn Ceremony, udo, and I do not know what that decision will be." Running Wolf gave his sister an angry stare, but there was also fear in his eyes. Then he turned and walked away.

The Green Corn Ceremony happened every year in midsummer when all local villagers gathered at the Town Creek ceremonial site to celebrate the harvest of the first green corn of the season. It marked the beginning of a new year and reminded the tribe members that all things could be reborn. At the ceremony, all criminal offenses committed by tribe members were to be confessed and then forgiven, with the notable exceptions of rape and murder.

The Pee Dee tribe observed the concept of Blood Law, where a murder had to be avenged by the murderer dying at the hands of the deceased's closest relative. If Red Willow were to speak out at the ceremony, Running Wolf would have to die at the hands of Eternal Blossom. This was the heart of Red Willow's agony. She could either be tormented by carrying the secret of her uncle's death or tormented by her brother's death at the hands of her aunt. It would just be a matter of which torture she could more easily endure.

Red Willow and Running Wolf trudged home in silence, oblivious to their surroundings. The birds were chirping throughout the forest, and the dogwood trees were beginning to bloom. It would have been a lovely spring morning had it not been for their heavy emotional burdens. Red Willow grieved for her brother, knowing he had experienced so much turmoil in his young life. It was hard for her to blame him for what he had done, but she knew that not turning him in for his crime would burden her with guilt for the remainder of her life. As for Running Wolf, he was back to feeling powerless again. The only difference was his sister was the one with the power this time. He remained hopeful that she wouldn't turn him in, but he knew in his heart she had to do what was right for her.

As Running Wolf and Red Willow approached home, they could see that their aunt and cousins were waiting. Running Wolf tilted his head back in frustration. These were the last people he wanted to see, given what had transpired in the woods. He stopped and stared while Red Willow pressed on.

She turned and looked back at Running Wolf standing in the distance. "You can't avoid everyone all the time," she shouted.

Running Wolf took a deep breath before hesitantly shuffling forward. Red Willow reached the hut first and exchanged an awkward hug with Eternal Blossom. Running Wolf ambled in slowly a few minutes later, and his little cousin came up and tightly grabbed his leg.

"Looks like your little cousin is excited to see you, atsutsa." Gray Dove beamed at the tender interaction.

"I think he has gotten more attached to men since his doda's death," Eternal Blossom said, a pained look on her face. "He looks up to you, Running Wolf. I'm glad he has you in his life."

Running Wolf's stomach flipped. The sight of this little boy, whose father he had murdered, hugging his leg made him want to vomit. The acute sense of guilt was almost too much. Running Wolf knew the pain of losing a father, and now he realized that he was the cause of that pain in another boy's life. The air felt thick, and he could barely breathe.

"Uh-huh," Running Wolf muttered. "I need to skin the rabbit we killed today, so I'll be outside." Running Wolf snatched up the rabbit carcass and excused himself.

"Why don't you take the ayolis down to the river to play and splash around for a little bit," Gray Dove said to Red Willow as she gestured the children forward. "Your agitlogi and I need some alone time."

Red Willow sighed deeply and rolled her eyes. She had been out foraging all morning and had just had the most difficult conversation of her life with her brother. But duty called, in the form of a mother with expectations. She begrudgingly rounded up the children and headed out.

"So, tell me how things have been, agilvgi?" Gray Dove gently stroked her sister's arm. "And be honest. It's just you and me here talking now. Say anything you want to say."

"I know what Howling Coyote did to you," Eternal Blossom's voice quivered. "I know that snake hurt you, and I never did anything. I'm sorry. I should have done more."

Gray Dove let out a deep sigh. Her sister's admission of Howling Coyote's wrongdoing moved her close to tears. She understood her sister's agonizing choice between the risk of acting and the regret of not acting and delicately reassured Eternal Blossom that she did not need to feel guilty.

"What exactly do you think you could have done, agilvgi?" Gray Dove looked deeply into her sister's eyes. "Could you have sent him away? You know the council would not have allowed it. Could you have put a knife through his chest? You would have faced your death then, according to the laws of the tribe. What he did was on him and him alone, not you. And he will have to answer."

"But you did not deserve what he did to you." Tears welled up in Eternal Blossom's eyes.

"We rarely get what we deserve in this life, agilvgi." Gray Dove's shoulders slumped. "The only weapons we have to combat that hard truth are perseverance and hope—hope that someone will right the wrongs and justice will eventually prevail."

"I just wish things had been different," Eternal Blossom said as she wiped away her tears.

"So do I, agilvgi, but we must find a way to work with what life gives us." Gray Dove placed her hand on Eternal Blossom's knee.

Eternal Blossom felt a lightness in her body that she had not felt in a long while. The two women set about preparing for dinner by chopping some freshly picked green onions and sassafras leaves for their rabbit stew. Running Wolf entered the house with the newly skinned rabbit and laid it on the table. The cooks grabbed the rabbit carcass and began cutting it into chunks for the stew. Running Wolf made his way quickly towards the door.

"Why are you off in such a rush, atsutsa?" Gray Dove asked loudly, trying to stop him before he was entirely out of earshot.

"My friends and I are going to practice our chunkey," he replied as he poked his head back through the doorway.

"Fine, but do not be late for dinner."

"Yes, Etsi." Running Wolf bolted out of the door.

"My son has not been himself lately," Gray Dove said to Eternal Blossom in a mother's intuitive voice. "Something is not right."

"Being with his agidutsi when he died must have shaken him up," Eternal Blossom replied, blissfully unaware of the truth. "No young atsutsa should have to witness such a terrible event."

"You might be right, agilvgi," Gray Dove squinted, "but it feels like something even deeper than that."

Chapter Three

Wysoccan

Running Wolf hurried off but *not* to practice his chunkey. Instead, he took a detour to the hut of the tribe's medicine man in search of something to give him some relief from his overwhelming guilt and anxiety.

The medicine man was an older gentleman with a long flowing mane of silver hair and leathery, sunbaked skin. He had long white stripes painted in rows down his chest and horizontally below his eyes. He wore a black-feathered headdress that came down to just above his eye line, casting a shadow on his face and giving him an air of mystery. The medicine man spent a large portion of his time out in the woods, communing with his mother nature and harvesting the plants needed to create his medical concoctions. All the villagers said he could talk to the plants, and they would answer him, providing him with the valuable information about their medicinal properties that he needed for his work.

Running Wolf gingerly shuffled through the door to the medicine man's hut, bowing his head. The medicine man was busy grinding up some herbs and did not even acknowledge his presence.

"Holy One?" Running Wolf called out timidly.

The medicine man continued grinding and still did not look up. Running Wolf stood silently, rubbing his forearms. The awkward silence was alarmingly uncomfortable, but he refused to leave, determined to see the medicine man and unsure of why he was being ignored.

Finally the medicine man spoke without turning his head. "You should not be here." He kept grinding.

"I need your help," Running Wolf implored, moving closer.

Slowly, the medicine man lifted his head and gazed at Running Wolf. "What makes you think I can help you?"

Running Wolf rubbed the back of his neck. "I heard you have some medicines that will take a person to the spirit realm."

"Those medicines are not toys for young men to play with," the medicine man scowled. "They are only for those whose true purpose is spiritual enlightenment."

"That's . . . that's what I want."

The medicine man squinted. "And just what makes you want spiritual enlightenment, ayoli?"

Running Wolf stiffened. "My father died when I was very young, and, as you know, my agidutsi died recently." Running Wolf wrung his hands. "I am struggling to understand these tragedies. I want the wisdom to understand and the peace to overcome."

The medicine man took a long look at Running Wolf, trying to discern if his motives were pure. He could tell the boy had a good heart but was greatly confused, and he took pity on him. Reaching high onto a shelf behind him, the medicine man pulled down a small pot with some dried leaves and handed a batch to Running Wolf.

"This is wysoccan." The medicine man stared intensely at Running Wolf. "It is potent medicine and is not to be taken lightly. When you are ready, take just a handful of these leaves and brew them up in a pot of boiling water. Drink the potion, and it will take you to the spiritual plane. There you will mingle with the spirits and learn from them what will become of your life." He paused, focusing his eyes directly on the eyes of Running Wolf. "Now, there are two things you must do when you take this drink. Make sure you are not alone when you drink it and give yourself a few moons to recover after your journey. This medicine will open your spirit but will greatly burden your body."

"Wa do, Holy One." Running Wolf bowed his head reverently as a gesture of thanks. The medicine man nodded his head and continued his grinding. Running Wolf left the hut with a bounce in his step, now eager to get to his chunkey practice.

Chunkey was the tribe's official sport, played by rolling a large smooth stone disk from a starting line where two competitors stood. The competitors would fire their spears in the direction of the rolling disk, hoping to land them near where the disk stopped. A judge awarded a point to the competitor whose spear landed closest to the stopped disk, and the game continued until one player reached twelve points. A big chunkey competition among all the young braves was to be held immediately before the beginning of the Green Corn Ceremony, and

Running Wolf had longed to be a champion ever since he was a little boy, watching the games with his father. Now he was at last reaching the point of his life where he could be competitive.

Running Wolf practiced his chunkey with his friends for most of the afternoon. The mental focus and the physical exertion that the game required provided him with the outlet he needed to deal with his powerful emotions. The chunkey field was the one place where he could clear his mind and let it all go.

After his afternoon practice, Running Wolf returned to the family hut for dinner. The family shared yet another meager meal and casual conversation. Running Wolf was unusually talkative during dinner, a fact that did not escape the notice of Gray Dove and Red Willow. When they had finished the meal and everyone was cleaning up, Running Wolf asked his sister, "Would you like to take a walk?"

Red Willow craned her neck and turned her ear towards her brother. "What did you say?"

"You heard me," he retorted.

Red Willow turned towards Gray Dove with a perplexed look. Gray Dove shrugged to indicate she was just as confused as her daughter. Red Willow stood up and pointed an open palm at the doorway, beckoning her brother to lead. Running Wolf strolled outside and Red Willow followed, turning back to look at their mother as she crossed the threshold.

"So, why am I out here with you?" Red Willow asked as they began their walk.

"I have something I want to show you," he replied, looking around to see if anyone was watching.

He opened a small satchel and showed Red Willow the leaves he had obtained from the medicine man. She was not impressed; she had seen plenty of dried leaves in her time.

"You brought me out here to show me leaves?" Red Willow asked Running Wolf in a mocking tone while poking him in the chest.

"It's not just leaves," he replied in a slow rhythmic tone for emphasis. "It is called wysoccan. It is supposed to provide me access to the spiritual realm."

"And why do you need to go to the spiritual realm?" Red Willow questioned. "Are you trying to escape the harsh truth in this realm with us?"

"No, I'm not trying to escape the truth." Running Wolf straightened his posture. "I am trying to find the truth. I feel that the spiritual realm might get me to the truth in a way that will give me some relief."

"And what about me, udo?" Red Willow vigorously pointed her finger at her chest. "Do you not think I could use some relief also?"

Running Wolf smiled. "I have enough for both of us." He pulled out the leaves, showing her how much he had.

"Why are you telling me all of this?" Red Willow furrowed her brow.

"The medicine man said I need someone with me when I take this medicine because it could be dangerous," he replied. "I want you to come with me on a 'hunting trip' to be my companion."

Red Willow looked down at the leaves again before staring into the distance. She was curious about this spiritual plane. Would she be able to reconnect with her long-dead father there? If so, the risk could be worth the reward. That thought alone was enough for her to agree to go with her brother. "I will go."

Running Wolf reached to hug Red Willow, but she rebuffed his offer. "Save that for another time, udo. I'm not in the mood."

The pair returned to the hut and began to make plans for their drug-induced spiritual quest. They knew they could not tell their mother, so they agreed to use the guise of a hunting trip. It took them a few days before presenting their plan to Gray Dove. One morning, the family was gathered around their breakfast area when Red Willow decided it was time.

"Etsi, Running Wolf and I would like your permission to go on a hunting trip to the hills," Red Willow asked as she fidgeted with her hands. "We hear there is much game there, and you know that we could use some more meat."

Gray Dove stopped eating and crossed her arms in front of her chest. The hills were a dangerous area, the home of ferocious coyote packs and often subjected to raids from enemy tribes, and she had no intention of letting them go. She looked intently at the children with pursed lips. "You can't be serious!"

"We are serious." Red Willow was stone-faced.

"What makes you think I would give you permission?" Gray Dove questioned.

"We need this," Red Willow implored. "Not only can we get some good meat, but it will be a good chance for Running Wolf and me to spend some time together. You're always saying how you wished that we would get along better. This trip can help us do that."

Gray Dove uncrossed her arms and leaned back in her seat. All she wanted at this point in her life was for her children to form a strong bond. Maybe Red Willow was right; this trip might be a good chance for them to grow closer. Gray Dove looked lovingly at her children. "You may go. But you must protect each other at all costs. I could not bear losing you."

"Wa do, Etsi." Red Willow grabbed her mother's hand to show appreciation for her relenting. "I promise you that we will stay safe, and we will come back with the best meat for the family."

The siblings left the breakfast area and began to pack their things for the hunt. It would be about a day's journey to the hills on foot, so they had to pack light. They brought two wooden sticks for making fire, a smooth stone for boiling water, deerskin pouches to hold their water, deer pemmican for food, bows and arrows for hunting, and an A-frame travois that Skye would pull to haul any game they killed. Most importantly of all, for their purposes, they had the wysoccan.

Red Willow and Running Wolf left together that morning after breakfast. They hiked all day before stopping to set up camp around dusk. Their first task at the base was to get a fire started. Red Willow directed Running Wolf to go into the woods and get some kindling and leaves for the fire. Running Wolf was feeling rambunctious that evening, so he decided to push back on his sister's demands.

"Why do *I* have to be the one to gather kindling for the fire?" he grunted.

"Because I will stay here and get things situated at camp," Red Willow replied as she unpacked their supplies. "And we will need some things to get a fire going."

"Why don't you go get the kindling while I stay here and get things situated?" Running Wolf crossed his arms in front of his chest.

"You can't be serious!" Red Willow rubbed her forehead. "You think I trust you to set up camp properly?"

Running Wolf lifted his leg and planted his foot firmly on the ground. "You think you are so much better than me at everything, but that's because I never get a chance to prove myself."

Her brother's misplaced brashness amused Red Willow. She thought this would be a fun opportunity to put him in his place. "I'll go get the kindling if you can wrestle me down and pin me to the ground," she said in a gruff voice. "I pin you down, you get it."

"Fine."

The two squared off. Running Wolf lunged at his sister, and they locked arms. They struggled for a bit, with Running Wolf acting as if he was giving it his all and Red Willow thinking she was toying with her little brother. Suddenly, Running Wolf threw Red Willow to the ground. Her attitude quickly changed from amusement to anger. Running Wolf pounced, trying to pin his sister to the ground, but she skillfully rolled away. They got up, dusted themselves off, and squared off again. This time, when Running Wolf lunged at his sister, they locked arms briefly before she drove him back with little resistance. Tripping over his backpedaling feet, Running Wolf fell to the ground with Red Willow landing on top of him. He squirmed for a moment before she finally made him succumb.

"Go get the kindling," Red Willow said to her brother as he lay helpless on the ground.

"You win this time, agilvgi," Running Wolf's voice was strained as he was still in Red Willow's tight grip, "but I will have my revenge soon."

Red Willow loosened her grip, and Running Wolf pulled himself up off the ground and dusted himself off. His pride was hurt, but that was all. He slunk away from the camp, defeated, and went to get the kindling. While he was away, Red Willow got out the firestarting sticks and fed

Skye a small handful of pemmican. Skye lapped up the pemmican, which consisted of dried deer meat and dried blueberries held together by duck fat. Pemmican was the primary nutrition source used by the Pee Dee on their extended trips, as it maintained its palatability regardless of the weather.

Running Wolf came back with the pine straw, and the siblings began the process of making their fire. Red Willow placed the pine needles in a bunch at one end of the long, hollowed-out firestarter stick. Running Wolf grabbed the other firestarter stick, which had a pointed end, and began to rub the point into the hollowed-out shaft towards the bunched needles. He rubbed more and more vigorously until sparks began to appear. Eventually, the sparks ignited the tiny nest of needles, and the duo had their fire. Nightfall soon descended, and the brilliant symphony of the stars was played into existence by the Great Spirit. Running Wolf and Red Willow lay down by the fire and gazed up at the glorious night sky. They both soon fell soundly asleep, cradled by the shimmering moonlight.

Red Willow awoke before dawn to find her brother still asleep. Rather than just sit and wallow in her thoughts, she decided to get her day started to take her mind off things. Grabbing her bow and arrow, she and Skye headed out into the woods. After some time, Red Willow found a fallen tree that was a perfect spot to watch and observe her prey. She sat down with her back lodged against the tree and broke off a piece of pemmican for both herself and Skye, waiting and watching. After about thirty minutes, she heard a rustling among the leaves. Skye's ears stood straight up, animated by the animal's sound in the distance. His snout was moving up and down rapidly, trying to ascertain the animal's scent. He arched his lips to show his ferocious canines and let out a low growl. Red Willow rubbed Skye on the back of the neck to calm him, then slowly raised her head above the edge of the log and looked out into the distance. Coming down from his roost was a beautiful tom turkey with striking bronze, copper, and green plumage. Red Willow gazed at the turkey with awe and wonder. She thought it would be a shame to kill this bird, but she knew why she was there and what she had to do. She pointed her bow and arrow across the top of the fallen tree, let fly, and her aim was true. The arrow pierced the bird through the stomach, and down he went. She sent Skye out to retrieve the bird, and the two headed back to their camp.

Red Willow arrived back at camp to find Running Wolf still sleeping. She stoked the fire and added some kindling to keep it burning. Annoyed at her brother's persistent ability to sleep, she decided to play a trick on him. She grabbed a small piece of the pemmican, rubbed it between her fingers, and then smeared a tiny amount onto Running Wolf's nose without waking him. The pemmican smell piqued Skye's curiosity, and Red Willow called him over to where her brother lay. Skye ran over, stuck out his sloppy saliva-laden tongue, and began licking Running Wolf's nose. Running Wolf awakened with fury and thrashed around, delighting his sister as she giggled furiously.

"What is your problem, agilvgi?" Running Wolf shouted in anger when he saw her giggling.

"The only problem I have is that you are such a lazy udo." She grabbed some of the pine straw and sprinkled it over his head. "I have been awake for a long time and have already killed a turkey while you slept the time away."

Running Wolf rubbed his eyes and then glanced around to see the turkey. He was impressed by the bird and congratulated his sister on being a good hunter.

"I don't need your flattery, udo, but I do enjoy it," Red Willow said as she stoked the fire. "Why don't you get up and have breakfast with me?"

The two sat together and shared some pemmican for breakfast as they sat by the fire. Skye walked around their campsite, smelling everything in sight and marking his territory. The siblings sat in silence, unsure of what to say to the other. Red Willow still felt pity for her brother and was starting to lean towards not turning him in. Running Wolf was unsure about his sister's decision, and he was trying hard to be on his best behavior. Red Willow finally broke the awkward quiet.

"Are you ready for your spirit medicine, udo?" Red Willow asked as she looked over at her brother.

"I guess so." Running Wolf stared down at the ground.

Red Willow pushed her brother on the shoulder to goad him into action. "You wanted to do this, udo. Now is the time."

"I thought you wanted to take it with me?"

"I'm not a fool," Red Willow shook her head. "I'll take it after seeing what it does to you. Besides, the medicine man said I needed to watch you to make sure you were safe."

"Fine," Running Wolf practically spat, "I'll do it first."

Red Willow and Running Wolf got out their large, smooth stone and placed it into the fire to heat up. After an hour, they pulled the stone out of the fire with their deer antler tongs and put it in their deerskin water pouch to heat the water. The dropping of the hot rock into the water let off a slight hiss. They added the wysoccan to the hot water and allowed it to steep for several minutes. Running Wolf said a prayer to the Great Spirit, asking for a blessing on his spiritual quest, and then took a large sip of the tea.

Immediately after ingesting the tea Running Wolf began to feel strange. His mouth dried up quickly like a sandy desert, and his vision became so blurry he could not distinguish one object from another. It was as if everything was bleeding into one unified reality. He began to feel nauseous and immediately crouched down next to the fire and vomited. The vomiting made him feel slightly better, although he began to sweat profusely. The wysoccan pulled his spirit away from his body, and he found himself looking down at his mortal shell. He drifted through the air, landing in disembodied form a mile away from the campsite in a dense forest. He looked up to see a squirrel hunched in the cleft of a tree branch glaring down at him.

"Come with me, Running Wolf." The squirrel jumped down from the tree and beckoned Running Wolf to follow him. "I will show you where to find what you are looking for."

A talking squirrel? All Running Wolf could do was laugh at the thought. The hallucinatory squirrel, however, was not laughing. He pulled back his tiny, clawed hand and smacked Running Wolf across his giggling disembodied face.

"Hey!" Running Wolf said as he rubbed his ghostly cheek. "What was that for?"

"This isn't playtime," the squirrel said. "We've got places to go and things to see. Less laughing, more moving!"

The squirrel pointed towards the east, and they set off together through the woods, conversing the entire time. Running Wolf was in disbelief at what was transpiring at first, but the further they got into the woods, the more comfortable he became with the talking squirrel. They entered a meadow at the edge of the woods and stopped short.

"Well, oginalii, this is as far as I can take you. The eagle will take you on the next phase of your journey." The squirrel bowed to Running Wolf and pointed to the sky.

A giant bald eagle swooped in and landed next to Running Wolf. He jumped onto the back of the eagle, and the eagle soared across an open meadow full of brightly colored fluorescent flowers aglow with light. The eagle stopped and landed at the edge of the field, where the sky abruptly turned from sunny and bright to the blackest of black nights. He dismounted the bird and stared into the dark void.

Running Wolf stood on the edge of the pitch-black nothingness, afraid of moving into the unknown abyss. Eventually, he noticed a pinpoint of light in the distance, which grew wider and wider as it moved towards him. It was a cluster of fireflies, and they soon buzzed up next to him with their lights flickering, motioning him to follow them into the dark emptiness. He reluctantly followed, staying with them until he came upon a flickering campfire and the silhouette of a man sitting on a log with his back turned. He strolled around the man to look at his face and was stunned to see his father, Hunting Bear.

"Hello, atsutsa," Hunting Bear said to the boy. "It is good to see you. Take a seat and let us talk."

Running Wolf weakly shuffled over to the log across from Hunting Bear, keeping his eyes locked on his father the entire time in disbelief. Then he took a seat. Tears welled up in Running Wolf's eyes, and he put his head down, unable to look his father in the eye. Hunting Bear took his hand and raised his son's chin.

"I know what you did, atsutsa, but I am not ashamed of you," Hunting Bear began. "What you did was wrong, but it was not unforgivable. When I was with you in life, I prized the value of knowing right and wrong with absolute certainty. But since I have been away from you, I have learned that the world is not so black and white. It is not always easy to do the right thing or even discern what is right and wrong. I now value forgiveness as much as, or even more than, justice."

Running Wolf wiped the tears from his eyes. He experienced a feeling of immense lightness in his body, something that he had not felt since the horrible event. His father's forgiveness lifted the weight of a thousand boulders off his shoulders. "So, I am free from my burden? I can let go of my guilt and fear of retribution?"

Hunting Bear leaned back on his log. "You are free to let go of your guilt and fear, uwetsi. But your actions have created a debt that must be paid, although it will be paid in a way that you do not expect. Just know that all will be well for you in the end. Go in peace."

A rush of wind suddenly snuffed out the campfire and Running Wolf's spirit was rushed quickly back into his body. He awakened in a haze beside the fire with Red Willow and Skye looking at him curiously. Red Willow waved her hands in front of her brother's face. "You have been passed out for hours, udo. We were starting to wonder if you were ever going to wake up."

Running Wolf was still dizzy and nauseous. He gingerly brought himself to his knees and tried to reorient himself to the earthly realm. Red Willow saw that he was still struggling, so she grabbed his water pouch and offered him a drink. Running Wolf took multiple large gulps from the bag and let out a huge "ahhhh" of thirst-quenched relief.

"So, what was it like?" Red Willow asked. "What did you see?"

"Too much to talk about right now." Running Wolf brought himself to his feet and stretched out his arms. His body was back on earth, but his spirit was still somewhere else. He walked around the campsite aimlessly for a few minutes before he decided it would be best if he lay back down for a while.

It was nightfall, and a cool spring breeze was wafting through the air. Running Wolf lay down in the grass and stared up at stars in the sky. He was either very much at peace or exhausted, and Red Willow could not tell which. Red Willow warmed herself by the fire and left her brother alone with his thoughts. Running Wolf was still dazed, but he was comforted by seeing his father's vision. He settled into hazy contentment, sure in the knowledge things would turn out alright for him in the end.

Red Willow awoke early again the following day, surprised to find that Running Wolf was up before her. He had stoked the fire back to good health and had already been down to the creek to fill their water pouches. Was this the lazy brother with whom she had grown up? She was still unsure what had happened to Running Wolf on his spiritual journey, but she was pleased to see the changes.

"So, can you talk about yesterday now, or are you still too weak?" Red Willow pushed Running Wolf on the shoulder a few times, teasing him.

Running Wolf moved his sister's hand away from his shoulder. "I will tell you if you stop messing with me."

"You are so sensitive, little udo," she replied. "Just tell me."

Running Wolf scratched his head. "I do not know where to start. There were lots of colors and sounds and talking animals . . . and I talked to Doda."

Red Willow's eyes opened wide. "Stop right there. You talked to Doda?"

"Yes."

"Get out your tea," Red Willow announced. "It's time for me to take a trip."

The duo prepared the wysoccan tea just as they had the day before, and Red Willow took a large sip. Her heart began to beat rapidly in her chest as if it were ready to burst right through her skin. She felt a tingling sensation move throughout her body like being stung by hundreds of tiny little bees. Everything around her was moving in slow motion. Since she had seen her brother vomit when he had taken his medicine, she prepared herself for her own round of throwing up, but it never came.

Suddenly a bright light enveloped Red Willow's spirit, and she was astrally transported to a high mountain top. On the ground next to her were a flute and the skeletal remains of a deer. A voice in the air beckoned her to play the flute. It was a strange request, considering she had no idea how to play. She picked up the flute and examined it, looking for any clues that might reveal how it worked. She fumbled around before putting one end in her mouth and awkwardly blowing into it. An awful noise emanated from the flute, but the noise was enough to lift one of the deer bones off the ground. Red Willow was confused by the oddity of the whole situation. Putting the flute back into her mouth, she blew out another hideous note, lifting a second bone off the ground. She played note after note, and the notes lifted one by one the deer bones until they finally formed a complete standing skeleton.

"You must follow me if you wish to get the answers you seek," the talking skeleton said to Red Willow.

Red Willow leaned into the weirdness and followed the skeleton. The skeleton led Red Willow further up the mountain, through an area where there was a foot of snow on the ground and howling winds.

The pair reached a cave on the side of the hill, and the deer skeleton beckoned Red Willow to enter. Upon entering the cave, Red Willow saw the figure of a man trapped in a giant block of ice. She could not make out the image of the man, so she approached to get a closer look. She was stunned to see that it was her uncle, Howling Coyote. A voice rang out deep from the recesses of the cave.

"I am as coldhearted in death as I was in life," the voice bellowed, echoing off the cave's walls.

Red Willow was not sure how to respond. The voice was her uncle's, but his mouth was not moving.

The disembodied voice continued to speak. "What I did to your etsi was wrong, and I face the consequences. But what your udo did was wrong as well, and two wrongs do not make a right. There must be a consequence for Running Wolf's actions, and I believe that deep inside you know that. You must confess your knowledge of my murder before the tribe. It is the only way."

"But I cannot send my udo to be sacrificed for his crime." Red Willow's voice quivered. "It would be too much to bear."

"There will be forgiveness for your udo, just like there will be forgiveness for me in time," the voice replied. "It is true that the tribe will demand a murder for murder because the idea of retributive justice is built into the nature of humanity, and there is no way around it. However, the spirit world is a different place with forgiveness for all. You have to believe that it will work out in the end."

The cave walls began to shake, and rocks fell around Red Willow. She covered her head and tried to get back towards the entrance. But before she could make it out, the entire mountain collapsed into a pile of rubble, burying Red Willow in the dark and leaving her unable to move.

Panic began to set in, and she screamed at the top of her lungs. She felt a stream of water smack her in the face and awoke to find Running Wolf sitting over her with an empty water pouch in his hand.

"You were screaming, agilvgi," Running Wolf panted. "Are you alright?

Red Willow lay motionless on her back and stared up at the sky. Skye walked up to her and licked her face. Red Willow didn't move a muscle, still in a catatonic state from her drug-induced journey. Running Wolf waved his hand in front of her face without a response then checked her breathing to make sure she was still alive. She was breathing normally, so he decided not to rouse her. Finally, after an hour or so, Red Willow sat up and asked for water. Running Wolf brought her water and a small piece of pemmican. She ate and drank.

Unlike Running Wolf's spiritual vision, Red Willow's did not leave her content but instead more confused than ever. Its message conflicted with her intuitive leanings of not turning in her brother, and she did not know which to trust. She knew she had to make a decision soon before it ate her up inside.

Running Wolf felt his sister was exhausted from her spiritual journey, and she needed time to rest and recover. He helped her into a comfortable position and fashioned his coat into a pillow where she could rest her head. Once she fell asleep, he decided to do some hunting. He headed off into the woods with Red Willow's rabbit stick and deer knife, searching for small game.

Deep into the woods, Running Wolf heard a piercing, high-pitched noise he recognized as the cry of a bobcat. He followed the sound stealthily, hoping to track down the animal and sneak up on it. Eventually, he reached a place where he could see it from a distance. The bobcat was standing near a hollow log, surveying the area. Running Wolf went around to the back of the log to try to make his move from behind. He perched beside the timber then jumped out quickly, simultaneously hurling the rabbit stick towards the cat. He struck the bobcat directly on its head, and it went down with a loud cry. Rushing over to the downed animal, he said a prayer of thanksgiving over it before slitting its throat.

Running Wolf was beginning to walk away with his catch when he heard a tiny cry coming from the hollow log. He looked inside the log and saw a baby bobcat kitten, instantly realizing what he had done. "I've killed this baby's mother." His heart sank into his stomach as he looked into the eyes of the youngling, devastated by what he had unknowingly done. Feeling he could not leave the defenseless little one alone in the woods, he tried to coax it out of the log. The kitten raised its fur and hissed, lunging at Running Wolf's outstretched arm. He pulled back, tempted just to leave it to fend for itself, but his conscience got the best of him. He reached into the log again, getting bit this time, and managed to pull the kitten out. It was fighting him the whole way, but he managed to grab the scruff of its neck and subdue it. He headed back to camp with the little one in one hand and the carcass of its mother in the other.

Upon returning to camp, Running Wolf found Red Willow awake and alert. He told her what had happened in the woods, and he showed her the little kitten. She scolded her brother for killing the kitten's mother and asked him to bring her the poor little thing. She took it from her brother and tried to cradle it in her arms. The cute little babe squirmed for a bit before Red Willow could soothe it enough to keep it calm. She immediately sensed a deep connection with the kitten.

"What should we name it?" Running Wolf asked.

"It has this beautiful red coat, like a blazing fire." Red Willow gently stroked the little female baby bobcat behind its ears. "We should call it Fyre."

Red Willow slept that night with the little one in her arms. They awoke and packed up their things the following day, including Fyre and their animal carcasses. They loaded up their travois, attached it to Skye, and headed towards home.

Chapter Four

White Owl

Upon returning, Red Willow and Running Wolf settled back into their usual routines. Their spiritual journeys had cleared their minds and allowed them to refocus as they waited for their time of revelation at the Green Corn Ceremony. Red Willow resumed her gardening. The corn she had planted in her garden mounds was nearly a foot high, and it was now time to plant the beans next to it. The newly growing corn would support the climbing beans as they rose towards the sky. She chuckled to herself as she planted the beans and thought about her immature little brother. In her family garden metaphor, she considered the beans like her brother because he was so mentally frail and needed so much support.

One day, as she was tending to her garden, Red Willow heard a sound rising in the distance. She stopped what she was doing and tuned into the noise. It was a beautifully haunting melody that danced in her ears like the music of the spirits. She turned to face the music and saw a young brave playing the beautiful song on his flute in the distance. It was her friend White Owl, whom she had known since childhood.

Red Willow stood and listened to the song in a trance-like state. White Owl played louder when he noticed his audience of one, hoping to keep her attention. When the melody ended, White Owl looked across the way at Red Willow with a gentle gaze and a playful grin. He bowed his head towards her respectfully and went on his way. Red Willow's heart quickened, and a feeling of warmth radiated through her body. It was a strange new sensation for her, and she shook her hands vigorously to try to snap herself back into reality. She tried to put these feelings out of her mind and get back to work on her gardening chores, but she could not focus and gave up quickly, heading back to her hut.

"How was your day, my ayoli?" Gray Dove asked Red Willow as she ambled through the doorway.

Red Willow plopped down on her hammock. "Something strange happened today. White Owl came up and started playing his flute while I was out in the garden. It was nice, but I didn't understand why he would do that."

Gray Dove looked at her daughter with a sly smile. "It sounds to me like he has affection for you."

"What do you mean? How is that possible?"

"I mean, he likes you and wants you to be his mate," Gray Dove smiled.

Red Willow dropped her back down into the hammock and stared at the ceiling. "I don't have time for that."

Gray Dove walked over and sat down on the hammock next to her daughter. "Don't be so hasty to close yourself off, my ayoli. You might want to give him a chance."

Red Willow let out a long sigh. "With Doda being gone, I have so much to do around here in this home with this family. I don't need any outside distractions."

Gray Dove stroked Red Willow's hair gently. "All I am saying is that you are becoming a woman, and you may want to have your own family one day. I will not always be here, and neither will your brother. It will be good for you to have a life of your own. Just let me speak to White Owl's mother to see his intentions, and then we can go from there. There will be no obligations."

Red Willow turned onto her side, with her back towards her mother. "If that's what you want, then fine."

The next day Gray Dove went to visit White Owl's mother. Red Willow went out to the garden for a little bit to putter around but could not get any real work done as she anxiously awaited her mother's return. Gray Dove returned after a few hours and sat down with Red Willow to talk to her.

"White Owl *does* have intentions of courting you, my ayoli," Gray Dove told her. "I had a good talk with his etsi, and I believe they are a good family, and he would prove to be a good partner for you. He is kind and fearless and strong, much like your father. His etsi and I have arranged a time for the two of you to sit down and talk so that you may get to know each other better. He is coming here next sunset to share a meal with us."

Red Willow began pacing around the hut. "I am not ready for that. What makes you think I need to have a partner?"

"Because you need more in your life than just your brother and me," Gray Dove responded. "You must find other people with whom you can have a caring and intimate relationship. You are more ready than you think you are. I can sense that."

Red Willow knew deep inside her soul that her mother was right. She did not have close relationships outside of her immediate family, finding it extremely difficult to let anyone in since her father passed. The pain of his loss created an emotional chasm that she found it impossible to cross. Red Willow let out a deep sigh and wiped a small tear from her eye.

Gray Dove hugged her daughter tightly. "I understand, my ayoli. You have been through so much, and I am proud of how you have handled it. It is OK to be vulnerable."

Red Willow rested in her mother's arms, soaking in the nurturing energy before Running Wolf barged into the door and interrupted the tender moment. "When are we going to eat?"

Red Willow scoffed at her brother, annoyed at his unwanted presence. "Whenever you prepare your own food."

Gray Dove released Red Willow. "I thought you two were getting closer," she said, shaking her head. "Running Wolf is right, though. It is time to start making dinner." Gray Dove proceeded to her dinner preparations while her daughter and son retired to separate corners of the hut.

The following day the preparations began for the special meal with White Owl. Red Willow and Gray Dove took out some turkey bones left over from the last hunt. They placed them in a pot with hot water over the central fire pit, added wild onions and sassafras leaves, and allowed the mixture to steep all day. While the broth was steeping, they went to work on the cornbread. They added water, chopped up some hickory nuts into a few handfuls of cornmeal, and kneaded the mixture together into dough. Then they dropped dough balls into a pot of boiling water and waited for them to float to the top. While they were waiting on the corn cakes to cook, Gray Dove asked her daughter how she felt about the dinner.

Red Willow rubbed her hands together anxiously. "I'm confused and frustrated and ready to get this over with. Part of me thinks I don't have time for nonsense like this, but another part is curious. I believe that you and Doda had a special bond before the Tuscarora took him from us, and," she hesitated, causing her mother to look at her more intently, "I want to see if . . . I can have the same. Red Willow's eyes widened as she gazed up at her mother. "But how will I know what makes a person the right partner?"

As Gray Dove pondered her daughter's question, a small rain shower made its way into the village. The raindrops pelted the house's thatched roof, creating a soft pitter-patter sound. Gray Dove thought back to the early years of her relationship with Hunting Bear and decided that the best way to answer her daughter's question was with a story.

"When your father and I were first married, I was unsure about him. I had not chosen him myself; he was chosen for me. And while he was always kind to me, I still found it difficult to let my guard down. Your father was a very patient man . . . probably because he had to be with a udalii like me. When I found out that my doda had died, I was obligated to attend his burial ceremony. The only problem was that he had become a member of the Tuscarora tribe after leaving our sidanela. Despite the strained relationship between our two tribes, I was still expected to go to the Tuscarora village and witness my father's burial. It would be a long trip, and I did not know what kind of reception awaited me. I told your doda about it, and I told him I would go on my own, that he did not have to spend his time away from the tribe or put his life in danger for my obligations. But your father refused to let me go without him. He insisted that my duties were his duties, no matter what kind of trouble it might cause him. Then and there, I knew he was the right partner for me. We were fortunate that the trip for my father's burial was uneventful, but the fact that your doda cared enough about me to go made me realize he was the one. That's how you know a good partner— when they do things for you that might not be easy, and you do the same. Love is not a feeling. It is a series of committed actions that two people do for each other."

✖✖✖

The cornbread popped to the top of the boiling water, letting the women know it was time to take it out. They removed the cooked cornbread and laid it out to dry. They checked the broth, and it had a pleasant rich taste, so they took it off the heat and set it on the floor to cool. Red Willow got out the special bearskin rug they used when they had company and spread it onto the floor. Gray Dove called out to Running Wolf to come in for dinner, as he had been outside with his friends practicing chunkey. The three sat down on their respective beds and awaited the arrival of White Owl.

"You look beautiful, ayoli," Gray Dove said to Red Willow as they waited for their guest to arrive.

"And stressed too," Running Wolf interjected.

"Don't start with me right now, udo!" Red Willow cut her eyes at her little brother. "I'm not in the mood."

"What did I say?" Running Wolf leaned back away from his sister. "I just speak the truth. Anyone with eyes can see that the anxious spirits inhabit you now. What is so important about this meal anyway?"

Red Willow shook her head. "You wouldn't understand. Just try not to mess it up."

Gray Dove winced in pain. "Can we please just have a pleasant meal without any bickering?"

White Owl strutted up to the hut's door, dressed in his finest headdress with his best blanket draped over his shoulder. In one hand, he carried a plug of tobacco and, in the other, a bunch of wildflowers. White Owl was above average in height and had broad shoulders, but he had thin and long arms and legs that made him a lanky man. However, his extreme confidence was enough to overcome any physical limitations he faced. Gray Dove struggled up from her seat when she saw White Owl in the doorway and shuffled over to greet him.

White Owl bowed to Gray Dove and presented her with the tobacco. "A gift for the head of the household. Wa do for allowing me the opportunity to visit your home."

Gray Dove gingerly bowed in return. "We are glad to have you with us, White Owl. Please come in and share our meal."

White Owl walked into the hut and turned his gaze to Red Willow. Her soft black hair shimmered in the ray of evening sun beaming through the hole in the roof. She gave him a glance and an awkward head nod to acknowledge his presence. He noticed a slight grin during the brief peek he got at her face and took it as a sign of her interest. Sensing her anxiety, White Owl approached Red Willow with conviction, hoping to ease her nerves.

White Owl handed Red Willow the wildflowers. "These are for you."

Red Willow immediately laid the flowers down on the bearskin rug. "Wa do."

Red Willow and White Owl stood next to each other in awkward silence while Gray Dove brought over the prepared food vessels and placed them down onto the rug. Everyone took their seats with their legs crossed. White Owl sat down next to Gray Dove and across from Red Willow. Running Wolf sat next to his sister. Gray Dove motioned to everyone that she was going to bless the food.

Gray Dove closed her eyes and bowed her head. "We thank the Great Spirit for the resources that made this meal possible. We thank the Earth for producing it, and we thank all those who labored to bring it to us."

Gray Dove served the meal of turkey bone broth and cornbread, and the four began eating.

"You know that Red Willow is responsible for this meal," Gray Dove said to White Owl. "She hunted the turkey that provided the broth, and she helped to bake the cornbread."

White Owl responded through bites of his food. "Red Willow is a woman of many talents. Any man would be lucky to call her his udalii."

Red Willow squirmed in her seat, uncomfortable with the conversation. She could no longer contain her anxiety and blurted out awkwardly, "Let's just get this out now. You think I'd make a good udalii, but what makes you think you would make a good uyehi? What can you provide for me that I can't provide for myself? Because as you've seen, I don't have any problem taking care of myself."

White Owl stopped eating and placed his fingers on his chin. He nodded his head while collecting his thoughts. "I don't think you need a provider, Red Willow," White Owl looked at her, "but I think you need a partner, someone to stand by you and for you. I don't believe there are a lot of men out there who are up for this role, but I believe that I am."

Red Willow lowered her head and suppressed a smile. This was what she was looking for in a partner: not a caretaker, but an equal.

"I'm glad someone is not intimidated by her because I know that I am," Running Wolf spontaneously exclaimed. "She's more of a man than I think I will ever be."

Gray Dove scowled at her son. Red Willow laughed uncomfortably as she glared at her brother.

"Red Willow has many great qualities that make her rise above the level of male and female," White Owl continued, unfazed by Running Wolf's strange outburst. "That's why I would consider her a worthy partner."

Gray Dove steered the conversation towards a different topic, hoping to avoid further embarrassment. White Owl had made a good impression on her, and she wanted him to marry Red Willow. She didn't want any strange family quirks to scare White Owl away. They finished the meal, and White Owl stood up to leave.

"Well, I must be going. I am grateful for your hospitality," White Owl said as he ambled towards the door.

"It was a pleasure to have your company," Gray Dove said as she motioned to Red Willow. "Why don't you see White Owl out?"

Red Willow stood up, fixed her dress, and straightened her hair. With a bounce in her step, she walked out ahead of White Owl. White

Owl grinned and followed her happily. When they were entirely outside and alone, he turned towards her.

"I know that you are a tough nut to crack," White Owl smacked his lips, "but I have eyes for you—and only you."

White Owl stared deeply into Red Willow's eyes and took her by the hand. Red Willow swallowed noticeably as White Owl squeezed her hand firmly but gently. They held hands for a timeless moment before White Owl released his grip and turned to leave into the night. Red Willow stood and watched as he left, letting out a deep sigh.

Once White Owl was entirely out of sight, Red Willow snapped back into reality and turned her ire towards her baby brother. She tromped into the hut, confronting Running Wolf and shoving him in the chest. "Why would you say something so mean at dinner?"

Running Wolf raised his hands in defense. "I just said what I felt. And besides, it's true. You *are* intimidating!"

Red Willow pointed her finger in her brother's face accusingly. "But what about me being manly? Do you have any idea how that might put White Owl off? You are trying to mess up my life at every turn!"

Running Wolf pushed his sister's finger away and stormed out. *Was* he trying to mess her life up? It wasn't his plan, but since their father died, he had considered himself the man of his hut. It never occurred to him that his mother or sister might have another man, like White Owl, around. He wandered around the village for a bit before heading down to the river, standing and quietly watching the water meander its way over the rocks. He picked up a handful of smooth stones from the riverbank and chucked them into the current.

One morning, a few days after their dinner, Red Willow discovered a sack of cornmeal sitting outside of their doorway. Yet another odd occurrence amid a series of bizarre events in her life lately. She lugged the sack into the hut, plopped it down in front of Gray Dove, and asked if she knew why it was there.

Gray Dove chuckled. "It is a proposal, my ayoli. Since I have not yet arranged for you to be married, White Owl knows that he can make the first move. It is customary for a young asgaya to leave a sack of cornmeal at the doorway of the agehya that he wishes to marry. She will make cornbread from the cornmeal and present it to him if she wishes to marry him. If she does not wish to marry him, then she will leave the cornmeal as she found it at her doorway. So," Gray Dove turned to her daughter, "it looks like you have a decision to make."

Red Willow squinted. "Why *haven't* you arranged a marriage for me yet, instead of making me go through this strange process? It worked for you and Doda."

"Whether or not to arrange a marriage is totally up to the agehya's sidanela," Gray Dove explained. "And since your doda is gone, I am the only utana left to make that decision. I believe with all my heart that the Great Spirit has plans for you, and I am not going to stand in the way of those plans by choosing for Him."

A sinking feeling developed in Red Willow's stomach, the cornmeal sack in front of her tangibly demonstrating the necessity of a choice. She still wasn't sure if she was ready for this level of commitment, and if it had been any other man, her answer would have been an easy "No." But White Owl had impressed her and aroused something within her that made her think twice.

Red Willow brushed her hair out of her face. "I'm bewildered, Etsi. What do you think I should do?"

"I cannot answer this question for you, my ayoli," Gray Dove whispered, trying to catch her breath. "You must follow your heart and the guidance of the Great Spirit. Whatever you decide, I will always be here to support you."

Red Willow plunked down on her bed and let out a giant sigh. She spent the next few days in a haze, trying unsuccessfully to get work done in her garden. During a restless night's sleep, the decision suddenly and without warning came to her. No matter how much she cared about White Owl, she could not be involved in a relationship until she had settled the matter with her brother. The following day she wistfully picked up the unbaked cornmeal and set it outside her door. The decision to reject the proposal was not easy, but it was much easier than the terrible decision she would have to make regarding her brother's destiny.

Chapter Five

The Gift

Eternal Blossom was well known around the village for her beautiful jewelry creations, and she was about to make the most essential piece of her lifetime. She wanted to create something special for Gray Dove to signify the special bond the two had formed amidst the trials and tribulations of their lives. Shell gorgets were her most prized works, and she had it in her mind to make the most stunning gorget ever seen.

Eternal Blossom headed down to the river, her pouch in tow. Her primary goal was to locate the perfect mussel shell for her sister's gorget, but she could also use the time to collect some mussels to feed her family. She cautiously approached the riverbank and waded slowly waist-deep into the water. She turned to face the bank and dipped her hands in upon reaching the proper depth, feeling around on the bottom with a sweeping motion. It was frightening to be dropping her hands deep into the murky river waters without knowing what she might encounter, but mussels were bottom dwellers, and that is where she needed to go. She continued to sweep the river bottom with her hands, all the while moving back towards the bank. About halfway back, she found her first mussel. It was not the beauty she had hoped for, but she knew it would still be edible. She tossed it into her tote and continued her search.

This process continued for a few hours as Eternal Blossom slowly headed down the river. She had a pouch full of mussels but still no prized specimen. Determined to get what she came for, she continued her search downriver. A couple of hours later, she finally found it—a beautiful large mussel with a shimmering array of green, yellow, and brown bands. She pumped her fists and danced a happy dance right there in the middle of the river.

Eternal Blossom's happy dance quickly morphed into something different. During one of her spins, she stopped dead in her tracks, realizing she had wandered to where the villagers had found Howling Coyote's body. She stood and stared at the eerily tranquil spot, pondering the juxtaposition of happy and sad, before deciding she was ready to move towards the good and leave behind the bad. She stuffed the alluring mussel into her pouch and headed for home.

Eternal Blossom was excited to share her bounty with family, so she brought the mussels to Gray Dove and asked her to help prepare them for a shared meal. Gray Dove was appreciative of her sister's gift, and the two boiled up the mussels and set them out for the family dinner. The families sat down together, thanked the Great Spirit for the bounty, and began to eat.

"I heard about your proposal," Eternal Blossom mumbled to Red Willow between bites of food. "It must be difficult for you. I'm proud of you for doing what you thought best for yourself. I wish I had had that opportunity myself when I was your age."

Red Willow sighed. "It is hard for me to say it was the right choice. White Owl is a good man and would've made a good partner. But I felt the spirits were leading me in a different direction."

Eternal Blossom clenched her jaw tightly and nodded her head in faux approval of her niece's decision. Truthfully, she was *not* proud of Red Willow for what she did . . . she was incensed. Her resentment towards her niece simmered. Red Willow had the chance to choose a life partner, who was by all accounts a kind and decent man, and she decided to say no? It made no sense to Eternal Blossom, who'd had neither a choice in who she married nor ended up with a decent man.

The family finished the meal, and Eternal Blossom and her children got up and headed for the doorway. Gray Dove walked with them and thanked her sister again for providing the mussels. Eternal Blossom gave her sister a tender hug and kissed her cheek. "I love you," she whispered into her sister's ear. She turned, gathered the children, and headed for home.

Back at home, Eternal Blossom put the children to bed and began working on her masterpiece. She cracked open the mussel and scooped out the insides, rinsing the shell in hot water to remove all the remaining bits and then laying it out to dry. The next night after her children were asleep, she began the painstaking process of smoothing out the shell to create the beautifully round shape. She grabbed a tiny stone flake and dipped it into some wet sand, using the stone to sand down the edges of the shell to begin the shaping process.

Night after night for one solid week, she sanded down the shell until it was as circular as the glossy nighttime moon. The next step was to drill two holes in the sanded-down surface so that she could braid a necklace through it. She grabbed her pointed stone drill bit tip and attached it to a short wooden rod. Stabbing the drill bit tip into the shell, she began to work it back and forth between her hands to open the hole.

The crowning jewel of this fantastic gorget—and what would make it a one-of-a-kind piece—would be an engraving on the shell's interior. Eternal Blossom grabbed her small, serrated carving stone and began to fashion the image of a pair of sisters holding hands into the surface. This was the most intricate part of the process as well as the most time-consuming. It would take her two weeks to finish the engraving, but she knew the effort was well worth her time. She admired her handiwork, then mulled over when she would present it to her sister, deciding that the eve of the Green Corn Ceremony would be perfect.

✖✖✖

Summer was rapidly approaching. The corn Red Willow had planted was starting to reach the sky, and the beans had begun their climb up the cornstalks. The recently planted squash spread out and would soon wholly shade out the weeds trying to steal valuable nutrients from the other plants. Her analogy for the family garden was now complete. She was the protector, fighting off those vile weeds. Red Willow looked out upon what she had helped create with a sense of pride and accomplishment. She lingered there, thinking about what was soon to come before heading back to the hut.

She entered the hut and found her mother sitting by the fire, taking sips of tea between labored breaths. Red Willow wrinkled her brow. "How are you doing, Etsi? Tell me the truth."

Gray Dove let out a deep sigh. "The truth is my body hurts, and I'm moving slower than I used to. I can't even do my usual chores. I'm not sure what is happening, but I know my body is betraying me." She forced a smile. "But it is nothing I cannot handle with help from the Great Spirit, and I don't want you to have to concern yourself with it."

Red Willow folded her arms in front of her chest. "But I am concerned, whether you want me to be or not. Promise me that you will go and see the medicine man."

"I promise," Gray Dove replied.

Running Wolf rushed into the hut from his morning fishing trip and laid his catch down by the fire. He quickly headed back outside, his mind on chunkey practice. He had become obsessed with the sport and achieving victory at the ceremonial games. It was helpful to distract himself from the looming Green Corn Ceremony.

"Where are you going?" Gray Dove asked in a frustrated voice. "You are always in such a rush. I feel like I never get to spend time with you anymore."

"I'm going to practice my chunkey, Etsi," Running Wolf replied, hurrying off. "You know that the big competition is coming soon, and I want to be the best."

Running Wolf arrived at the field to find that White Owl was already practicing. He stood for a minute watching White Owl, sizing up his potential competition. White Owl was a naturally gifted chunkey player, having great velocity and accuracy with spear throwing. He also had the most beautiful and well-crafted spear that Running Wolf had ever seen. Running Wolf was impressed by both skill and spear as he watched White Owl's intense practice.

"Can I join you?" Running Wolf asked White Owl as he walked up to the field.

"All are welcome on the field of play, Running Wolf," White Owl replied.

Running Wolf grabbed his spear and took the rolling stone from White Owl. He rolled the rock down the field and then let his spear fly. The spear landed with a sharp thud about twelve inches away from the stone. White Owl was excited with Running Wolf's first throw, so he decided to take a break and watch Running Wolf for a few minutes.

Running Wolf continued his practice throws. He rolled the stone and tossed his spear, landing it even closer than his first toss. After several successive rolls, each ending with his spear closer and closer to the stone, he landed it so close to the stone that it created sparks as its tip grazed the stone on his final practice toss. White Owl, who had been watching from afar, came strolling up to the field.

White Owl stretched his arms out in front of his chest and then behind his back, puffing his chest out. "It looks like you are warmed up, Running Wolf. How about a little friendly competition?"

Running Wolf cracked his knuckles. "Fine by me."

White Owl walked closer to Running Wolf. "I think it would be more fun if something were at stake. If I win, you put in a good word with your *agilvgi* for me. She did not accept my proposal, but I haven't given up."

"What's in it for me if *I* win?" Running Wolf tilted his head to one side.

White Owl planted his spear into the ground next to him. "What do you want from me?"

Running Wolf stared intently at the coveted spear. "How about that?" he said, pointing to it.

White Owl turned towards the spear and looked lovingly at his prized possession. "It would be a heavy price to pay, but I'm feeling pretty confident, so let's go. I win; you help me out with your agilvgi. You win; you get my spear."

The two bowed to each other to acknowledge their wager, then began the match. They rolled the stone, and each threw their spears. Running Wolf's spear landed about a foot closer to the rock than White Owl's, giving him a one to zero lead. White Owl won the next frame, tying the score at one apiece. The match went back and forth for multiple frames until Running Wolf tied the score at eleven.

"You either win here or lose here," White Owl said to Running Wolf before rolling out the final stone.

White Owl rolled the stone, and the competitors threw their spears. Running Wolf took off down the field after the spear, trying to coax it into the best possible location. His spear landed in a beautiful spot about six inches from the stone. He watched as White Owl's spear came flying in and landed within one inch of the rock about five seconds later . . . game over!

White Owl rushed in with outstretched arms, elated with his win. "You played well, oginalii," White Owl said boastfully, "but the Great Spirit was with me today. The results might be different the next time we meet, but today's victory is mine and with it my prize. Time for you to pay up and put in a good word with your sister for me."

"I will do what I can," Running Wolf shrugged, "but she will do what she wants, not what I tell her."

Running Wolf left the field, saddened that he could not win the spear he coveted, and made his way home, hugging the riverbank. He strolled into the house, head hung low, to find his sister and mother preparing for dinner.

"How was your practice?" Gray Dove asked.

Running Wolf tossed himself down into his hammock. "I ran into White Owl on the field, and he beat me in a competition."

Red Willow stopped what she was doing when she heard her brother mention White Owl. She had not been able to put him out of her mind since rejecting his proposal and was eager to get any information she could gather about him. She walked over to her brother and stood next to the hammock.

"What did he have to say?" Red Willow asked Running Wolf as she studied his face intently.

Running Wolf took a bite of some dried persimmon that he had stored in a clay pot under his hammock. "He wants you to accept his proposal. He said he's not giving up on you."

Red Willow paused, surprised to hear that White Owl was still pursuing her. Had she made a mistake by rejecting his proposal? She figured he would give up and move on to the next girl after her rejection but was flattered by his continued pursuit. Could he be the one the Great Spirit meant for her to be with after all?

"I admire his persistence," Gray Dove chimed in. "He seems to know what he wants and is willing to take a risk."

"So, what should I tell him, agilvgi?" Running Wolf asked, still munching on his persimmons.

Red Willow walked away from her brother. "Tell him that if he wants to talk, he knows where to find me. He doesn't have to use my udo as his messenger."

The women completed their dinner preparations, and the trio sat down to eat. They finished their meal without much fanfare, and they each went their separate ways. Gray Dove fired up her tobacco and sat down to meditate while Running Wolf and Red Willow retired for the night. Gray Dove's thoughts quickly turned to her illness. She feared the worst and prayed to the Great Spirit that He would keep her around long enough to see her children get to a place in life where they were stable and well cared for before she left the earth.

The next day Gray Dove decided to see the medicine man, as she had promised Red Willow she would. Taking the scenic route to delay her arrival, she meandered through a garden of mint plants. The intense, sweet aroma of the mint tickled her nostrils and temporarily lifted her spirits. She was hopeful that the medicine man would give her positive news.

"Osda sunalei, Holy One," Gray Dove said as she walked through the entrance to the medicine hut. "Do you have time to see me?"

The medicine man looked up, surprised to see Gray Dove. "Is this about your son's visit? He was here not long ago, and I gave him something to help him with his troubles."

Gray Dove's eyes squinted, and a worried look crossed her face. "My son? Is he not well?"

"He is fine, just confused and seeking answers, as many young men his age do. What troubles you, my agilvgi?" the medicine man asked, quickly changing the subject.

"I have been in a lot of pain recently, and I have noticed that my body is changing in strange ways," Gray Dove said softly.

The medicine man rolled his tongue in his mouth pensively. "Show me where your body is changing."

Gray Dove removed her clothes and revealed her breast and underarm to the Holy One. On her left breast was a swollen hard nodule and in her armpit were a few small acorn-shaped nodules as well. The medicine man let out several low-pitched grunts as he examined Gray Dove's body. Gray Dove looked up at the hut's ceiling, tapping her feet nervously and wishing she were anywhere else in the world but there.

"I have seen this situation before," the medicine man nodded. "I'm afraid to say that it does not usually end well. I have something that may help . . . so we will try that."

He went to his storage shelf and retrieved some Witch Hazel stems. "Take these and boil them to create a tea for yourself. Drink it once per moon."

Gray Dove put her dress back on and thanked the medicine man. Stunned by his words, she slowly shuffled out of the hut. The phrase "it usually does not end well" reverberated in her mind. She knew what it signified and was not yet ready to leave her children. Reuniting with Hunting Bear was one thing, but orphaning her children was another. As she reached her family hut, she paused outside the doorway and took a long look as tears welled up in her eyes.

Chapter Six

Raiding Party

One morning while Running Wolf was out on a fishing excursion, he noticed a nice stand of wild blackberries on the opposite side of the river. The river formed a natural boundary between the Pee Dee and the Tuscarora. While the Tuscarora did not live directly adjacent to the water, the territory on that side was a no man's land where the tribal rules and etiquette did not apply. Running Wolf knew it would be unwise to cross the river, but the allure of the succulent wild fruit was too tempting. He walked down the riverbank to find a spot where he could cross without much difficulty. Coming upon a shallow site with some rock outcroppings, he crossed over to the other side.

Upon reaching the berries, he was delighted to find that they were plentiful and ripe. He ate handful after handful and gave thanks and praise to the Great Spirit for the gift. Running Wolf was so wrapped up in the blackberries that he did not notice the band of Tuscarora raiders lurking in the trees beyond the stand. They rushed upon him without warning and grabbed him by the arms. Startled, he flailed his arms and made a momentary escape. But as he ran towards the river and cried for help, the raiding party caught and tackled him. They tied his arms up, blindfolded him, and headed off with him into the distance.

Running Wolf's cries of distress were heard by one of the other villagers, fishing down at the river. The villager caught a glimpse of Running Wolf and his captors leaving. Frantic, the man rushed back to the village to inform Red Willow and Gray Dove what had taken place.

"Tuscarora raiders have taken Running Wolf!" the villager exclaimed through panting breaths. "I was down at the river fishing when I heard a cry for help. I rushed to see what it was about, and I saw the kidnapping."

Gray Dove dropped the water jug she was holding and froze in a panic. Red Willow saw the frightened look on her mother's face, which strangely made her calm and focused, immediately knowing what she had to do. "I've got to go. There is no time to waste," she thought to herself. She called Skye and asked the villager to point out the raiders' direction. She and Skye rushed out and took off to chase after the raiders. On her way out, she ran into White Owl, who had seen the frantic villager headed to Red Willow's house and knew something was wrong.

"What's going on?"

"They took Running Wolf, and I have to go find him," Red Willow exclaimed.

"I'll join you," said White Owl, a firmness in his voice. I don't want you to have to do this alone."

Red Willow was so focused on her mission that she didn't respond. She just headed towards the river to begin her search for her brother, along with Skye and now White Owl. The group arrived at the initial site of Running Wolf's capture and stopped so that Skye could pick up Running Wolf's scent. Once Skye had the smell, they resumed their pursuit. They walked briskly throughout the day before coming upon the captors, who had begun to set up camp for the night.

Red Willow, White Owl, and Skye stopped along the edge of the tree line, away from the camp, to survey the scene. Still tied up and blindfolded, Running Wolf was next to the campfire, being watched by one of the raiders. Three more raiders were stationed in a circle around the camp's perimeter. Red Willow began plotting her strategy for retrieving her brother.

"I'm sure they will be fine." Eternal Blossom was with Gray Dove, rubbing her back and trying her best to comfort her sister. "Red Willow will bring him home; Hunting Bear trained her well."

Gray Dove slumped over, head in hands. "I have seen so much heartache; I don't know how to make it end. I want my children to be safe. I want to know they are safe, and then I want to leave this world."

Eternal Blossom lifted Gray Dove's head out of her hands to look her in the eye. "You don't mean that, agilvgi. You have lived a hard life, but there is a purpose, even if it is unclear."

Tears streamed down Gray Dove's face. "I just don't feel that way right now . . . all I feel is exhaustion. I need rest, but I can't have that until I know things will be alright."

Eternal Blossom reached in to hug her sister, and as she squeezed her tightly, she felt the lump on her sister's breast. Eternal Blossom pulled away from the hug with a concerned look. "What is going on with you, agilvgi?"

Gray Dove inhaled deeply through her nostrils, trying to suck up the mucus that accompanied her tears. "My usdis are in danger! What do you think is going on with me?"

"No, I mean the strange lump." Eternal Blossom pointed to Gray Dove's chest.

"Oh, that." Gray Dove wiped her nose. "Just one more problem. The medicine man said he'd seen it before and 'it usually doesn't end well.' I think my time is coming."

Eternal Blossom's stomach clenched like it was in the paws of a mighty bear. She took a deep breath and rubbed her sister's arm gently. "Wait here," she said. "I have something I want to give you." Eternal Blossom had been waiting for the Green Corn Ceremony to give Gray Dove the gorget she had made for her, but she felt like now was the right time.

"Where am I going to go right now?" Gray Dove replied.

Eternal Blossom returned to her hut to retrieve the gorget. "I made this for you," she said as she held the gorget in front of Gray Dove's face. "I was saving it for a special time, but it feels like now is when you need it the most."

The gorget radiated a sparkling glow in the light of the hut. Gray Dove was mesmerized by its beauty, taking it from Eternal Blossom and clasping it tightly in her hand. "You made this for me? It looks like it was handcrafted by the Great Spirit Himself."

Eternal Blossom beckoned Gray Dove to turn the gorget over. "Take a look on the other side."

Gray Dove turned the gorget over to see the beautiful engraving of the two sisters. She opened her mouth wide and looked up at Eternal Blossom. Eternal Blossom smiled down at her big sister, tears welling up in her eyes. Gray Dove stood up, grabbed her sister by the neck, and pulled her close, hugging her tightly with no intentions of ever letting go.

Back at the raider camp, Red Willow was still trying to devise a strategy. Outnumbered by her enemies, she would need to even the odds. A plan came to her as she noticed a large mob of deer on the edge of the tree line about one hundred yards from her position. If she could just flush them out towards the raider camp, it would create enough of a distraction to allow her and White Owl to retrieve Running Wolf. White Owl and Skye moved behind the deer to drive them out towards the raiders while Red Willow moved towards the backside of the camp to take advantage of the diversion.

Skye and White Owl crept up slowly behind the deer then rushed them at the last moment, screaming and barking. The startled herd stampeded straight towards the camp. Taking the group by surprise, the charging deer sent most of the raiders rushing to the front of the camp, leaving just one guard behind. Sensing her opportunity, Red Willow crouched low to the ground and stealthily moved into the lightly guarded camp. As she drew closer to the unsuspecting sentry, she spotted a jagged stone caressing the dirt next to her. Digging the rock out from its earthen home, she sprinted towards the oblivious raider. At the last moment, the man turned, but it was too late. Red Willow pulled her arm back, stone in hand, and flung it forward onto the side of his skull. It landed with the thump of a watermelon falling to the ground, and the raider collapsed in a heap. Red Willow untied Running Wolf and removed his blindfold.

Running Wolf grabbed his sister by the forearm, glad to see her but sorry for what had happened. "Uyo ayelvdi, agilvgi. I didn't mean to put you in this situation."

Red Willow lifted her brother from the ground and spun around to check their surroundings. "There is no time for apologies now, udo. We must move."

By this time, the other raiders had taken notice and were rushing back towards camp and letting loose their arrows. Running Wolf and Red Willow ran across the field, dodging a hail of arrows as she directed him to a large boulder. Red Willow dove behind the boulder and turned to see her brother trip and fall just a few feet away. Running Wolf tried desperately to crawl on his belly to the safety of the boulder. Red Willow noticed Running Wolf's struggle and lunged out to grab his arms and pull him in just as an arrow landed on the ground a few steps away.

Red Willow and Running Wolf leaned against the backside of their sheltering rock, their pulses racing and heaving for breath. The arrow fire suddenly ceased, raising Red Willow's suspicions. She slowly raised her head over the top of the boulder to get a look at what was happening. Seeing nothing of note in the distance, she knelt back down behind the boulder and wondered if it was time to make a run for it. Suddenly, a loud thud reverberated on the other side of the boulder. She peered over and staring her in the face was a Tuscarora raider with a tomahawk. The raider drew his tomahawk to strike, but before he could swing it downwards, White Owl came rushing in and tackled him to the dirt.

The raider's bow and arrows fell to the ground in front of Red Willow as White Owl and the raider tumbled down behind her.

Red Willow grabbed the bow and arrows and began to scan the area for the two other raiders. One was approaching quickly on her left and the other on her right. She launched an arrow at the raider on her right then spun and launched another at the one on her left. Both arrows hit their mark, and the two raiders fell. White Owl and the other raider were still wrestling, and there was a large amount of blood in the grass below them. Then she noticed a giant gash on the left side of White Owl's torso. She knew she had to act quickly, so she rushed towards the melee and threw her body into the raider to knock him off White Owl. Running Wolf followed, jumping on top of the raider and choking the life out of him.

Red Willow went to tend to White Owl, who was shaking uncontrollably. She looked down at the large, gaping wound in his side and her eyes grew as wide as the full moon.

"It's bad, isn't it?" White Owl asked.

Red Willow put her hand on his lips. "Don't speak. You will need all the energy you can muster to heal your wound. Just focus on that." Red Willow applied pressure to the gash to try to control the bleeding.

Running Wolf staggered over and noticed White Owl's wound. He put his head into his hands and let out an agonized scream, sending a flock of birds scattering from the nearby trees.

"Go into the woods and find me some goldenseal," Red Willow barked.

Running Wolf clenched his fists tightly and swung his arms towards the ground. "Now!" Red Willow shouted again.

Running Wolf took a deep breath and hurried into the woods to search for the goldenseal. He soon found a large stand of plants, harvested the leaves, and brought them back to Red Willow. She took the leaves, wrapped them together into a compress, and pressed them down on White Owl's wound. She then ripped off a piece of her clothing and used it to bandage the outside of the injury.

"We have to get him back to the village as quickly as possible," Red Willow said to Running Wolf, who could see the fear in her eyes.

The trio and Skye set out back towards the village. They struggled to make their way through the darkness, only stopping for a few water breaks. White Owl leaned heavily on Red Willow and Running Wolf the entire way, barely able to move his legs. The group arrived back at the village just before dawn and headed straight to the home of the medicine man. Red Willow and Running Wolf dropped White Owl off and nearly collapsed from exhaustion.

"You have to help him, Holy One. He is badly injured," Red Willow pleaded.

The medicine man removed the blood-soaked makeshift bandage to examine the wound. A look of dismay crossed his face. Grabbing a jug of clean water, he quickly rinsed the wound and brewed some wysoccan. He knew he would have to put White Owl through some pain to keep him alive, and he wanted White Owl somewhere else in spirit when he did it.

The commotion had stirred the entire village, and word about the group's arrival made its way to Gray Dove and Eternal Blossom. When Gray Dove realized what was happening, she ran towards the medicine man's hut. Finding her children there safe and sound, she was overjoyed. She fell onto the ground next to them, and they shared a group hug.

The medicine man was distracted by the ruckus. "Take your sidanela back to your house. I will handle things here."

Running Wolf and Red Willow lifted themselves and dusted off their clothes. They reached down in tandem to pick up their mother. Gray Dove stood in between her children and put her arm around their necks. Together, they shuffled out of the hut. Red Willow turned to get one last look at White Owl. She gazed at him lying there, so badly wounded and in so much pain, and she felt pity for him. But it wasn't only pity that she felt. It was something much more profound.

After the family was gone, the medicine man went to work. He administered the wysoccan tea to White Owl and waited for him to pass out. Once he saw that White Owl had been in the spiritual realm for a sufficient time, he picked up his spear and placed the head into a pile of hot coals in his fire pit. He removed the searing hot spear from the coals and cauterized White Owl's wound. Then he placed a goldenseal poultice on the newly cauterized wound and bandaged it. White Owl twitched, but only slightly, as he was still deep into his spiritual journey.

When White Owl finally awakened to feel the extreme pain in his side, the medicine man was ready. "You must rest for a long while, my young brave," he said. "The pain will be intense, but you will pull through."

Exhausted by their ordeal, Red Willow and Running Wolf spent the day resting. The following day Eternal Blossom came over to check on them. As she neared the hut, she noticed Skye sitting attentively next to the entrance, eagerly scanning the horizon for signs of his best friend's return. She gave the faithful canine a gentle stroke on the crown of his head, before entering to find Red Willow and Gray Dove sitting with their morning tea as Fyre played with a dead mouse on the floor next to them.

"Where is Running Wolf?" Eternal Blossom asked.

"He is down at the river fishing," Gray Dove replied.

Eternal Blossom curved her eyebrows. "I'm surprised he went back out so soon after what happened."

Red Willow teased Fyre with the dead mouse. "He had to get out and do something to relieve his troubled spirit."

"What do you know about his troubled spirit?" Gray Dove squinted her eyes as she stared at Red Willow. "First, the medicine man tells me Running Wolf is troubled, and now you tell me he is troubled. Am I the only one who doesn't know the source of my own atsutsa's troubled spirit?"

"I guess he's just troubled by Howling Coyote's death," Red Willow said as she darted her eyes back and forth.

"There is more than that at work here," Gray Dove replied, "and I will find the answer even if no one will give it to me."

Eternal Blossom quickly changed the subject. "How are you doing, Red Willow?"

Red Willow walked over to the doorway and stared out at nothing in particular. "I'm worried about White Owl. I should've told him not to come with me to save Running Wolf."

White Owl's injury wracked Red Willow with grief. She blamed herself for what had befallen him. If he weren't interested in her as a partner, he would not have gone with her and nearly gotten himself killed.

Eternal Blossom sighed, still envious of Red Willow and her suitor. "You are blessed to have someone in your life who cares enough about you to put himself at risk to save someone you love."

Red Willow knew her aunt was right. White Owl cared about her, but that kind of affection was almost too much for her to bear. The pain of losing her father had led her to keep everyone at a distance, preventing her from experiencing any genuinely intimate relationships. She sighed deeply and wondered if it might be time to let that pain go and let someone special into her life.

Running Wolf was down at the river with thoughts of his own. He was feeling guilty again, not just for the murder of his uncle but also for getting himself kidnapped and putting his family—and White Owl—in danger. The desire to run away loomed large in his mind as he figured his family would be better off without him. Only his father's promise to him in the spiritual realm that all would end well enabled him to resist the temptation to flee. For now, he would have to deal with his guilt and hold out hope that things would work out. He grabbed his spear and hurled it into the water towards a group of fish swimming in the shallows, managing to hit one in the process.

Back at the hut, the women had begun weaving some pine straw baskets. Red Willow resented being there as she loathed basket weaving. But her mother and aunt forced her to be present, knowing there would come a time when this skill would be necessary. Red Willow was still at the novice stage, as evidenced by the many pinpricks she had given herself while threading the needle through the bundles of pine straw. She was not even halfway through with her basket, while her mother and aunt had already finished. Gray Dove got up and took the children outside to play, leaving Eternal Blossom to help guide Red Willow through completing her work.

"Don't worry usdi, your skills will improve with time," Eternal Blossom said.

Red Willow threw her tools down. "Maybe I'm just not cut out for basket weaving."

Eternal Blossom placed her hand on Red Willow's back. "You've had so much to do since your father died that you haven't had as much time to hone your skills as your etsi and I did when we were younger. In time you will be weaving your baskets as quickly as we do."

Red Willow snatched her supplies back up, and begrudgingly started weaving again. "I doubt that."

As she watched Red Willow slowly fumble her way through the weaving, Eternal Blossom thought it might be a good time to bring up the thorny subject of Gray Dove. "I know about your etsi. She told me about the pain she has been having and the visit to the medicine man. I want you to know that If things get tough, you will be able to count on me."

Red Willow abruptly stopped and turned to face her aunt. "What visit to the medicine man?" she asked.

Eternal Blossom moved her fingers to the bridge of her nose and let out a deep sigh. "I guess she hasn't told you yet," she replied, unable to look her niece in the eye. Another deep sigh arose from her chest. "It's not my place to tell you, but since I messed that up already I might as well. She went to see the medicine man about her recent health issues and he gave her some unfortunate news."

"Unfortunate news?" Red Willow snapped, her heart rate ramping up. "What do you mean?"

"He does not think . . ." Eternal Blossom looked downward, shaking her head, ". . . he does not think it will be long for her in our world."

Red Willow slowly dropped her tools and hunched over, burying her face in her palms. Eternal Blossom moved in close and gently rubbed her back. The two shared an infinite moment of sadness, squeezed into only a few minutes of silence.

Eternal Blossom finally spoke, her voice wistful. "Sometimes the best thing we can do for our hurting loved ones is just be there. And I plan to be there for all of you."

Her aunt's reassurances warmed Red Willow's heart. She lifted her head to reveal moist red eyes and sniffled away the remaining tears. Eternal Blossom hugged her tightly, sending a fleeting feeling into her soul that she should share her secret. But how do you tell someone that your brother murdered their husband? And how would her aunt react? She knew Eternal Blossom did not like her late husband, but it might be too much for her to hear that her nephew had murdered him. The feeling of wanting to share slipped away as fast as it had come, leaving Red Willow to hold her secret a little while longer.

Red Willow finished her basket just as Gray Dove returned to the hut with the children. Gray Dove was panting heavily. "They wore me out. I had to come back in and rest."

"We just finished up here," Eternal Blossom smiled. "Why don't I take the children home and give you some time to rest."

The following day Red Willow awoke with intentions of checking on White Owl. It had been a few days since the ordeal, and she thought he might be more settled in and able to take visitors. She cautiously ambled over to his hut and poked her head through the doorway.

"May I enter?" Red Willow asked White Owl's mother.

White Owl's mother greeted Red Willow and waved her into the hut. White Owl stirred and turned around to face Red Willow. The two exchanged an awkward greeting, Red Willow looking down at the wound on his side to see how it was healing. It was still mangled, filled with dried blood and pus.

Red Willow rubbed her hands together anxiously. "I'm sorry for what happened to you. I wish you had not gone on the rescue mission."

"I don't regret what I did, and I would do it again if I had the choice," White Owl replied. "The wound will heal in time, but you cannot replace your udo."

Red Willow swayed her body gently from side to side. "You risked your life to save ours, and I am eternally grateful for it."

White Owl's side was starting to hurt, and he readjusted himself in the hammock. "So, how is your udo?"

Red Willow ran her hands through her hair. "He's still a little shaken. Hopefully, he will not cause any more trouble. We've had quite enough of that recently."

"Well, it was not his fault that he got kidnapped," White Owl replied.

Red Willow drew her lips tightly to her face and her eyes began to dart around the room, pausing a few seconds each time they landed on White Owl's mother sitting in the corner. White Owl sensed that Red Willow had more to say that couldn't be said in the presence of his mother.

"Etsi," White Owl said with a nod of the head to his mother. "May Red Willow and I have some time alone?"

White Owl's mother clenched her teeth and let out an aggravated grunt. She pushed herself up slowly from her seat and indignantly shuffled out of the hut. Once she was comfortably out of earshot, Red Willow relaxed her face and released a heavy sigh.

"It *is* his fault that he got kidnapped! If he had not crossed the river, none of this would have happened. And that's not the only thing he has done."

White Owl furrowed his brow. "What do you mean?"

Red Willow interlocked her palms and began gently massaging them together. She was hesitant to reveal what Running Wolf had done, but she knew she needed to build trust with the man who had saved her brother and wanted to be her husband. "If I tell you, you must promise to keep it a secret. Can you promise?"

White Owl nodded in agreement. Red Willow leaned over and whispered, "Howling Coyote's death was not an accident."

White Owl turned his head sharply and craned his neck. "Howling Coyote fell and drowned in the river."

"No," Red Willow said quietly, "that is not what happened." Her face was flushed, and she began shaking. White Owl reached over to comfort her, but she pushed him away.

White Owl folded his arms. "If he did not fall and drown, then what happened."

"My udo . . ." Red Willow's voice trailed off.

"Your udo what?"

Red Willow slumped her shoulders and turned away. "Running Wolf killed Howling Coyote. He struck him with a rock, then pushed him in the water and drowned him." This all seemed to come out in one breath.

White Owl's mouth was agape. He could not fathom the idea of young Running Wolf being a cold-blooded killer. White Owl wondered what kind of family situation he might be getting himself into by courting Red Willow.

"But everyone, even Eternal Blossom, believes that Howling Coyote's death was an accident," White Owl said, still stunned by what he had heard.

"Yes, that's what everyone thinks. But I know differently." Red Willow turned back to face White Owl. "I saw with my own two eyes."

White Owl's eyes went wide. "You *witnessed* the murder?!" He could not believe what he was hearing.

Red Willow nodded softly. "I know what you are thinking. Please don't judge my udo. He had reasons for doing what he did. Our agidutsi was not a good man. He hurt my etsi, and Running Wolf just wanted to protect her."

"What do you mean that your agidutsi hurt your etsi?"

Red Willow's breath quickened. "He hit her on a regular basis. His anger was often out of control."

White Owl turned his head and stared into the distance, taking in the intense stream of information from Red Willow. "I guess that makes it easier to understand. But murder is still murder. If the tribe finds out what happened, they will demand a life for a life. What are you going to do?"

"I think the right thing to do is confess it at the Green Corn Ceremony," Red Willow whispered. "I'm uneasy about doing it that way, but I had a vision that things would work out if I told the truth. I don't know what that means, but I think I have to trust it."

White Owl raised his voice in defense of Running Wolf. "If you tell the truth, that will spell doom for your udo."

"Maybe not," Red Willow replied. "Maybe the tribe is ready to show mercy. Maybe that's what the Great Spirit has in mind."

White Owl let out a deep sigh. "I do not envy you, Red Willow. It is a difficult situation. I pray for you that things will go in the best way possible."

"Thanks," Red Willow replied. "So that you know, you are the first person with whom I have shared this. That is how much I trust you."

White Owl nodded, his eyes closed. "I appreciate your trust. It makes me feel good to know that you trust me in this way."

White Owl and Red Willow sat awkwardly for a moment before White Owl changed the subject. "I have something I want you to give your udo." He pointed to his chunkey spear, the one that Running Wolf had coveted. "He seemed to be very fond of it when we met on the field for a game earlier this moon cycle. I won't be able to use it at the games this year."

White Owl's offer warmed Red Willow's heart. "I'm sure he will appreciate it. Wa do," Red Willow replied with gratitude, "for everything." Red Willow leaned over and kissed White Owl on the cheek before leaving. White Owl immediately felt a rush of adrenaline throughout his body, temporarily blunting his pain.

Chapter Seven
Soaring Eagle

S ummer had arrived, and the garden growth was in its dynamic phase. Ears of corn were cropping up, bulging out from the stalks. Tiny pods peppered the beanstalks, with small beans beginning to bulge out—like a little fetus in a pregnant belly. Blooms arose left and right on the squash plant, with fruit swelling from the tips. It was almost as if the Great Spirit were painting a beautiful piece of art with the growing plants. The corn was nearly ready for harvest, which meant it would soon be time for the Green Corn Ceremony. But before the Green Ceremony came the annual chunkey competition.

Running Wolf had been pouring his heart into practicing with the new spear White Owl had given him. His obsession grew more intense as the competition drew closer.

"How are you feeling about the games, son?" Gray Dove asked Running Wolf one night as he returned from practice to eat dinner with his family.

Running Wolf did not look up from his food. "Good."

Gray Dove grunted, annoyed by her son's inattentiveness. "I'm sure you will do well. But whatever happens, know that we are proud of you."

Running Wolf wanted so badly to feel that his family could be proud of him, but his secret shame kept the feeling from soaking into his soul. A win at this year's games would give his family a reason to be proud. Thoughts of the impending contest flooded his mind, leaving him unable to think about anything else.

"May I be excused to go practice?" Running Wolf asked.

Gray Dove was agitated that Running Wolf was asking to leave yet again. "Didn't you just get in from practicing?"

"Please?" Running Wolf asked again.

"Just go," Gray Dove huffed. "But no practice after the next sunrise. You need to clear your head for a day."

"Fine." Running Wolf rushed outside.

Gray Dove turned her attention to her daughter. "How are things with White Owl?"

Red Willow sighed lightly. "He's still in a lot of pain, but his wounds are healing."

Gray Dove prodded her daughter for more information. "I notice you have been going to see him almost every day."

Red Willow squinted, aware of Gray Dove's probing mission. "I just want to check on him to make sure he is healing, that's all. And besides, he needs some companionship. He has to sit around all day doing nothing while he recuperates. It is incredibly boring for him."

"Well, I'm glad to hear that he is improving," Gray Dove said. "Have you reconsidered his proposal?"

Red Willow leaned in towards her mother. "He hasn't proposed again," she snickered, before quickly changing the subject. "How about you? How are you feeling?"

Gray Dove pursed her lips. "The pain never stops, and I have some strange new growths around my shoulder. And I am always so, so tired. But rest always helps."

Her mother's confession of her deteriorating health sent uneasy feelings radiating throughout Red Willow's body. Her stomach clenched and her heart sped up, as she was petrified at the thought that she might soon lose her mother. Knowing that she needed to be strong when her mother couldn't, Red Willow slowly regained her composure. She put her arm on her mother's shoulder, gripping it reassuringly. Gray Dove took her daughter by her hand and kissed it. "Bless you, my little ayoli. I think I'm going to lie down now."

Competition day arrived, and Running Wolf was pacing around the hut and pumping his fists in a strange mixture of excitement and anxiety. In just a few short hours, the villagers would be gathering in the town courtyard to watch sixteen young braves compete to see who would be crowned this season's chunkey champion. The competition consisted of a series of head-to-head matchups, with the winner of each match advancing until only one competitor was left standing.

Gray Dove stepped in front of Running Wolf and grabbed him by the arms. "Slow down, uwetsi. You need to relax before the competition." She pulled out her tobacco pipe and asked Running Wolf to sit with her. "Let us give our prayers to the Great Spirit for a successful day."

She packed the pipe with tobacco and said a short prayer before lighting the tube and taking a big inhale. She then passed it to Running Wolf, and he repeated the exercise. Running Wolf felt the Great Spirit weaving the powers of intense focus directly into his soul. His anxiety slowly faded, replaced by a deep feeling of attentive readiness.

The family headed to the town courtyard for the start of the games, entering to the sound of loud drumbeats and chanting that vibrated the earth underneath their feet. The rhythmic and pounding pulse of the drums resembled the beating of one giant heart, representing the collective heartbeat of all the Pee Dee souls. The competitors gathered at one end of the courtyard, with the crowd on the opposite side. Running Wolf took his spot among the competitors just as the tribal council leader stepped into the middle of the area.

The crowd drew eerily silent. "We gather here today for this competition to honor the Great Spirit, who gives us courage and strength," the leader's voice echoed into the near-silent courtyard. "These competitors will use these gifts to battle and see who will emerge victoriously. Let the competition begin."

An uproarious cheer from the crowd shattered the silence, and the first two competitors took the field. Running Wolf's match was the last one of the first round. He used the delay to scout his potential opponents, but his anxiety crept back in as the first-round matches wore on and his time drew closer. The penultimate game ended, and it was now his turn to play.

Running Wolf entered the field of play with his heart racing and all eyes in the village on him. The crowd placed wagers amongst themselves, and murmurs rose from within their ranks. Running Wolf walked up and stood face to face with his competitor, and the two combatants exchanged greetings by placing their hands on each other's shoulders. Then they nodded, released their hands, and moved to their separate sides. The tribal council leader grabbed the stone and rolled it down the center of the field. Running Wolf watched the stone rolling, trying to gauge its trajectory, and waited for the precise moment to send his spear flying. He cocked his spear behind his head and flung it with great force. Unfortunately, his grip was too tight, and he held the spear much too long on his follow-through, causing it to land embarrassingly short of the target. The murmurs among the crowd started to get louder as they wondered aloud if the young brave was ready for this level of competition.

Running Wolf grabbed his spear and walked back to the starting line, banging his head with his fist in frustration. The public embarrassment that he had just endured multiplied his feelings of inadequacy. He closed his eyes and imagined himself sitting across from his father and hearing how proud Hunting Bear was of him, and this temporarily helped him regain his composure.

The next stone was rolled, and Running Wolf waited patiently for a few seconds before he cocked his spear back and sent it flying. This time his throw was pure, and he landed a dart, very close to the stopped stone, but his competitor had an equally impressive throw. The judge came out for the measurement and found Running Wolf's spear slightly farther away. Running Wolf had dug a quick two-point deficit for himself in the early stages of the contest, and he was going to have to find a way to dig himself out.

In round three Running Wolf found his footing, throwing a tight spiral within inches of the stone, cutting the deficit to one. The two competitors then exchanged points for the rest of the match until the score was tied at eleven points apiece, leading to a winner-take-all round. Running Wolf was intensely focused as the council leader rolled the stone, and the competitors aimed. The spears were launched through the air and swooped down at their targets like eagles swooping down upon their prey. The two spears landed almost precisely next to each other within a foot of the target. It would take a judge's ruling to determine the winner. The judge came out and studiously made his measurements. By a width of an eagle's feather, he declared Running Wolf the winner. Running Wolf pumped his fists in the air in celebration. As a show of respect, he turned to his competitor, placed his hand on the man's shoulder, and bowed. He walked off the field, feeling confidence like he never had before.

Building on the momentum from his first victory, Running Wolf won his next two matches with relative ease. The wins put him into the final match against Soaring Eagle, son of the tribal council leader and the defending champion from last year's games. Soaring Eagle was a haughty competitor who considered himself above all others. He was privileged due to his father's status, and he wanted everyone to know it.

Soaring Eagle was also physically imposing in every way save for one, an inadequacy that gave him much difficulty with the women of the tribe. He had a wild, unkempt mane of hair and smoky green eyes. Contrary to most of the tribe, he had splotches of hair sprinkled across his jawline as if he were some sort of ungroomed animal.

As he entered the field of play, Soaring Eagle refused to greet Running Wolf. Instead, he stretched out his arms to the heavens and stood facing the crowd. He was both revered and reviled. He lifted his spear above his head and plunged it straight down into the ground, indicating that he was ready for the match to begin.

The council leader rolled the first stone, and the competitors released their spears. Running Wolf's throw was true, landing just inches from the rock. Soaring Eagle's spear landed much further away, giving Running Wolf the early lead. Soaring Eagle stared down Running Wolf, almost to remind him that he had no business winning this match. The next stone was rolled, and Running Wolf had an excellent throw, landing closer to the stone than Soaring Eagle had, increasing his lead by another point. Soaring Eagle was furious that this little young brave was beating him.

The third stone was rolled, and Running Wolf's throw came closer yet again. By this time, Soaring Eagle had had enough. As the pair walked up the field to retrieve their spears, Soaring Eagle "accidentally" stepped on Running Wolf's spear, splintering it near the base. Examining the damage, Running Wolf found the spear to be unusable. He furiously shouted curses at Soaring Eagle, but Soaring Eagle paid him no mind. Running Wolf begged the judges to intervene, but none of them dared to call out the unfair behavior of the council leader's son. Running Wolf's only recourse was to grab his backup spear and continue the match.

With Running Wolf frustrated and using his backup spear, Soaring Eagle managed to run off eight consecutive points and take a commanding lead. Running Wolf rallied to win one more point before Soaring Eagle put him away with four successive points to score a twelve to four victory. A triumphant Soaring Eagle pumped his fist in the air as he stomped around the courtyard, shoving Running Wolf to the ground on his final pass.

Gray Dove watched from the crowd and saw her son's face in a way she had never seen it before, an angry scowl emanating from it like a predator stalking its prey. Running Wolf pushed himself quickly up from the ground and ran at Soaring Eagle, tackling him from behind. A crowd soon gathered to watch the emerging brawl. The two wrestled back and forth on the ground before Soaring Eagle managed to elbow Running Wolf in the ribs and loosen his grip. He then tossed Running Wolf to the side and towards the crowd's edge. Red Willow fought her way through the crowd to get to Running Wolf and pull him away before the melee escalated further.

"If you ever want to fight for yourself without relying on your agilvgi for help, come find me," Soaring Eagle shouted at Running Wolf as his father pulled him away.

Red Willow shot a glaring look towards Soaring Eagle. "Why don't you just take your victory and walk away, you evil snake."

Soaring Eagle began walking towards Red Willow. "What did you call me?"

Red Willow stood her ground. "You heard what I said."

Soaring Eagle walked directly up to where Red Willow stood and looked down at her. "You should not speak to your superiors with disrespect. You must learn your place."

Sensing the tension developing and wanting to prevent the situation from escalating, Soaring Eagle's father approached the group. He stared at Soaring Eagle with a steely gaze, indicating his disapproval. Soaring Eagle found himself under the spell of his father's critical nature once again, and he skulked away, head bowed.

✖ ✖ ✖

Soaring Eagle and his father had always had a complicated relationship. After Soaring Eagle's mother passed away while giving birth to her daughter when Soaring Eagle was two, his father was ill-equipped to deal with raising both an infant and a toddler. So, he sent Soaring Eagle and his infant sister to live with their aunt and uncle. His aunt and uncle were not overtly cruel; they just paid him very little attention. He was allowed to roam without boundaries, and worse, to misbehave without consequences.

Soaring Eagle's father only occasionally checked in on him, even though he lived nearby, on the other side of the woods. On the occasions that Soaring Eagle's father did manage to visit, he was always aghast at his son's erratic behavior and never afraid to let Soaring Eagle know what a source of shame he was to the family. This combination of neglect and shame created a toxic stew in the cauldron of Soaring Eagle's personality development.

✖ ✖ ✖

Red Willow and Running Wolf left the field with a smoldering anger and stomped back to their hut. Gray Dove sensed Running Wolf's frustrated disappointment and tried to console him. "I'm sorry you lost today. But I am still proud of how you competed."

Running Wolf scoffed, "How could you be proud of me? I lost."

"Life isn't always about wins and losses," his mother replied. "Life is about competing, even when the competition is difficult."

When they got home, Running Wolf violently punched his fist into a support post, startling Gray Dove and Red Willow. "Take it easy, udo," Red Willow said as she grabbed her brother's arms. "You don't want to hurt yourself."

"Oh, I don't want to hurt myself?" Running Wolf shouted. "Maybe I want to hurt that snake, Soaring Eagle!"

Gray Dove moved towards her enraged son. "What Soaring Eagle did today was wrong. But you can't let your anger towards him control you."

Running Wolf pulled away from Gray Dove and raised his palms into the air. "So, I'm just supposed to let him walk all over me and intimidate me?"

"No. You are supposed to stand up for yourself," Gray Dove spoke softly but firmly. "But the best way to do that is to recognize your internal strength and dignity and ignore other people's stupid and weak behavior. You are better than Soaring Eagle on the inside, but it will take time for you to realize it."

Running Wolf exhaled sharply, trying to rid himself of those internal spirits that provoked his anger. Gray Dove gingerly walked over and embraced him tightly. Skye lumbered over to the pair, trying to get his share of the affection, and the family shared a tender moment.

Chapter Eight
Ceremonial Preparations

The ears of corn in the garden had begun to ripen, and the Green Corn Ceremony was just around the corner. The newborn corn signaled to the tribe that it was time for rebirth, renewal, and a new year. A time to cast aside old things to make room for new and for all tribe members to confess their sins and forgive each other for their wrongs. Murder, however, was considered unforgivable, and therein lay Red Willow's problem. She had decided, based on her vision, to confess her uncle's murder, and to let the consequences play out, hoping for the best. And now that she'd made up her mind, there was no turning back.

On the day the ceremonial preparations were commencing, Red Willow decided to approach her brother to see if she could gauge his spirit. Gray Dove was outside washing their deerskin rug while Red Willow and Running Wolf were lying in their respective beds. Red Willow called out to her brother from across the room. "So, udo, how are you feeling about the ceremony?"

Running Wolf stared up at the ceiling, gently stroking Fyre's fur. "I'm fine," he said with a strangely carefree attitude. "Doda told me things would work out well for me in the end when I saw him during my spiritual journey."

Red Willow ran her hand slowly through her hair, surprised by her brother's revelation. On the surface, their spiritual visions were incompatible, hers telling her to turn Running Wolf in and his telling him that things would be fine. Red Willow had hoped that the tribe would show mercy to her brother for his crime if she revealed it, but that hope had been fading recently. If what her brother said was true, and their visions somehow aligned, mercy might be possible.

Gray Dove entered the hut and tried to rouse the children. "Let's go," she snapped, "we've got a lot to do."

Fyre instantly jumped down from Running Wolf's lap at the sound of Grey Dove's shrill voice. Red Willow and Running Wolf sluggishly pulled themselves out of their beds and listened to their mother bark orders. The first step in preparing for the Green Corn Ceremony was to discard all worn-out items that the family used daily. Running Wolf grabbed his old and tattered clothes and tossed them into the fire. He stood and watched as the flames consumed the pants he had worn on the day he killed Howling Coyote, wondering if his life, too, would soon be in ashes. Red Willow seized last year's leftover cornmeal and scattered it into the woods, looking on as a flight of pigeons swooped in quickly and devoured it. The image of the tossed-out supplies burned in her brain as she contemplated that she might have thrown away her only chance at romance. Gray Dove snatched up her old, leaky clay pot and smashed it into pieces. As she buried the shards in the ground, she considered her situation much like the pot. She was falling apart, losing her usefulness, and was likely to be buried soon.

After the family had discarded all the old things, Gray Dove placed a bundle of cedar sticks onto the central fire. The cedar smoke wafted through the air, filling the room and cleansing everything as it went. The spirit of purification permeating the atmosphere led Gray Dove to ask the children if they had anything they needed to confess in order to purify their souls. Running Wolf and Red Willow looked at each other out of the corner of their respective eyes, each wondering what the other was thinking at that moment. It took her a minute, but Red Willow answered her mother's question with a gentle shake of the head. Running Wolf looked on as his sister refused to disclose the secret they shared, and he knew his turn was coming. It should have been an easy "no" for him as well, save for one small detail—he was afraid to lie to his mother.

Gray Dove turned to Running Wolf. "What about you, uwetsi? Do you need to confess anything while we are here together? You know that anything can be forgiven . . . I mean most things anyway."

Running Wolf hesitated and began to curl his toes nervously. "I might have something to admit to," he said, looking down at his twitchy feet.

"You can tell us, uwetsi." Gray Dove reached out and took Running Wolf by the hand. "It will be fine, I promise."

Running Wolf closed his eyes and massaged the back of his neck. "I . . . I . . . I killed Howling Coyote," he blurted.

Red Willow's eyes opened as big as a luminous full moon. With the health issues Gray Dove was experiencing already, the last thing she needed was to hear this shocking news. She turned back towards Running Wolf and shoved him on the arm. "Have you lost your mind?"

"I'm done holding onto this secret," he said, flailing his arm violently, "and I want you to be done, too."

Gray Dove turned to Red Willow with a fiery gaze. "You *knew* about this?!"

Red Willow stammered for a bit, but the words would not come. Gray Dove refocused her attention back to Running Wolf. "Do you know what kind of danger you put yourself in?"

Running Wolf shrugged, as if nothing concerned him. "Doda told me in a spiritual vision that everything would work out fine, so I'm not worried."

"A spiritual vision? Ahh, that is why you sought out the medicine man. What exactly did Hunting Bear tell you?" Gray Dove asked, eyes focused on her son.

"He told me that the debt for the murder would have to be repaid but that all would be well in the end."

Gray Dove dropped her head into her hands. "I do not know how all can be well. The tribe will not stand for this if they find out. I need some time to make sense of everything I have heard. Leave me . . . both of you!"

Red Willow and Running Wolf went outside to sleep. Gray Dove sat down by the fire and filled her pipe. Lighting it, she sent the smoke up as an offering to the Great Spirit, along with prayers for her son's forgiveness and petitions for guidance on what she should do next. She sat motionless in the smoke-filled room, the weight of Running Wolf's admission slowly dropping on her shoulders like a heavy travois. She breathed a heavy sigh when no immediate answers to her prayers were forthcoming. It seemed as though she was going to have to go it alone when facing the monumental decisions that awaited at the upcoming ceremony.

Gray Dove fell into a light sleep and found herself dreaming, as she often did, about the child that she had lost. Her stillborn child appeared to her as a toddler in the dream, running around, laughing, and playing. In previous dreams, she had tried and failed to get the attention of her unborn son, but this night's dream was different. For the first time Gray Dove could remember, the child stopped its play and toddled over to her. Staring up at her for a moment, the child recognized Gray Dove's sadness and reached out to embrace her leg. She placed her hand on his shoulder and held him tight for what felt like an endless moment before releasing him to let him continue his play. A lightness of being filled Gray Dove's spirit, and she slept peacefully and easily the rest of the night. She awoke at daybreak to the sounds of chirping cicadas.

Soon after, Red Willow and Running Wolf ambled in from their night spent outdoors. "How did everyone sleep?" Gray Dove asked with a surprisingly cheerful tone.

Red Willow and Running Wolf exchanged confused looks, unsure why their mother was suddenly so tranquil. "Not great honestly," Red Willow snapped. "It seems like you slept good, although I don't see how that is possible."

"I didn't think it was going to be possible either," Gray Dove replied peacefully, "but the Great Spirit sent me a message in a dream that brought me immense comfort."

"At least one of us is feeling comfortable," Red Willow replied as she massaged her forehead.

"I don't know," Running Wolf chimed in, "I'm not feeling too bad either."

Red Willow rolled her eyes back in her head and stomped her foot. "I can't deal with you people right now. I'll be off in the garden. Come and get me when it is time to go."

It was the final day of preparation for the ceremony. The family's first task was a ritual bath in the river to cleanse and purify their bodies. They meandered down to the water, passing by many lush gardens filled with budding corn stalks. The dew-covered plants glistened in the sun's rays, radiating their particular brand of spirit-driven energy. Soaking in the plants' essence provided the family a mental clarity that was sorely needed. They reached the river to find many of the tribe already gathered; among their number was White Owl.

Delighted to see Red Willow, White Owl rushed over to greet her. "How are you doing?"

Red Willow shrugged her shoulders. "I've been better. I see your wound is healing nicely," she said as she gently rubbed her hand across his scarred torso.

White Owl looked down at Red Willow's hand caressing his disfigured trunk. "It will always be with me. But I take pride in it, carrying it as a symbol of my bravery in combat."

Red Willow squinted at White Owl and placed her palm above her eyebrows, trying to block out the streaming sunlight. "So, what are your plans now that you are returning to normal life?"

"I was given a vision of my future during my time in the spiritual plane after the medicine man administered the wysoccan," White Owl replied.

Red Willow interlocked her hands behind her back and rocked back and forth on the balls of her feet. "Was it a . . . good future?"

White Owl looked down at her and smiled. "It was everything I ever wanted."

Red Willow embraced White Owl tightly, and they held each other for a captivating instant before Red Willow let go. She turned and headed back towards her family, looking back and smiling at White Owl as she went. White Owl smirked and awkwardly raised his hand to bid her farewell.

Once the tribe members arrived at the river, the medicine man separated them into two groups, men in one and women in the other. Each group went to separate parts of the river, where the villagers undressed and entered the water one by one. An assistant to the medicine man was waiting for the people as they waded in, dunking the naked villagers and rubbing cedar ash on their foreheads. Upon completing this ritual bath, the villagers put on their new clothes for the year and returned to their huts.

Back at the hut, Gray Dove and the children completed their preparations. They put out their old central fire to make way for the new flame they would be getting at the ceremony and harvested a portion of their newly ripened corn as a gift offering. They gathered the belongings and dutifully trudged to the town courtyard in front of the temple. The entire tribe gathered inside the walled enclosure, each clan in a different spot. Gray Dove and the children gathered with the other bear clan members, including her sister Eternal Blossom, who threw her arms around Gray Dove as she entered the gathering. "How are you feeling?"

Gray Dove chuckled awkwardly. "Sick and tired. But I am glad to be here."

The clan members exchanged pleasantries and then began preparations for a shared meal. The clan leader, Spotted Turtle, gathered the clan's collective bounties, each family contributing as they were able. People donated turkey carcasses, fox meat, turtle soup, fresh blackberries, and plenty of corn. The women of the clan gathered the food gifts and began preparations for the luscious feast, leaving the men to sit and exchange stories about their hunting and fishing adventures. It took a few hours until the meal was fully prepared and ready to serve, but when it showed up there was no doubt it was worth the wait.

The group sat together in a large circle and partook of the dinner. The food was passed, smiles were shared, and pats on the back were plentiful. It was the kind of joyful and cohesive time that most everyone loves, save for one person—Red Willow. She was still burdened by the weight of the family secret, a burden that neither her mother nor brother shared. She looked on as the both of them participated in the revelry, her lips pursed in frustration.

The head of the clan, a burly man named Spotted Turtle, addressed the clan members as they were eating. He reminded them that all transgressions were to be confessed for the tribe to get a fresh start for the new year. The announcement was a stark reminder of what lay ahead for Gray Dove, Red Willow, and Running Wolf. The clan members shared a tobacco pipe as an offering to the Great Spirit and then retired for the evening.

Chapter Nine

The Green Corn Ceremony

At dawn on the ceremony's first day, each of the four clans built a large teepee-shaped wooden tower in the four corners of the courtyard. The four towers represented the four stages of life—birth, youth, adult, death—and reminded the tribe members that their lives were seasonal, just like the crops that sustained and nourished them. The towers were set on fire and left to burn throughout the ceremony, their rising smoke forming a large black plume tickling the highest clouds.

The women of the tribe began their preparations for the first ceremonial dance, adorning their legs with mussel shell rattles and filling gourds with dried beans to use as shakers. Red Willow and Eternal

Blossom participated this year, but Gray Dove was too weak to dance. The women gathered around the central area of the courtyard, where there was a large fire pit. They stomped their feet, shook their shakers, and chanted as they moved in a circular motion around the fire pit, forming a mighty chorus. Red Willow went through the motions at first, but the more she danced and chanted, the more swept up she became. With each successive stomp and chant, a tiny part of her individuality floated away, pushing her toward an ecstatic merger with the whole.

The men of the tribe looked on with reverence, holding the women in high regard as the life-giving energy of the tribe. Their dance around the fire pit was central to the ceremony, as it symbolized the pouring out of their enlivening spirit into the new year's fire. Symbology, however, was the last thing White Owl had on his mind as he watched the dance. Red Willow's body captivated him as she twirled around the fire, and he could barely restrain himself from jumping into the circle and dancing the day away with her.

After about an hour of dancing, exhaustion replaced ecstasy, causing Red Willow's motions to slow. Her breathing labored, her calves burning, she wondered if the dance was ever going to end. But before Red Willow was literally on her last legs, the dance leader called the women to a halt, deciding they had adequately prepared the pit to receive the new fire. Red Willow gingerly stumbled back to her clan and sunk down to rest. The village looked on as the medicine man lit the central ceremonial fire. The flame quickly set the giant brush pile in the middle of the pit ablaze, generating an impressive inferno. As the fire spread outward along four different brush pathways to each of the outer fire towers, it formed a flame hub with spokes radiating in four directions, symbolically burning away the old year.

After the women's dance, the men gathered to share the white drink. The medicine man prepared the white drink by boiling the leaves of the yaupon holly tree in a giant pot, producing an emetic concoction that the men would drink to cleanse themselves of the previous year's impurities. The tribal council leader was usually the first to partake, but he had fallen ill, and his son took his place. Soaring Eagle stepped up to the pot, dipped his cup, and took a big gulp. He then turned to the crowd of men, raised his arms as a show of dominance, and spit into the pot to "mark" his territory. The medicine man immediately grabbed a cup to scoop out the spit and chastised Soaring Eagle for disrupting the drink's purity. The rest of the men took turns partaking, with Running Wolf near the end of the line.

This was Running Wolf's first time, as he had finally come of age. He had heard stories about the white liquor, but nothing prepared him for what he was witnessing. Each of the men ahead of him was puking, most within mere feet of each other. The smell of the vomit was nauseating, and Running Wolf almost upchucked before even reaching the pot. When it came to his turn, he dipped his cup gently, taking only a tiny amount of the noxious liquid. He carefully sipped it before the medicine man encouraged him to tilt his head back and down it in one gulp. His throat burned as the tea moved down his esophagus, and his stomach uncontrollably cramped when it reached his gut. Those effects were relatively mild, however, compared to what came next. Running Wolf felt the contents of his stomach moving back up the same route that the tea had taken down before they erupted violently from his mouth. He bent over, put his hands on his knees, and wiped a tiny amount of leftover vomit from the corner of his mouth before another eruption came. By this time, Running Wolf was sweating and panting, waiting for another heave that never came. He now understood the true nature of purgation.

The women gathered for their ritual purification ceremony, forming a long single-file line in one corner of the courtyard. At the head of the line, holding an alligator garfish jawbone with exposed serrated teeth, stood the wife of the bear clan leader Spotted Turtle. As each woman approached the leader, she dragged the sharp and jagged teeth down their backs, creating several small gashes. Red Willow dutifully took her turn, stepping up to the head of the line and offering her back. The initial sting of the teeth caused her to arch her back in pain. As the woman raked the teeth down her back, she could feel the warm liquid beginning to drip from her wounds. An instant of pain, followed by a satisfying sense of relief.

The afternoon arrived, and it was time for the confession of wrongdoings. The villagers regrouped into their clans and sat in a circle around their respective fires. Spotted Turtle gave a speech, reminding the bear clan members of the importance of treating each other with respect and honoring the tribe's values, which formed the basis for their survival as a group. After his uplifting speech, he encouraged the clan members to speak out about any grievances or wrongs they had committed against the tribe. Several people spoke up about minor offenses they had perpetrated, such as stealing and lying. Spotted Turtle promised them that the Great Spirit would forgive them.

After a moment of silence, Spotted Turtle asked if any others needed to confess anything. Red Willow trembled like a leaf in the wind, as she knew the time had come for her to speak out. Running Wolf was eyeing his sister, observing her agitated state, and hoping she would not say anything. Suddenly an afternoon thunderstorm rolled in. Just as the skies darkened, and the thunder clapped, Gray Dove stood up swiftly.

"I have to confess to the murder of Howling Coyote." As she spoke, the rain began to pour.

A look of horror crossed Red Willow's face, and she grabbed her mother, trying to pull her to the ground. "What are you *doing*?!"

Gray Dove looked down at her daughter with an oddly serene visage. "You know that sinners must confess all crimes, my ayoli, no matter who committed them. Your doda believed this, as do I."

Running Wolf rocked back and forth on the ground. "You can't do this, Etsi!"

Gray Dove placed her hand on her son's shoulder. "We must do everything we can to keep our family safe. Your doda showed us how important that is and now I am following in his footsteps."

The clan was abuzz at the startling revelation. Spotted Turtle wasn't sure he had heard Gray Dove correctly, so he asked her to repeat herself. "I killed Howling Coyote," she shouted. "His death was not an accident."

Spotted Turtle had no time to reflect on Gray Dove's confession, as the shocked clan members started to grow unruly. He had to take control. He summoned two men to take Gray Dove into custody, and they escorted her to a small hut outside the walled courtyard. As the guards were whisking her away, she passed her stunned sister. "I'm sorry it had to be this way, agilvgi. Please forgive me."

Eternal Blossom swelled with a rage she could barely contain. She was angry not with her sister but the system of retribution that would pit her and her beloved sister against one another. She knew her husband had been a scoundrel who got what he deserved, but she was not ready to face the task laid out for her by her sister's confession. How could she ever be ready to take her sister's life, even as justice for the murder of her husband? The rain was pouring now, lightning and thunder crashing. The tribe members searched for cover, except for Running Wolf, Red Willow, and Eternal Blossom. The three stood together, oblivious of the downpour, a frightened family exchanging looks of incomprehension.

At dawn on the second day of the ceremony, the clan leaders gathered at the temple mound to discuss matters of tribal importance. Presiding over the council meeting, due to his father's illness, was Soaring Eagle. Also present were Spotted Turtle, the leader of the beaver clan, Walking Squirrel, and the leader of the deer clan, Proud Robin. The agenda for the meeting was this year's corn crop status and a request for additional fencing to provide a better defense against raiding parties.

After the council had discussed all the other business, Spotted Turtle cleared his throat and rose to speak. "There is also the matter of a murder confession that I received from one of my clan last night."

Soaring Eagle immediately chimed in, eager to discuss retributive punishment. "Yes, we have heard about Gray Dove. Astonishing for a woman to confess murder. But our laws are clear. The punishment for taking a life is that you will have yours taken. There cannot be harmony within the tribe as long as Howling Coyote's spirit roams the earth in anguish while his murderer walks free."

Proud Robin stroked his chin before delivering a measured response. "I fear we must not be so hasty. We haven't had to deal with a murder in a very long time, and never, to my knowledge, by a woman. Laws are meant to do more than punish; they are meant to hold our tribe together. We must meditate on this before making a decision. The law also says that we may banish the murderer from the tribe if we so choose."

Spotted Turtle nodded vigorously. "I agree. Not only is Gray Dove a female. She is also sick with perhaps very little time left. It doesn't feel right to me to sentence her to death."

Soaring Eagle looked directly at Spotted Turtle. "Doesn't *feel* right? Your feelings are not important. The council must uphold the law of the tribe if we are going to survive. She must be put to death, even if she is a female and even if she is already dying."

The sycophantic Walking Squirrel sidled up to the source of his admiration. "I have to say that I side with Soaring Eagle. It is foolish to ignore the laws of the tribe just because they make us feel," he sneered at Spotted Turtle, "uncomfortable. They are there to protect us, and the council must uphold them. We should sentence Gray Dove to death for her crime."

"Looks like it's two against two," Soaring Eagle shot a glance at Spotted Turtle. "You know how we settle tie votes."

Spotted Turtle closed his eyes and nodded his head. It was an uneasy feeling for him to leave the fate of one of his clan members to chance, but rules are rules. "Summon him."

Soaring Eagle sent Walking Squirrel out to get the medicine man and then stomped to one corner of the tribal council hut. He retrieved a small clay saucer containing one black rock and one white rock and returned to where Proud Robin and Spotted Turtle were seated. The group sat together in awkward silence as they awaited the arrival of the medicine man. After a few moments, Walking Squirrel reentered the hut, with the medicine man close behind.

"I hear that you need the assistance of the Great Spirit," the medicine man grumbled.

"I'm sure you have heard by now that we have a murderer among us, Holy One," Soaring Eagle said as he paced the floor. "The council cannot reach a decision on how to handle this situation. Some of us want to go against our common laws," he said, focusing his gaze on Spotted Turtle.

The medicine man turned to Spotted Turtle. "Is this true?"

Spotted Turtle leaned back in his seat. "Something does not feel right about this situation. I am not ready to sacrifice one of my clan members to satisfy blood lust . . . and I believe my fellow council member Proud Robin is with me." Proud Robin nodded his head affirmatively.

The medicine man looked towards Walking Squirrel. "And you?"

Walking Squirrel looked up at Soaring Eagle, ensuring him of his unwavering support. Then he turned to the medicine man. "I side with Soaring Eagle. I believe Gray Dove should be put to death for her crime as our laws clearly state. It shouldn't even be a question."

The medicine man rubbed his face gently. "If you all truly cannot agree, we will let the Great Spirit decide. Bring me the cup."

Spotted Turtle handed the medicine man the saucer containing the differently colored rocks. "So that we are all clear, there are two options. A drawing of the black rock means that Gray Dove will be sentenced to death and a drawing of the white rock means that Gray Dove will be sentenced to banishment from the tribe."

The men nodded their heads in agreement. The medicine man looked upwards and whispered a barely audible prayer to the Great Spirit, asking that His will would be done. Then he cupped his hand over the top of the saucer and shook it vigorously. Reaching his hand gently into the bowl, he pulled out a rock, and grasped it in his fist tightly. The men stared intently at the rigidly clenched fist, waiting to see what the will of the Great Spirit would be. The medicine man slowly released his grip, revealing black.

A maniacal smile crossed Soaring Eagle's face, while Spotted Turtle slumped his shoulders in defeat. "The Great Spirit has spoken," the medicine man bellowed before turning to leave.

Soaring Eagle hastily stalked past Spotted Turtle, bumping him in the shoulder. "At the setting of the sun, we will have an execution. Send word to your clans."

Spotted Turtle left the council meeting dejected and uneasy, returning to his clan to deliver the devastating news. He gathered his people together in a semi-circle, standing front and center, and took a deep breath. "The council has reached a decision about our sister Gray Dove. Under much protest, she has been sentenced to die. The execution will take place under the moonlight tonight."

Running Wolf felt a sharp pain explode in his stomach as if a stampeding deer had kicked him. He collapsed to the ground in a heap and pounded his fists repeatedly into the earth. Eternal Blossom's motherly instincts kicked in and she rushed over to comfort him, even as she was completely unraveling. Red Willow's blood raced as she shook her head, refusing to accept the reality of the situation. She bolted from the group, hoping to discover her mother's whereabouts, frantically rushing from place to place. She finally stumbled upon her mother's makeshift prison and begged and pleaded with the guards to free her mother. But the guards were unmoved, and Gray Dove remained in captivity. Crestfallen, Red Willow sat down on the ground and placed her head between her knees.

The tribe gathered around the central fire pit for the men's stomp dance late in the afternoon. Before the dance, Soaring Eagle stood up in front of the crowd to announce Gray Dove's execution. "It is my unpleasant duty to report that we have a murderer among us," he said in a voice befitting the disingenuous politician he was becoming. "Gray Dove has confessed to the murder of Howling Coyote. The council will punish her according to the laws of the tribe following the end of the stomp dance. Please pray to the Great Spirit during the dance that He will use our steps to cleanse the tribe."

Murmurs and whispers spread throughout the crowd, silenced only by the intense rattle shaking of the dance leader, signifying the start of the dance. A drummer pounded on a large drum, echoing and amplifying the beat. The men shuffled and stomped their feet in an alternating rhythmic pattern as they circled the ceremonial fire. The male dance leader let out a bellowing chant, which the other men echoed. The coordinated stomping and shuffling continued as the sun moved its way further down the horizon, inching closer to the moment of awful truth for Gray Dove and her sister.

The men's dance stopped when the fiery reddish-yellow sphere was within a mere few feet of dipping below the horizon. *The time had come.* The villagers gathered in the courtyard, eager for a blood sacrifice. Soaring Eagle made his way up the steps to the top of the temple mound and called down for Eternal Blossom to join him. Eternal Blossom slowly made her way to the mound's base, head held low to conceal her tears from the crowd. She lurched up the steps, her body shaking the entire way. When she reached the top of the mound, she nearly collapsed as Soaring Eagle gave her a devious smile and head nod. Eternal Blossom shuddered in revulsion and searched for a spot far away from Soaring Eagle's menacing presence.

Soaring Eagle began his oration, seeming oddly gleeful to be presiding over such a solemn event. "Blood has been spilled by the hands of one of our tribe members. It has created an imbalance in the life force of our tribe, and the spirit of one of our tribe members now roams the earth without peace. Today, we are here to restore balance to our tribe and send Howling Coyote's spirit to the afterlife where he can rest in peace."

Soaring Eagle called to his guards to bring forth Gray Dove. She appeared, standing straighter and looking more robust than in weeks. Eternal Blossom and Gray Dove locked eyes. Suddenly Gray Dove pushed away from the guards and lunged towards her sister, trying to console her. But the guards held her tightly, and she was able only to tilt her head at Eternal Blossom. The moment's agony was too much, and Eternal Blossom burst into tears. Gray Dove whispered into her sister's ear, "It will be alright."

Eternal Blossom wiped her eyes, struggling to catch her breath. The sun was now halfway beneath the horizon, its scattered light beaming through the temple in a panorama of reflective colors. The guards placed Gray Dove on a stone bench in front of the temple and bound her feet and hands. With a light in his eyes, Soaring Eagle pulled out a deer antler dagger and offered it to Eternal Blossom. "Take this weapon and shed blood for the blood that has been shed so that the tribe will be whole again."

Eternal Blossom stood motionless.

"Take the weapon," he repeated, thrusting the handle towards her.

A look of misery crossed her face as she took the dagger and gazed down at her sister, lying exposed and helpless in front of her. Around Gray Dove's neck was the gorget Eternal Blossom had made for her.

Gray Dove noticed Eternal Blossom eyeing the gorget. "I want it with me when I arrive in the afterlife. I am proud to have such a fine piece of jewelry to display. I think Hunting Bear will love it."

Eternal Blossom's lip quivered as she struggled to find words. "You did . . . what you had to do. I forgive you."

"You have given me all I could ever want in a sister," Gray Dove continued, "and now you must do what you must do."

Eternal Blossom turned away from Gray Dove and gazed out at the crowd, their eyes fixed on her, some waiting with glee, others trembling with fear. She looked for her own children but found no sign. Red Willow had taken them back to the clan campsite so they would not have to witness what was about to unfold, and for that, Eternal Blossom was grateful. In the front row of the crowd below her stood Running Wolf, visibly trembling. She pitied her young nephew and wished desperately to comfort him.

"What are you waiting for?" Soaring Eagle shouted.

Eternal Blossom looked back at Gray Dove, whose eyes were closed and whose mouth whispered a prayer. There was no choice; if she did not do the unthinkable, Soaring Eagle would do it himself, she was sure of that. Better for her to do it mercifully than for her sister to die under Soaring Eagle's rage. Eternal Blossom lifted the dagger slowly over her head, suppressing the unbearable scream crying out inside her. With the blade at its apex above her head, she paused, hopeful there would be some interruption from the Great Spirit. A stiff breeze blew across the courtyard, knocking her slightly off balance.

"Now!" Soaring Eagle screamed.

Gathering herself again, she raised the dagger above her head. But before she could begin to bring it down, a voice cried out from the crowd.

"Stop!"

It was Running Wolf. "You cannot do this. She is innocent. I killed Howling Coyote."

The dagger dropped to the ground from her limp hand as a stunned Eternal Blossom turned towards the boy. In the confusion, Gray Dove thrashed about on the stone and freed herself enough to look down on her son as he walked up to the temple's base with the sunlight surrounding him in a full-body halo.

Soaring Eagle glared down at Running Wolf, furious at the interruption. "What is the meaning of all this?" He moved to pick up the dagger.

Gray Dove turned towards Soaring Eagle, trying to distract his attention away from her son. "Pay no attention to the atsutsa. An evil spirit possesses him. My blood is the blood you want."

"Silence!" Soaring Eagle barked as he motioned his guards to tackle Running Wolf. "Bring the atsutsa here to me."

Gray Dove watched in horror as the guards grabbed Running Wolf and brought him to Soaring Eagle. The two stood face to face. "Are you telling the truth, atsutsa?" Soaring Eagle asked Running Wolf, examining him closely. "Are you a murderer?"

"Yes. You have to let my etsi go." Running Wolf's gaze turned towards his mother, who was still bound and kneeling next to the stone.

Gray Dove shook her head towards Running Wolf and pleaded with Soaring Eagle. "Do not listen to him. He is lying."

Soaring Eagle clenched his teeth as the veins in his neck started throbbing. He growled, and then a look of contentment came over his face. "I have the answer. Since neither of you can agree on who the murderer is, then we will kill both of you."

The crowd gasped in unison. Spotted Turtle, who had been sitting quietly in the background watching the events unfold, finally spoke up. "No! That is not how the law works. The taking of two lives creates another imbalance. Only one life must be taken for the balance to be restored. You cannot . . . and *will not* kill them both."

Soaring Eagle threw his arms up in the air. "I must uphold the law. Someone must die here. What do you suggest I do?"

Proud Robin interjected from his seat next to Spotted Turtle. "The only alternative to death is banishment. If we do not know the true identity of the murderer, then we have no cause for killing, but we must remove the murderer from our presence to rebalance the life force in our tribe. If we banish them both into the wild, it will be up to the Great Spirit to decide the murderer's punishment."

Soaring Eagle picked up the dagger, switching it from hand to hand. Seeking a vote he knew would be in his favor, he turned to Walking Squirrel. "What say you, Walking Squirrel?"

Walking Squirrel stared timidly at Soaring Eagle. His instinct was to support him, but something buried deep within his spirit came forward. "I think we should banish them rather than execute them."

Soaring Eagle stomped his foot in anger before relenting to the will of the other council members. "Then," he said, throwing the dagger to the ground, "banishment it will be."

He called for his guards to release Gray Dove and escort her and Running Wolf out of the village. The pair were blindfolded and marched back down the steps towards the gathered crowd. The crowd jeered as they approached. Some even spat on them as the guards paraded them through the throng. Eternal Blossom watched from the top of the temple mound with tears as the guards led her beloved sister and nephew out of the village. Soaring Eagle dismissed the crowd back to their clan encampments with a reminder that the ceremony would continue at sundown.

Exhausted, broken down, and emotionally shredded, Eternal Blossom returned to the bear clan camp. Red Willow rushed out to meet her. "What happened?" she demanded.

Eternal Blossom stared blankly at Red Willow, incapable of providing her anything more than the bare facts. "Banished. Both of them."

Red Willow grabbed Eternal Blossom by her shoulders and looked her directly in the eyes. "What do you mean 'both of them?'"

"Your mother and your brother."

Red Willow let go of her aunt and clutched her hand to her chest. "That . . . that can't be possible."

Eternal Blossom nodded. Red Willow grabbed a clod of dirt and flung it into the distance. Then she began stomping around in circles. Her blood boiled. "I must do something," she screamed at her aunt. *But what?*

Red Willow rushed to the end of the courtyard but found Soaring Eagle had placed it under heavy guard to prevent any further disturbances from disrupting the rest of the ceremony. Looking for another way out, she hurried towards the fence and desperately tried to climb it. Unable to get a tight enough grip, she could not pull herself over. As a last-ditch effort, she tried to squeeze between the fence posts, but she could not find an opening through which she could fit. She screamed and kicked at the fence in frustration until she exhausted herself.

At dusk, all the clans gathered around the central ceremonial fire for the burning of the green corn. Each villager brought forth their newly harvested corn and chucked it into the fire as an offering to the Great Spirit to ensure a successful harvest for the upcoming season and to purify the tribe from last year's transgressions. The smoke from the fire grew higher and higher from each successive addition of corn until the last bit was added and the smoke reached into the very arms of the Great Spirit. The men dressed in their brightest plumage and performed the feather dance around the enormous blaze to signify that all things had been refreshed and made new. They danced well into the night while the women began preparations for the fast-breaking meal.

Meanwhile, Gray Dove and Running Wolf were being led, bound and blindfolded, deep into the woods. When the moon reached its apex, the guards stopped marching, left the two alone, and returned to camp. Sensing that the guards were gone, Running Wolf managed to free himself from his bonds and then unbound his mother. They found themselves together in the pitch-black of the deep forest, with no sense of direction.

Running Wolf looked at Gray Dove with shame in his eyes. "I'm sorry I messed up, etsi. I've ruined everything." Gray Dove did not care what her baby boy had done wrong; all that mattered was that he was still alive. She threw her arms around him and embraced him tightly.

Chapter Ten

Into the Wilderness

At dawn on the third day of the ceremony, all the clans came together and broke their fast with a shared meal of corn cakes and deer roast. Everyone at the feast was in a celebratory mood, except Eternal Blossom and Red Willow. They were present in body but absent in spirit, standing off to the side and not partaking. After the villagers finished the meal, the renewal of the household fires completed the ceremony. Each female head of household gathered a long piece of kindling and went to the central ceremonial fire to take a flame from it to rekindle their household fires. Eternal Blossom knew the importance of the new fire and summoned the motivation to participate, though she moved slowly, as if a great weight rested on her shoulders. She tried to rouse Red Willow. "You are now the head of your household. You must get the newly consecrated flame for your home."

Red Willow waved her off. "I have no home . . . and I have to protect my family."

"Tell me you aren't thinking about rescuing them? If the council catches you, they will punish you harshly."

Red Willow stared into the distance. "I will do what needs to be done."

Eternal Blossom sighed, knowing she was powerless to stop Red Willow, and went with the other women to obtain her flame. Once all the women had their flames, they led a grand procession of all the tribe members out of the courtyard and back to their homes. Soaring Eagle watched the parade from the top of the temple mound.

"Keep an eye on Red Willow," Soaring Eagle said to his guards as he looked down upon the crowd. "Make sure she doesn't try to do anything that would go against the council's decision."

Red Willow returned to her family hut to find Skye and Fyre waiting. Intent on going into the woods to find her mother and brother, she gathered some supplies and hurried to leave the hut. But the instant she crossed the threshold, she noticed Soaring Eagle's guards watching her. She stomped back into the hut and threw her supplies to the ground.

Then it dawned on her that the guards watched her, but they weren't watching Skye. If she could just get Skye to her family with some supplies . . . Red Willow took her provisions, bundled them up, and saddled them onto Skye. Then she grabbed Running Wolf's spear and Gray Dove's pottery paddle and let Skye smell them so he could pick up their scent. She could tell Skye was eager. As he left the hut in one direction, she took off in the other, figuring the guards would track her and not notice Skye.

Soaring Eagle returned to his father's hut to check on him and finish what only he knew he had started. The medicine man greeted Soaring Eagle as he entered the house. "It is not looking good," the medicine man said, placing his hand gently on Soaring Eagle's shoulder. "If you have anything to say to your father, say it now." The medicine man left, leaving Soaring Eagle alone with his father.

Soaring Eagle's father was struggling to catch his breath. With a strangely unconcerned look, Soaring Eagle leaned over and whispered, "I hate to see you like this, doda. I wish it didn't have to be this way."

His father grunted.

"But in the end," Soaring Eagle smiled, "you were just too weak to lead this tribe the way it needs to be led."

His father's eyes widened.

"It was time for some new blood, Doda, so," Soaring Eagle's smile turned into a grin, "I poisoned your tea with a heaping amount of honeysuckle berries before the ceremony."

Again, his father tried to say something but could only emit a choked breath.

"But you can sleep well knowing that the tribe is in good hands—the hands of a leader who will make the tough decisions when they need to be made."

Soaring Eagle slowly placed one hand tightly over his father's mouth and pinched his nose with the other. His father's eyes grew even wider as he stared at his son in horror, too weak to fight back. His body shuddered and sputtered until it went still. Removing his hands from his father's lifeless body, Soaring Eagle gazed down at the corpse. He pursed his lips tightly, and a single tear trickled down his cheek. *What was this strange sadness?* He used all his energy to push it back down and forced his mouth into a satisfied smile. He had learned the hard way that his emotions were not to be trusted.

✖✖✖

Deep in the forest, after a fitful night's rest, Running Wolf and Gray Dove were still trying to orient themselves and figure out how to survive. Running Wolf sat on the ground, nervously rocking back and forth. "We have to find our way back to the tribe."

"No!" Gray Dove shouted. "They will kill us both if we try to return!"

Running Wolf rubbed his hand across his nose as he continued rocking. "So, what now then?"

The wheels began to turn in Gray Dove's mind. "We are going west . . . to the Catawba tribe." She knew that the Catawba were hospitable, and their village was within a feasible walking distance. Still, it would be an arduous journey, especially with her physical limitations, but they might be taken in as refugees if they could only make it to the town.

Running Wolf turned to his mother with a concerned look. "You aren't serious? You will never make it there with the shape you are in."

Gray Dove looked at her son reassuringly. "I'll be fine," she said, knowing full well that she would not be. "We will need some food and water, so let's not waste any more time."

Gray Dove and Running Wolf remembered that they had heard the sound of running water on their march through the forest. They retraced their steps for about an hour before happening upon a small stream. The flowing water fell gently over large, flat rock outcroppings, and the trickling sound created a sense of calm and peace as they refreshed themselves with a cool drink.

By now their hunger pangs were kicking in, and with what energy they had remaining, they embarked on a mushroom foraging foray. The pair set out deep into the woods, searching for decomposing logs, which were prime habitats for the fungi they needed to sustain themselves. Running Wolf was several steps ahead of his mother, who was having trouble keeping up, when he stumbled upon a rotting log that was home to many mushrooms. Desperate with hunger, he grabbed some of the mushrooms and brought them to his face. As Gray Dove caught up with him, she stopped him with a shout. "Don't eat those!"

Running Wolf dropped the mushrooms and stared at his mother. He didn't understand why she was so angry.

With a stern voice, Gray Dove admonished him to stay close to her so that she could point out which mushrooms were edible and which were poisonous. He now learned the concept of being selective in what you ate in the forest, and he trembled for some time over how close he had come to death. They continued foraging until they found a log with some edible mushrooms, which they brought back to their spot beside the stream. There they sat by the rippling water and fed their ravenous hunger with the delectable fungi.

With the sun now low in the sky, Gray Dove suggested they set up camp where they were rather than pressing on. She did not tell her son how utterly exhausted she was. They rested peacefully for an hour or so before being disturbed by rustling leaves in the distance. Running Wolf's heart began thumping and he quickly grabbed a large stick to defend himself and his mother from whatever wild animal was approaching. He listened intently as the sound came nearer and nearer. Then he glimpsed something in the distance that made him think his eyes were playing a trick on him, but as the object got closer, he was overjoyed to see that it was no trick. Running Wolf rushed to meet his best friend Skye and gave him the biggest head rub ever. Skye jumped up onto Running Wolf's chest and licked him on the face. Gray Dove was happy to see Skye but even happier to see the supplies he had with him. She knew her son would need as much help as he could get on the next leg of the journey.

Gray Dove and Running Wolf lay down next to the stream, thoroughly spent. Running Wolf lay on his back, looking up at the moonlight scattered through the tree canopy. Gray Dove was on her side, with her back facing Running Wolf. He was still too troubled to sleep and had some questions rolling through his mind that he could no longer contain. "Why did this have to happen?"

Gray Dove yawned, dismissive of her son's serious question, and badly in need of sleep. "The Great Spirit wills it."

"Did the Great Spirit also make you suffer so much at the hands of Howling Coyote?"

Gray Dove tried again to shut the conversation down. "Some things are difficult to understand, uwetsi."

"What is so difficult to understand?" Running Wolf sniffled and wiped a few small tears from his eyes. "Howling Coyote deserved to die. That's what I understand."

Gray Dove sensed her son's guilt and sadness, and she turned to face him. "It's not your fault that we are here, atsutsa. I know you meant well."

"They were going to sacrifice you for something you did not do, something *I* did. So, it was my responsibility to come forward."

"But I was willing to let them sacrifice my life because I love you, uwetsi."

Running Wolf sighed deeply. "The tribe did not even want to know the truth about why Howling Coyote had to die."

"They are not about the truth, atsutsa," Gray Dove scoffed. "They are about balance. Whether what you did was just or unjust did not matter to them. Blood was spilled, and more blood had to be spilled to rebalance things. It is how the world works."

"I just wish it didn't have to be this way," Running Wolf lamented.

Gray Dove huddled up next to her son and put her head on his chest. "Me too, uwetsi. Me, too."

After a restful night's sleep, the newly formed trio set out on their westward trek. Coming upon a deep river, Running Wolf stopped, running his hands through his hair in frustration. "We can't cross here; it's too deep."

Gray Dove placed her hands on her hips, knowing that she had no time for detours. "Well, we have to find a way to make it work. Go back and look in the woods to see if you can find a fallen log that will be big enough for us to float across. I will look for a branch that we can use for paddling."

Mad at himself for not thinking of this, Running Wolf ran off to explore the woods in search of a suitably large log. Finding a good chunk of wood, he dragged it down to the riverbank and showed it to Gray Dove for her approval. She looked the log up and down and shrugged. "Let's give it a try."

Running Wolf positioned the log halfway into the water, straddled it, and slowly moved on, trying to stay steady. The front of the log began to sink a bit as he put more of his weight onto it, but he secured his grip and managed to stay upright. Gray Dove handed him the tree branch paddle and tried to direct Skye onto the log. Skye dug his large paws into the ground, mightily resisting any attempts by Gray Dove to move him. Gray Dove mustered what remained of her strength, picked up the reticent dog, and placed him on the log, following closely behind. The log found its level once Gray Dove and Skye were on. Running Wolf pushed them away from the bank and began to paddle, moving them out into the river.

It was a wobbly, precarious ride. About halfway in, Gray Dove lost her balance. Running Wolf watched in horror as she tumbled into the water, then scrambled to help. "Don't move!" Gray Dove shouted. "You're going to tip it over!" Waving off Running Wolf, she struggled to make her way back to the log. Grabbing hold of a branch sticking out, she yelled, "Keep paddling!" Then she rode the rest of the way across the river, holding on to the back of the log, as she lacked the energy to pull herself back up. They made it safely, and Running Wolf pulled his soaking mother onto the bank.

Gray Dove bent over with her hands on her knees and looked up at her son. "That was fun!"

"Fun?" Running Wolf stared at his mother. "You almost drowned!" She gave him a sly smile, and he began to laugh. She laughed back before patting him on the shoulder. It was a welcome moment of levity after all they had been through.

Chapter Eleven
Breaking Bonds

A week had passed since the Green Corn Ceremony, and things had started to settle into a routine for most Pee Dee villagers, except for Red Willow and Eternal Blossom. Red Willow found she could not bear to stay in her old family hut by herself, so she moved in with Eternal Blossom and her children. Soaring Eagle's guards were still keeping an eye on her, preventing her from leaving to search for her family. She had just about given up hope of ever seeing them again, and her primary source of comfort now was Fyre, her constant companion.

One day, after she had finished working in the garden, she returned to her aunt's house to find White Owl waiting. He had asked Eternal Blossom's permission to eat dinner with the family, hoping to catch up with Red Willow, and Eternal Blossom welcomed him in. Red Willow was pleasantly surprised to see him and was glad to have a friend. Even after all that had transpired, White Owl still found her captivating. The family and White Owl sat down and shared a meal of corn cakes and squash stew.

After dinner, White Owl and Red Willow sat outside and took turns puffing on a tobacco pipe. "I'm glad your agitlogi allowed me to come over," White Owl said between tokes. "I've wanted to see you and talk to you. So, how are you doing?"

Red Willow rubbed her eyes with the tips of her fingers. "Well, things turned out worse than I could've imagined at the ceremony. Instead of losing one family member, I lost two. It hasn't been easy."

White Owl blew a puff of smoke into the air. "I can only imagine how unbearable this must be for you. I want you to know that you have been in my prayers every day."

"I feel so powerless," Red Willow sighed. "I keep wondering if there is something I could've done differently. All night long, every night, it is all I think about it. Sleep is impossible, and I am so tired."

White Owl looked Red Willow directly in the eyes. "There was nothing you could have done differently that day," he said. "Once your etsi spoke out, the crowd was going to do what the crowd would do. And as much as you want to find your etsi and udo and help them, you know how it will end: you will end up lost and shunned by the tribe, just like them."

Red Willow looked out into the distance. "Maybe I want to be lost and shunned by this tribe."

White Owl turned away and took a deep breath. "There are good things in this tribe that are worth staying for even if you can't see them now. It will take time for you to heal from what has happened but do not give up on those still here who care about you."

Red Willow nodded and looked kindly at White Owl. Then she leaned over and put her head on his shoulder. Her tender, soft skin electrified him, warming his heart. She felt safe and comforted by his presence, which she had not felt since before the ceremony. He put his arm around her, and they stared off into the moonlight.

✖ ✖ ✖

Gray Dove, Running Wolf, and Skye continued westward at a snail's pace towards the home of the Catawba tribe. Gray Dove's worsening sickness slowed them to a crawl. She knew she was not long for this world but desperately wanted to hold on for her son, and she did her best to hide the severity of her condition from him. She hoped they might reach the Catawba village in another few days. One night, Gray Dove pulled Running Wolf aside at camp for a serious talk.

Gray Dove wheezed as she spoke, causing Running Wolf to stare at her with concern. "I have something that I need to say to you, uwetsi. No matter what happens to me, do not give up. Follow the setting sun every day until you reach the Catawba village. Remember what I have taught you about mushroom foraging and getting fresh water."

Running Wolf looked at his mother with a puzzled face. "What to do you mean, no matter what happens to you?"

"My time is short," she whispered tenderly. "And I want to make sure that you will be well."

"I know you are tired. But you can't leave me to do this alone!" Running Wolf pleaded.

Sensing his fear, Gray Dove put her arm around her son and stroked his hair. "I would never leave you if I could help it, uwetsi." Tears trickled down from Running Wolf's eyes. Gray Dove embraced him tightly and gently rubbed his back. They lay down together for the night, snuggled up tightly.

In the morning, Running Wolf discovered his mother's lifeless body next to him. She had expired in the middle of the night, unable to catch her breath because of the disease's toll on her lungs. Running Wolf tried vigorously to rouse her, but his efforts were in vain. He fell to his knees next to his mother's body and let out an intense cry of agony as he pounded his fists into the ground. He knew he had set this chain of events in motion when he raised the rock over Howling Coyote's head, and he wished himself dead instead of his mother. He had now lost everything and was facing the world utterly alone, with the exception of the only living soul he trusted completely. His ever-faithful companion, Skye, tottered over and nuzzled up under Running Wolf's exposed underarm. Running Wolf grabbed Skye by his scruff and collapsed onto the forest floor.

Running Wolf spent the day paralyzed by his sadness and guilt, not eating or drinking. Well into the day, an overwhelming feeling of thirst finally forced him to take a small sip of water from his deerskin pouch. He rubbed his red, puffy eyes and fed Skye a small chunk of pemmican, still unable to eat himself. Nightfall was approaching, and he lay down to rest, more emotionally and physically exhausted than he had ever been in his life. He fell asleep quickly.

But Running Wolf's sleep was short-lived. A distant howling sound woke him a few hours into his slumber, and he noticed Skye's ears standing at full attention. The howling sound echoed in the night as Skye growled fiercely. In moments, Running Wolf found himself encircled by a pack of wolves. His heart thumped inside his chest as he grabbed a club he had fashioned from a hickory branch, swinging it wildly back and forth. The wolves were not intimidated, and they moved further into the campsite, heading for his mother's corpse.

Horrified, a massive rage flooded his spirit and, without concern for his safety, he barreled into the wolf pack. He swung ferociously, knocking the animals off his mother's body in a frenzied attack. The wolves slunk away into the night, soundly defeated. The power he felt coursing through his body was much like the power he felt when he'd killed his uncle. It was an energy he felt only when deeply provoked and one he could not easily control. If he could ever harness it in productive ways, he might be able to use it to his advantage. He lay down next to his mother's body and tried to calm himself down, eventually falling back to a fitful sleep, worried that the wolves might come back.

In the morning, he awoke with a renewed sense of purpose, knowing that continuing his journey was what his mother would have wanted. But he had to make sure her body would be safe from scavengers. It was the custom of some tribes to place their dead high in the trees for just that purpose. Traditional resting places of this type usually included a platform and burial clothes, but those things were unavailable. He took off his leggings and wrapped them around his mother's head and shoulders. As he did so, he noticed the gorget Eternal Blossom had made and removed it from his mother's neck and placed it around Skye's for safekeeping.

After choosing a suitable hickory tree, Running Wolf draped Gray Dove's lifeless body across his shoulders and began to climb, slowly. Hunger and exhaustion sapped much of his strength. He continued up the tree until he reached what he thought to be a safe height and placed his mother's body in a fork of the branches, giving her one last look before saying goodbye. Memories came flooding back. He knew he'd been her favorite child, even if she'd never said it, and the two had come to rely on each other intensely since his father's passing. He wept bitterly before squeezing her hand one last time.

After collecting himself, Running Wolf descended from the tree, never looking back. When he made it down to the tree's base, he stripped off some bark and carved his mother's initials into the trunk. Exhausted, he struggled back to his makeshift camp and finally ate a large piece of pemmican. Any further processing of his grief would have to wait; now, he had to press onward. He packed his things and called for Skye to join him.

✖✖✖

Back at the village, Soaring Eagle's father had been laid to rest in the ceremonial burial hut. As the new tribal council leader, Soaring Eagle wasted no time trying to implement his agenda. He was hungry for war and was planning to use the council's will to make it happen. He called an impromptu council meeting to present his plan, with the four clan leaders gathering at the lodge.

Spotted Turtle sat with his legs spread apart, arms resting on his thighs. "So, tell me again Soaring Eagle. Why did you call us here today?"

Soaring Eagle leaned back and muttered to himself briefly before beginning his diatribe. "I'm glad you asked, unalii. I'll tell you why I brought you here. We have lost our status in the land because of our recent cowardice. It is time to stop our tribe's slow decline into irrelevance and to reassert our dominance with a show of force."

Proud Robin rubbed his chin before responding. "You mistake prudence for cowardice, young asgaya. We haven't had a reason to go to war in a long time, and we still don't now."

Soaring Eagle chuckled. "You edudas are so stuck in your ways; you have no vision for the future. We can go on the offensive and make things happen instead of waiting to respond to what happens to us."

"And you want to do this now?" Spotted Turtle asked incredulously. "When we are so close to harvest time?"

"The harvest will be fine," Soaring Eagle scoffed. "You need to think bigger."

Proud Robin and Spotted Turtle exchanged concerned looks. "This is a bad idea," Spotted Turtle stared at Soaring Eagle, "and I believe my fellow councilmember agrees." Proud Robin nodded affirmatively.

Soaring Eagle turned and glared at Walking Squirrel. Feeling guilty for going against his friend in the prior decision, Walking Squirrel quickly voted to support Soaring Eagle's scheme. Spotted Turtle and Proud Robin were left holding their heads in their hands, unable to believe that they were in another tie vote situation.

"I think we all know what this means," Soaring Eagle said as he sent Walking Squirrel to get the medicine man and retrieved the clay saucer with the colored rocks.

The medicine man came and performed the rock ceremony once again. When he drew the rock, it again turned up black, giving Soaring Eagle the go-ahead for his war party. "I guess we know whose side the Great Spirit is on," Soaring Eagle said smugly to a dejected Spotted Turtle as he dismissed the meeting.

The following day, Soaring Eagle gathered the tribe in the courtyard and addressed them from the temple mound. His terrible countenance overlooked the villagers congregated below. Soaring Eagle wore his father's brilliantly adorned headdress, with feathers so tall and brightly colored that it could be seen for miles from the top of the mound. He began to shout his address to the onlookers.

"Today, I come before you all to offer a new way. It has been our tradition to conduct warfare only when we want to train our young men in battle or when we want to capture prisoners to replace our lost souls within the tribe. I have a vision where we conduct warfare to intimidate and cause fear in our enemies but only a great war party can fulfill that vision. I call on the young braves of this tribe to come forth and volunteer to take part and become great heroes. Each of your clan leaders agrees that now is the time to create this warring party and establish our dominance. If you are a willing and able participant, report to them by next sunrise and await further instructions."

A small round of enthusiastic chants went up, mostly from within the wolf clan. But the rest of the men remained silent, looks of consternation covering their faces. The next day arrived, and only a few young braves of the tribe met soaring Eagle's request; most were unwilling to participate. Soaring Eagle was roundly disappointed, knowing there was no way he could achieve his goals with this trivial force. He convened the council again to see if they had suggestions for how to increase the turnout.

Soaring Eagle paced around the temple as he addressed his fellow council members, "This low turnout will not work for my purposes. Can someone explain to me why I did not have more volunteers?"

Spotted Turtle looked stoically at Soaring Eagle, continually surprised at his arrogance. "The men of the tribe do not believe in your ways. They follow the paths of their ancestors."

"The men of the tribe are too stuck in the old customs," Soaring Eagle replied angrily. "How can we change their minds?"

"There are two reasons a tribe will go to war," Spotted Turtle explained, "either to train our young men in battle or to collect prisoners to replace lost members of the tribe. Creating fear and intimidation is of no interest to our men. If you want volunteers, you must approach them with one of these two alternatives."

"Or I could just threaten them with death if they fail to comply with my wishes," Soaring Eagle scoffed.

Spotted Turtle pursed his lips and squinted his eyes. "If you do that, your time as council leader will be very short. The men will not accept threats without fighting back. You should be careful how you handle this situation. You do not have the power that you think you have."

"Do not underestimate me," Soaring Eagle pointed his finger at Spotted Turtle. "I will try it your way this time. But one way or another, I will have my war party."

Soaring Eagle stalked away and began enacting his plan to manipulate the men into going to war. He crept sneakily through the village to see Eternal Blossom as she was outside her hut grinding corn. Her stomach sunk as he approached. Arriving, Soaring Eagle taunted her, saying, "Poor, poor Eternal Blossom. It's been a tough time for you lately. You must be so sad."

"I am sad about many things," Eternal Blossom replied without looking up from her corn grinding, "including the loss of your father. He was a great man."

Soaring Eagle crossed his arms. "Indeed, I have experienced loss just as you have."

Eternal Blossom looked up at Soaring Eagle. "Your father's loss was a loss for the whole tribe. We will miss his leadership."

Soaring Eagle now understood the insulting subtext, but he ignored it. "We should stop talking about loss and do something about it. If someone advocates for it, our men will go to war to replace our lost souls. You would be the perfect person to inspire our braves, since so many people in your life have gone missing."

Eternal Blossom tried to hide her shock. "You want me to push for a war party? Why would I do that—or anything—for you?"

Soaring Eagle turned his menacing gaze towards Eternal Blossom's children. "You wouldn't do it for me. You would do it for you, for your family. Little ayolis can be lost so easily. You wouldn't want to feel the sting of yet another loss, would you?"

A dark look crossed Eternal Blossom's face as her mind filled with terror. She knew Soaring Eagle would not hesitate to carry out his threat. "I will push for your war party, but you will not lay a finger on my children if I do. And that is the last thing you will ever ask of me. I want nothing more to do with you once this is done."

Soaring Eagle nodded smugly. "You will have no further quarrel with me if I get what I want. But if I don't, well . . . there will be a price to pay." He left her to finish her corn grinding and returned to his hut, eager to put his plan into action.

Chapter Twelve

Sitting Deer

Running Wolf was three days further into his now unbearably lonely journey towards the Catawba village, and his dwindling food supplies left him physically weakened. He was walking wounded, and the temptation for him to capitulate and join his mother and father was real. The only thing fueling his fire was the promise he'd made to Gray Dove to continue on no matter what.

Running Wolf set up his temporary campsite by a stream with a meager campfire, portioned out the tiny bit of pemmican left to Skye, took a small handful of hickory nuts for himself, and lay down to sleep, not realizing this would be his last night hungry and alone. In the morning he awoke to find three strange men standing over him, and he quickly rolled onto his knees into a defensive posture. Skye growled, but the men stared blankly; nothing seemed to phase them. Finally, one of the men spoke, "Your dog seems friendly." The other Catawba chuckled, breaking the tension.

The one who appeared to be the leader chimed in, "Who are you, and what are you doing here?"

Running Wolf stammered, knowing he could not tell the truth. "I am from the Pee Dee tribe. I was . . . part of a hunting party with some of my other tribe members, and . . . we got separated. I have been alone in the woods for days. Can you help me?"

"You are not worth our time, atsutsa," the sarcastic Catawba man laughed, "but we could use your animal for sure."

The group's leader stood with his legs crossed and his body resting against his bow. He studied Running Wolf, trying to size him up. Something about Running Wolf spoke to him, but he couldn't put his finger on it. The stirring of his soul led him to want to discover more about this strange youth. He looked straight into Running Wolf's eyes and said, "You can come with us."

The other men of the group scrunched their faces and swapped befuddled looks. One of the men spoke out to the leader, "Are you sure about this?"

The leader looked back at his subordinate. "I'm never sure about anything I do. But I know when to trust the spirit that speaks within me. We can at least give Sitting Deer a chance to meet this boy and decide what to do with him."

The men grumbled, less than thrilled about having a naive foreigner under their charge, but the words of their leader had settled the matter. Running Wolf stood, dusted himself off, and took his place with the group, with Skye trotting behind. The sarcastic man called out gruffly to Running Wolf, "You better pull your weight, young asgaya. We're not here to take care of you like your etsi."

Just hearing the mention of the word "mother" cut Running Wolf like a knife. He took a deep breath, trying to hold back his tears. It would take every ounce of his strength to continue, but he owed his mother nothing less.

✖ ✖ ✖

At the Pee Dee village, Red Willow continued her harvest by collecting the dried beans from their corn stalk trellises. She had also begun to collect sunflower seeds from the wild sunflowers around the village to provide another source of sustenance during the coming cold season. Despite all the darkness in her life, Red Willow still managed to find delight in the bounty that nature and the Great Spirit provided at this time of the year.

Red Willow's relationship with White Owl was growing closer. The loss of her family had created a giant hole in her heart, and White Owl's companionship filled it, at least partially. But she knew only one thing could truly fill the emptiness inside her, and that was something that required White Owl's assistance. One day as they were taking a walk, she expressed her feelings to him. "I have something to tell you. I have reconsidered your marriage proposal. If you will still have me, then I will marry you."

White Owl stopped dead in his tracks, stunned by what he had just heard. He did not know if this was real or if he was in a waking dream. "What did you say?!"

Red Willow stopped alongside him and looked into his eyes. "I cannot stay forever with my agitlogi. I want to have my own family, and that is why I want to get married."

White Owl's head was spinning, still unable to comprehend what was happening. "I think I need you to slap me in the face."

A confused look came across Red Willow's face. "Are you alright?"

White Owl doubled down on his request. "I need to know that I am not dreaming. Slap me in the face. I'm serious."

Red Willow slapped White Owl directly across the cheek, although not as hard as she could have, and waited for his response. He rubbed his face and examined his surroundings, confirming that he was not dreaming. Then he grabbed Red Willow by the waist and lifted her off her feet. "Of course we can get married, but we have to do it the right way."

The next day White Owl brought a sack of cornmeal and placed it outside of Eternal Blossom's hut. Eternal Blossom returned to find the bag and immediately realized what was happening: White Owl was proposing to Red Willow again, even though she had previously rebuffed him. Eternal Blossom sighed, still envious that her niece had found what appeared to be true love. She entered the hut, where Red Willow was playing with the children, and said flatly, "There's something outside for you."

Red Willow peeked her head outside the door. Noticing the cornmeal, she grabbed it and dragged it into the house. "Is that what I think it is?" Eternal Blossom asked.

"Yes. White Owl said he would propose to me the right way, and he has been good to his word."

Eternal Blossom began her dinner preparations. "I hope you will make the right decision this time."

Red Willow looked carefully at her aunt. "I did not realize you thought I made the wrong decision the first time."

Eternal Blossom sighed. "It's just that . . . I wish for you to be loved in a way that I was not."

Red Willow sensed her aunt's envy and felt pity for her. "I'm sorry that Howling Coyote was such a terrible partner. You deserved so much better."

Eternal Blossom sniffled, tears welling up in her eyes. Red Willow walked over and rubbed her aunt's back gently. "There is still time for you to find someone special."

Eternal Blossom wiped her face dry. "That might be true, but I know that you have someone special waiting for you now, and I will do anything to make sure that you two come together."

Her aunt's heartfelt concern touched Red Willow. The two shared an embrace as the children played on the floor next to them.

Running Wolf found himself an outsider within the Catawba hunting party. A few days into their trek, they still hadn't warmed up to him, only giving him small scraps of their food and small portions of their water. Running Wolf knew he had not proved his worth to the group yet and was waiting for the chance. It came one night when he heard leaves rustling in the distance. Skye began barking in the direction of the rustling and raced off. Running Wolf grabbed his bow and arrow and chased after Skye, following him to a tall hickory tree base. Running Wolf looked up into the rustling branches and saw a furry creature with large black circles around its eyes and sharp claws clinging to a branch. Hoping desperately to prove his mettle to the Catawba men, he grabbed his bow, loaded it, and sent an arrow flying into the tree. The arrow pierced the neck of the raccoon, and it came tumbling to the ground. He thanked the Great Spirit for the gift, snatched up the animal, and returned to the campsite. The men, awakened by the commotion, were surprised to see that Running Wolf was returning with some game. He threw the dead raccoon onto the ground in front of the men, proud of his catch.

"Perhaps this atsutsa is not as useless as we thought," the sarcastic Catawba man remarked.

"Good job, atsutsa," the Catawba leader exclaimed. "Now get some sleep. We have a long final leg of our journey, and we want to reach the village by sundown."

Running Wolf lay back down, but, given the excitement of his hunt and the anxiety of visiting a new place, he knew it would not be easy to fall asleep. His mind raced for a few hours before he finally succumbed to his exhaustion. After a nearly sleepless night, the men prodded him to wake him so they could begin their long journey home. They added his raccoon to the other animal carcasses they had collected during their hunt and set off.

After a long day's journey, the hunting party arrived at the Catawba village as the sun was setting. From a distance, the sight of the town reminded Running Wolf of his home, with a long wooden palisade surrounding a large courtyard and several buildings. But as they entered the town proper, Running Wolf was acutely aware that he was not in Town Creek anymore. Every other man Running Wolf encountered had a long, triangularly shaped forehead that came to a point at the apex. It was the strangest sight that he had ever seen. He did not realize it at the time, but he later learned that the people of the Catawba tribe practiced ritual head flattening, a process accomplished by binding the skulls of their newborn baby boys.

Not only were the men of the Catawba tribe different, but the women were as well. While the Pee Dee women were attractive in a certain way, they usually dressed plainly and only wore makeup on special occasions. On the other hand, the Catawba women dressed in beautiful, brightly colored skirts and painted their faces in bright colors throughout the year. Running Wolf made his way through the town, his young member standing at full attention, plainly evident through the makeshift deerskin loincloth that the Catawba hunters had given him. The villagers took notice and snickered at the boy for his inconvenient erection. Running Wolf turned away from the villagers and tried to cover his groin with his hands as he awkwardly followed his hunting companions.

The hunting party leader took Running Wolf back to his hut to get him some food and water, while the other two began organizing an impromptu council meeting to decide what to do about the boy. The meeting took place late that night in front of a roaring fire at the council lodge. The leaders of each tribal clan were there, along with a tribal priest named Rolling Cloud. An eccentric old shaman, Rolling Cloud had a thick head of silver hair that he wore in a puffy ball on top of his crown. His oddities were generally accepted without qualms among the tribe because he was such a loving and loyal spirit. He would often wander the woods around the village, eyes closed, sharpening his sixth sense to be in higher communion with the Great Spirit.

The council was presided over by a burly chief named Sitting Deer. His flat forehead was weather-worn and wrinkled, and his long gray hair was braided and hung down on each side of his head. With small, narrow-set eyes, he appeared to be perpetually intoxicated, and he wore a peaceful smile.

One of the hunters brought Running Wolf before the council, and Sitting Deer stared at him for a few tense minutes before breaking his silence. "Your presence here is a great surprise for us. Please enlighten us about who you are and how you got here."

"My name," he mumbled, "is Running Wolf."

Sitting Deer put his hand up to his ear mockingly and chuckled, "Speak up, atsutsa, so that we can hear you."

"My name," he practically shouted, "is Running Wolf. I am from the Pee Dee tribe. I got separated from some of my tribe members on a hunting journey. I ended up lost and alone in the deep woods and feared losing my life until some of your tribe members stumbled upon me and rescued me."

Sitting Deer leaned in towards Running Wolf. "I suppose you are eager to return to your tribe then."

Running Wolf froze, realizing he had not thought through his story. He, of course, was not eager to return to his tribe, but he could not let the Catawba people know. If they found out he had been banished, there was no way they would let him stay. But he had come too far to be unsuccessful, so he bought himself some time to figure out his next move. "I do miss my people very much. But it is a long and hard journey back, and I am not sure I am ready to make it just yet. If you would be so generous to let me stay, I would be forever in your debt."

Sitting Deer leaned back in his seat and stroked his chin. Something felt strange to him, and he sensed the boy might be lying, but he honored Running Wolf's request out of curiosity. "Out of our hospitality, we will allow you to replenish yourself here for a few moons before your return journey. And we will provide you with the necessary provisions you need once your journey begins. Make yourself at home in our tribe while you are our guest. The matter is decided."

Running Wolf bowed to Sitting Deer, and the council was dismissed. Running Wolf breathed a sigh of relief as he watched the council leaders disperse one by one. He quickly followed them out and found Skye waiting for him in the town square. Stroking his furry friend gently behind the ears, he whispered, "I think we have found our new home . . . for now."

✖ ✖ ✖

Back at the Pee Dee village, Red Willow and Eternal Blossom were preparing to host White Owl's family for a meal to discuss the couple's pending engagement. Red Willow wanted to make everything perfect to impress White Owl's parents. She poured her heart and soul into preparing a feast of deer stew, roasted squash, and corn cakes.

"Everything smells so delicious," Eternal Blossom remarked as she walked into the hut from her corn grinding chores to find her niece in her most delicate new dress with elegantly braided hair. "And you look magnificent, young one."

"Wa do," Red Willow replied. "I need everything to go perfectly tonight. I think White Owl's parents have doubts about me, and I want to show them that I will make a good udalii."

"Nothing in life is perfect," Eternal Blossom quipped. "If White Owl's parents can't see all you have to offer a uyehi, they are more blind than a cave full of bats."

Red Willow appreciated her aunt's encouraging words, which eased her anxiety as the hour for the meal quickly approached. All that was left for her was to add a few finishing touches and wait for their arrival. She made sure that her pipe was clean and that she had enough tobacco for the two families to seal the deal over a fresh offering to the Great Spirit.

White Owl and his family arrived shortly after she had finished her final preparations. Eternal Blossom invited them into the hut, telling them to make themselves at home. The group sat down, with White Owl and his parents facing Red Willow, Eternal Blossom, and her children. They thanked the Great Spirit for allowing them to gather together and began to partake of their meal.

The dinner was pleasant, with light-hearted banter and no discussion of the possible marriage. After the meal was finished, White Owl's parents asked Eternal Blossom, as expected, if they could speak with her in private. Eternal Blossom told Red Willow to take the children outside to play for a little bit, and White Owl's parents asked him to join them.

White Owl's father crossed his arms in front of his chest before beginning the conversation. "You should know that White Owl's etsi and I were very concerned when we heard of White Owl's intentions to propose marriage to Red Willow. With all the . . . recent events surrounding your family, we don't see any way she can be a good udalii to our atsutsa. We believe that bad behavior still stains her."

Eternal Blossom's blood boiled. How dare this man judge her niece like that! He had no idea of the truth behind the story. She wanted to punch him in the face, but she knew that for the sake of Red Willow she had to maintain her composure. She quickly gathered her thoughts before responding. "I hear your concern, and, of course, we all want what's best for our children. But I think that Red Willow is a very strong young agehya to have endured all she has. That strength will serve an uyehi well."

White Owl's father's face was unmoved. "But there is a moral defect within her family. Either her etsi or her udo is a murderer."

Eternal Blossom placed her hands on the ground and leaned in to face the father. "Do you believe that our laws are just and fair?"

White Owl's father leaned back, appearing slightly intimidated by Eternal Blossom's aggressiveness. "Yes."

Eternal Blossom lifted her hands and leaned back. "Then you should consider the matter settled. My uyehi's death has been avenged twofold. There is no need to punish Red Willow further by keeping her from being with your son, whom she cares about deeply."

"You may be right about those things," White Owl's father replied, "but since she has lost all her family, she has nothing of material value to offer us if we were to accept this union. The burden would fall on us to give them material support as they begin their shared life."

Eternal Blossom had had enough. She leaped to her feet and clenched her fists. "You are wrong to say that she has nothing to offer. She can give you HERSELF! She will always work hard. She will never be a burden to you or your son, just as she has never been a burden to anyone. If you stand in the way of this union, you are hurting both White Owl and Red Willow!"

As White Owl's father crossed his arms in stubborn refusal his wife put her arm on his shoulder and gave him a stern look of disapproval. Sensing that she was overruling him, he relented and gave his permission for the marriage to occur. Eternal Blossom brought out her pipe and her finest tobacco, and the new family shared a ceremonial smoke before bringing in Red Willow and White Owl to share the news.

Chapter Thirteen

Forging Bonds

Running Wolf was enjoying the hospitality of the Catawba while he could, still pondering his next move. But unbeknownst to him, his next move was being planned for him. Rolling Cloud was roaming the woods well past midnight one evening, trying to connect to the spirit of the night when a vision of Running Wolf seized him and burned itself deep into his soul. His first impulse was to rush to his chief, Sitting Deer, and share what he had seen, but he knew the chief would be sound asleep. So, he held onto his spiritual manifestation until dawn.

At daybreak, Rolling Cloud went straight to Sitting Deer's hut, unable to contain his excitement. Passing through the doorway, he found a half-awake Sitting Deer, but that didn't stop him from launching into his rant. "The Great Spirit communed with my spirit in the middle of the night and showed me the destiny of our young guest. In my vision, impassable waters filled with ferocious garfish trapped our people on many separate islands. All the people were in great distress because of their inability to reach out to each other. The atsutsa came in and, with great strength, killed all the garfish. Then he harnessed the waters and cast them aside, allowing people to cross and connect. Their newfound connections led the people into an era of prosperity and harmony. I believe that this atsutsa in our midst is important for our future, and you should not allow him to leave."

A groggy Sitting Deer rubbed his eyes and shot a confused glance at the wild-eyed priest. "Say that **again**," he instructed the shaman.

Rolling Cloud rolled his eyes in frustration that Sitting Deer had not heard. "The atsutsa is *important*! Do not let him leave until you know more about him," he replied before departing from the hut to get a daytime nap.

Sitting Deer stretched his arms and legs and pulled himself up out of his hammock. He went behind the hut to relieve himself and pondered what Rolling Cloud had shared. Of course, he had heard Rolling Cloud relay his story, every last word, but it was fun to irritate his fanciful friend. Sitting Deer had presumed that the boy would be a minor inconvenience for a short time and then would be out of his life forever. Now, with this revelation, he would have to reconsider who the boy was and what role he might play in the life of his tribe. Rolling Cloud's hallucination might have meant something, but Sitting Deer would need more than a vision before he could accept the boy as one of their own.

Sitting Deer kept a close eye on Running Wolf for a few days as he interacted with the other Catawba in their daily lives. He saw nothing special in the boy during these observations. Running Wolf just seemed like an ordinary awkward teenager. He was polite and helpful, but he did not demonstrate anything that made him seem like a savior. Given this, Sitting Deer decided that he should send the boy back to his home village. He invited Running Wolf to share dinner with him one night in the tribal council hut to inform him of his decision.

"Have you enjoyed your stay with our tribe so far?" Sitting Deer asked after they finished their meal.

"Yes. Your people are very nice."

Sitting Deer brushed some crumbs from his hands. "I'm glad to hear it. So, do you feel refreshed enough to begin your journey home? I'm sure your family is missing you."

Running Wolf's heart began to flutter, his eyes darting around the room as he searched for a safe reply. "Well, the truth is . . ." Running Wolf stammered, "the truth is I was not lost from a hunting party. I . . . I ran away from my home."

Sitting Deer sat straight as an arrow and squinted his already narrow eyes. "You mean you lied to me and my tribe? You disrespect me, young one, and you disrespect my people. Explain yourself."

Running Wolf sighed deeply, ready to release the emotional torrent of his life story. Everything came out in a rush. "I lost my father when I was young, and since then, nothing has felt right for me. I had no male that I could learn from, no one to teach me how to be the best man I could be. My agidutsi could have been an example for me, but he was an evil man who hurt my etsi. After watching this for a while, I couldn't stand it anymore, so I smashed his head in with a rock near the river and made it look like he had drowned. At our Green Corn Ceremony, I confessed my sin to the tribe, and they banished me. I cannot go back. I have no home."

"And your etsi?" Sitting Deer asked.

"She is . . . she is dead," Running Wolf replied, not wanting to add another layer of complication to his story.

Sitting Deer relaxed his stance and looked tenderly at Running Wolf, knowing himself the pain of loss that Running Wolf had experienced. Sitting Deer's first-born son had succumbed to a sudden illness at a young age some years ago. Looking at Running Wolf, Sitting Deer could almost picture the son he had lost. He wondered if this serendipitous meeting was a gift from the Great Spirit, a chance for both of them to enjoy a relationship they had missed. He also knew that accepting a murderer into the tribe would be frowned upon, yet he could not bring himself to let Running Wolf go.

Sitting Deer fixed his eyes on the boy. "You may make your home here in our tribe. But you must always work hard and prove yourself to be loyal and trustworthy. The first time you make me feel I can't trust you is the last. I will send you out into the woods to starve and let the wolves eat you."

Running Wolf nodded, hiding his fear as he knew Sitting Deer was serious. "Wa do for your generosity. I will not let you down."

Sitting Deer pointed his finger at Running Wolf, "And one more thing . . . your history stays between you and me. No one else needs to know."

✖✖✖

At the Pee Dee village, preparations were underway for the marriage ceremony between Red Willow and White Owl. Red Willow was busy harvesting blackberries for the traditional purple bridal blanket she would wear on her wedding day. To begin the dyeing process, she took a deerskin blanket and submerged it into a pot of hot marsh water over a simmering fire. In a second hot pot, she placed the blackberries into river water and waited for it to extract the juices. After the blackberries simmered for an hour, she smashed the pulp and pushed it through a strainer, leaving a purple liquid. Then she took her deerskin blanket out of the marsh water and placed it into the blackberry liquid overnight to let it soak up all the purple dye.

Tradition called for the bride to wear a multicolored necklace, and the task of its creation fell to none other than the acclaimed jewelry maker, Eternal Blossom. She had all the supplies she needed to make the different colored paints: crushed blue sunflower seeds, dried and crushed yellow squash blossoms, and dried and ground green elderberries. She cracked open three duck eggs into three different small clay dishes and resuspended the different powders into the viscous egg mixtures. Dipping a grass-tipped twig into her freshly created paints, she applied the various colors to many clay beads. Once the paint had dried, she fashioned the beads into her finished necklace.

As the eve of the wedding ceremony arrived, anticipation peaked in Eternal Blossom's hut. Red Willow was pacing the floor, wondering if she needed any last-minute preparations or had forgotten any necessary tasks. Eternal Blossom stopped her niece and presented her with the necklace she had crafted. "You are going to need this for the ceremony."

Red Willow took the necklace and held it gently in her hands, then smiled up at her aunt. "It is lovely." She slipped the necklace over her head and around her neck.

Eternal Blossom grabbed the purple blanket from the floor and wrapped it around her niece's shoulders. "You look beautiful. You remind me so much of your etsi."

Red Willow sighed. "I wish she could be here to present me to White Owl."

The two women exchanged a look of sadness, knowing they would almost surely never see Gray Dove again. "Her spirit will be there," Eternal Blossom said softly as she pulled Red Willow in close for a hug. "It lives in both you and in me," she whispered into her niece's ear. They shared a long embrace, sending a feeling of warmth coursing through their blood—the same blood that once flowed through the veins of their beloved sister and mother.

After a few minutes, Eternal Blossom released her grip and beckoned Red Willow to take a seat next to the smoldering embers of the hut's central fire pit. Eternal Blossom retrieved a small cup and dipped it into the clay bowl filled with warm water that was suspended above the fire. She grabbed a handful of ground skullcap leaves and tossed them into the cup before handing it to Red Willow.

"Drink this," she said with a tender smile. "It will help you get some sleep before your big day."

Red Willow took the cup and peered down into the murky brown liquid. "I could drink a creek full of this stuff and still probably not be able to sleep."

Eternal Blossom let out a soft chuckle. "I get it. I was once like you. A young agehya, on the verge of being married, full of doubts and questions about what my new life would be like." She paused for a moment and stared wistfully into the distance. "And I am not going to lie to you. Being with one asgaya for the rest of your life is going to be hard. You will face many trials and tribulations, but along with those challenges you may find the incredible reward of deep companionship. Sometimes, as with your etsi and doda, it works out perfectly; and sometimes, as with me, it does not work at all. I pray that it will work perfectly for you and White Owl."

Red Willow ran her free hand lightly through her hair. "That's very nice of you to say agitlogi. But I'm really just nervous about laying with White Owl. I've heard stories about what that's like, but I don't know what to believe and what not to believe."

"Ohh," Eternal Blossom exclaimed as she nodded her head understandingly. "THAT . . . will be awkward and uncomfortable at first. But with time you may grow to enjoy it."

"How do I know if we are doing it right though?" Red Willow asked.

Eternal Blossom pondered the question for a moment. "Like with most things in life, the Great Spirit will guide you through it when the time is right."

Red Willow was frustrated with the lack of a direct answer to her question. "But when is the right time?"

"White Owl's body will change . . . down there," Eternal Blossom said as she pointed to Red Willow's midsection, "in a way that will allow the two of your bodies to become one."

Red Willow scrunched her face tightly. "That sounds very strange to me."

"I guess it is strange," Eternal Blossom replied. "But it is nothing you need to fear. It is just another part of your life journey."

Red Willow sipped her tea and stared at the wispy smoke rising from what was left of the day's fire. "Wa do, agitlogi. I appreciate your wisdom."

"I'm glad I can be here for you ayoli," Eternal Blossom said as she got up from her seat and walked over to rub Red Willow's shoulder. "Now finish your tea and let's try to get some sleep." Red Willow nodded her head and tipped back the cup to pour the remaining liquid down her throat. She wiped the excess liquid from her mouth and stood up from her seat to make her way to the bed. Plopping herself down into her hammock, she tried her best to get comfortable. It was a night filled with tossing and turning, and nearly devoid of sleep. Red Willow awoke at daybreak, her stomach still aflutter with anxiety. She went down to the river to bathe in the cool water to wake up fully and calm her nerves. Fyre followed her down and splashed around, pawing at the minnows playfully as they swam by.

Feeling refreshed and fully awake, Red Willow returned to the hut to get dressed. She put on her most delicate new dress and leggings, placed the multicolored necklace around her neck, and draped her purple blanket around her shoulders. She painted her face with stunning red circles surrounding her eyes and two white streaks on each cheek. Eternal Blossom informed her that it was time for the ceremony to begin. Red Willow took a deep breath, grabbed the corn she had set aside as an offering to White Owl, and set off for the sacred marriage circle. They arrived to find the medicine man awaiting them in front of the holy fire. He greeted them and asked Red Willow and Eternal Blossom to stand inside the circle next to the flames.

White Owl and his family arrived shortly afterward. White Owl was dressed in his finest regalia: a large red and white feathered headdress and a large necklace made with many red and white porcupine quills. He also had his own purple blanket draped over his shoulder. The medicine man asked White Owl to stand inside the circle with his mother. White Owl gave Red Willow a look of confidence and care that eased her worries.

The medicine man said prayers of blessing for the couple, and the elders who had gathered to witness the ceremony sang. Red Willow brought her corn offering to White Owl, symbolizing her willingness to provide nourishment for their household. In turn, White Owl brought an offering of deer meat, signifying his intention to be a provider for their family. Then the medicine man removed the purple blankets from Red Willow and White Owl and asked them to stand side by side. He placed a new white blanket around them together to symbolize their union, after which the elders sang again. Following the ceremony, the medicine man retrieved a special jug and filled it with water. It was a single jug with two handles and two openings. Red Willow took one handle of the jar, and White Owl took the other. Together they each drank from the pitcher, further symbolizing their new bond. Everyone then celebrated with a sumptuous feast of bean bread and deer stew.

After the feast's conclusion, Red Willow and White Owl returned to her original family hut to spend their first night together as a married couple. As they walked through the entrance, memories flooded Red Willow's mind. She remembered the shared meals, the long talks, and, of course, the rivalry with her brother. Exhausted from the long and highly emotional day, she sobbed uncontrollably and collapsed into White Owl's arms. It was a much-needed moment of release, as she had held onto so many things for so long. White Owl laid her down on their new blanket and held her close until she fell asleep.

The following morning, Red Willow awoke on the blanket beside her husband, feeling rested and energized after her first good night's sleep in weeks. They lay face to face, playfully rubbing their noses together, the affectionate touching sending blood coursing heatedly through their veins. White Owl rubbed Red Willow's back gently to let her know that she was safe with him. Red Willow felt White Owl's erect manhood poke hard against her thigh. This was it—the moment her aunt had described to her. Her heart pounded like a drum, a mixture of anxiety and ecstasy pulsing in her spirit. Instinctively, as if the Great Spirit was guiding her just as Eternal Blossom had said it would, she slowly climbed on top of him and placed his manhood inside her warm body. It was painfully uncomfortable, but she saw the ecstatic look in his eyes, and she pressed on, awkwardly bouncing around on top of him for a minute or so before he released his seed forcefully, letting out a loud grunt. They lay back on the blanket and basked in the afterglow, content in a way they had never dreamed possible.

Chapter Fourteen

On the Warpath

The ranks of Soaring Eagle's war party had swelled considerably with more than eighty young braves volunteering. It was a sizable number, representing a third of the men from the tribe, and was more extensive than had ever been seen before among the Pee Dee. The first task of the men was to forge their weapons of war. The older men among the group taught the younger men how to shape arrowheads from flint, string their bows with deer sinew, craft their knife blades from deer bone, and create their shields with deer hide. Soaring Eagle was overseeing the entire operation, pushing the men to work long hours to be ready to go to war before the cold season set in.

After a month of training his warriors and preparing his war supplies, Soaring Eagle decided it was time to set out on the warpath. He gathered his warriors in the village square and had them bid their families farewell. Mothers said goodbye to their sons and sisters to their brothers. The impending march filled the villagers with a sense of both pride and anxiety. They realized that it was an opportunity for some young braves to prove themselves worthy in battle, but they also knew that it was the peak of the harvest season, and the harvest might suffer from the lack of laborers. Soaring Eagle gave no thought to the crops; his focus was solely on warfare.

Red Willow was glad that White Owl did not volunteer to be a part of the war party. She enjoyed her time with her new husband, and she did not want to be apart from him. They spent all their time together harvesting, hunting, and making love. Red Willow was seemingly fine on the outside, but the loss of her family still deeply troubled her. She had not given herself enough time to grieve, and her unresolved grief was working its way to the surface.

She had grown so close to White Owl that she began to irrationally fear she would lose him too, just as she had lost the rest of her family. On more than one occasion, she considered running away to save herself from any future heartache but stopped herself each time by reminding herself that things could be different this time. It was a constant internal struggle, and one she knew she must overcome if she wanted to maintain her sanity.

✖ ✖ ✖

After heading out, Soaring Eagle's war party hiked for an entire week without seeing any signs of human life. The men were beginning to get antsy, wondering if they had prepared so intensively and traveled so far for nothing. Finally, things took a turn on their eighth day away from home. A small Tuscarora settlement came into view on the horizon.

Soaring Eagle brought the men to a halt and called for his scout team, sending three scouts towards the village to get a closer look, while the rest of the men stayed back and waited for the scouts' report.

After an hour, the scouts returned. The village was small, housing only twenty or so families, and it would be no problem for the large war party to overtake it. Several men were itching for a fight and ready to go, but Soaring Eagle instructed the party that they would be waiting until nightfall to make their advance.

As darkness descended, the warriors made their way stealthily towards the settlement, with Soaring Eagle trailing at a distance. The group stopped together at the settlement's perimeter, waiting for the order to attack. Nervous excitement rose up in the warriors as they held their positions. One of the undisciplined warriors could not control himself, and he rushed into the settlement before the rest of the group, alerting the settlers to the war party's presence. A settler's arrow quickly downed him. The initial killing prompted the rest of the war party to charge the encampment, resulting in a hail of arrows. The women and children of the settlement took shelter in their huts, while the men tried in vain to stave off their attackers.

The battle was over quickly. Soaring Eagle then demanded his warriors bring out all the women and children. The warriors gathered them and brought them before Soaring Eagle, trembling and afraid. He paced back and forth, looking them up and down as he went. Grabbing one of the women, he pulled her away from the rest of the group. She begged him to spare her children and take her life instead. Her pleas triggered memories in his mind of growing up without a mother, and, for a brief second, his humanity arose. He ordered one of his warriors to take her children away from the group. Then he held the woman close to his side and ordered his men to fire their arrows upon the remaining women and children.

It was a bizarre order to give, considering the supposed goal of the party. One of the confused warriors spoke out, "I thought this mission was to provide us with replacement souls for our tribe. Why are we not taking these people hostages and returning home?"

Soaring Eagle gazed up at the moon as if he were trying to harness all its radiant energy. "The time is not right. There is more work to be done. Now finish these people, or I will do it myself."

Some men refused to comply with the order, knowing this was an unnecessary waste of life. But others were more compliant and stepped forward, letting loose their arrows into the row of women and children. The woman Soaring Eagle had in his grasp screamed in horror as she looked on at the chilling sight of the mass murder. Soaring Eagle whispered into her ear, "Go and tell your Tuscarora people what you have seen. Let them know that Soaring Eagle and the Pee Dee people are on the move."

Soaring Eagle released the woman and her children and ordered his men to burn the settlement, including the fallen bodies. For some of the men, this command was the breaking point. A group of about ten dissenters refused the order and demanded they be allowed to return home, as this was not what they had signed up for. Soaring Eagle mocked them as cowards but allowed them to leave. The remaining warriors torched the village with glee. Soaring Eagle looked on, the ever-expanding flames reflecting in the smoky green of his eyes.

Soaring Eagle and the war party continued their raids on small outer Tuscarora settlements for the next few weeks, never once accomplishing what they had set out to do. Sometimes they took entire settlements, and sometimes they made quick strikes then fell back, but never once did they take any hostages. It was, in the eyes of several in the party, a chaotic and fruitless mission.

Cooler weather was just beginning to set in, and the men were moving further away from their homes with fewer rations. There was increasing dissatisfaction among the group, and many abandoned the party to head back to their homes. Those left were tired and hungry and pleaded with Soaring Eagle to end the fighting. He begrudgingly relented and vowed to end the campaign but only after one final raid.

The party approached their last Tuscarora target and waited until nightfall, as they had done successfully before. Once again, the war party crept quietly towards the community, with Soaring Eagle trailing. When they came upon the edge of the encampment, they were surprised to find no signs of life. The fires were lit, but the people were nowhere to be found. The party moved further into the settlement to get a closer look. Seemingly out of nowhere, the Tuscarora surrounded the gathered Pee Dee warriors, stepping out of the shadows in full force with war clubs drawn. They clubbed the warriors savagely and mercilessly, slaughtering them. Soaring Eagle watched the massacre of his men from afar, with a sinking feeling in the pit of his stomach. He quickly turned away from the scene of defeat and death, making his retreat into the dark and starry night.

Soaring Eagle withdrew deep into the woods, overtaken by a breathless panic. He was all alone with no food, no water, and no help—days away from the Pee Dee village. Finding a fallen log for shelter, he lay down and closed his heavy eyelids. His total failure weighed heavily on his mind as he heard his father's shaming voice repeating itself in his brain. It would've been better for him if the villagers had just killed him alongside his men, he thought to himself. Shivering, he finally fell into a restless sleep.

Awaking the following morning with an intense need to empty his bladder, Soaring Eagle pushed himself up from the ground and urinated beside the fallen log where he had slept. He gathered some of the plentiful acorns on the earth and used a nearby rock to crack them open, feasting on the tiny morsels inside. It did little to relieve his hunger, but he took what he could get. Using the sun as his guide, he began his trek westward in the direction of the Pee Dee village. Around midday, he reached a small stream and took a drink of the refreshing water to quench his severe thirst.

It took him multiple days of slow and arduous travel, but Soaring Eagle finally made it back to his tribe. He stumbled into the village, exhausted and haggard, bearing the look of a broken man. Those who witnessed his shameful entrance were surprised to see him alone. The same mothers and sisters who had bid farewell to their loved ones all those weeks ago were now greeting Soaring Eagle with angry questions about their relatives' whereabouts. He made up a story about how they had all gone into the Tuscarora encampment together, with himself leading the charge, of course, only to be ambushed. In his fictional narrative, he fought his way valiantly out of the melee and was only able to escape by the grace of the Great Spirit. Whether his story was true or not was of no consequence to the tribe's women; the only thing that mattered was that their loved ones were gone. The women's cries and moans reverberated in Soaring Eagle's head, compounding the shame he was already feeling.

After allowing him a few days to recover, the villagers brought Soaring Eagle before the tribal council to give a full accounting of his actions. The atmosphere in the temple was thick with anger. Not only had Soaring Eagle's mission been a total failure but the harvest had suffered due to the loss of labor during his extended absence, and the tribe was now in danger of running low on food during the winter months. Soaring Eagle entered to see the other tribal council leaders seated, their faces grave, in the middle of the room. He shuffled gingerly over to where the group was sitting and stood facing the three men.

Spotted Turtle took a few deep breaths before he opened the meeting. "You are still the council leader . . . for now. So, why don't you *lead* us in trying to understand what is happening to our tribe," he said, focusing his gaze on Soaring Eagle.

Soaring Eagle looked back at Spotted Turtle with dead eyes. "It seems the Great Spirit has turned His favor away from our tribe and left us to suffer."

Proud Robin adjusted himself in his seat. "That is one way to look at things. Another way would be to say that the Great Spirit has turned his favor away from *you* only, and all these bad things happening to the tribe result from *your* bad leadership."

The harsh criticism stung Soaring Eagle, and he lashed out fiercely. "You have no right to blame me for all that has gone wrong! I did the best to bring our warriors home safely, but it was not meant to be."

Spotted Turtle leaned forward and pointed his finger at Soaring Eagle. "But it was your idea to take the warriors out in the first place, and that has cost us greatly. Can you not take any responsibility for the situation we face?"

"I made a decision, the people supported it, and it did not work out," Soaring Eagle replied calmly. "At least I chose to take a risk instead of doing the same thing season after season since the beginning of time."

"And look at where that got us," Proud Robin responded. "There is a reason that we follow the rhythm of the seasons. Because it sustains our lives!"

"You have been silent, Walking Squirrel," Spotted Turtle interjected. "Do you have anything to say?"

Walking Squirrel stroked his chin as he eyed Soaring Eagle. "The atsutsa made a mistake. I'm sure it won't happen again."

Spotted Turtle was visibly frustrated at this point, wanting to strip Soaring Eagle of his council membership immediately. He knew he could count on Proud Robin to side with him but was sure Walking Squirrel would lean the other way, and without a unanimous vote, Soaring Eagle could not be removed. It would take some political cunning to cajole Walking Squirrel into siding with him, but Spotted Turtle was adept at quickly coming up with a plan.

"Leave us so that we may discuss your fate," Spotted Turtle snapped at Soaring Eagle.

Soaring Eagle stormed angrily out of the temple, glaring at the men as he left. Spotted Turtle turned to Walking Squirrel. "Proud Robin and I are ready to remove Soaring Eagle from the council. We need your vote to do it. Are you with us?"

As expected, Walking Squirrel maintained his lenient stance towards his friend. "I said he made a mistake, and I don't hold it against him. He deserves no further punishment."

"Would it change your mind if I offered you the title of council leader in exchange for your support?"

Walking Squirrel's eyes widened. It did not take long to change his mind, as the prospect of being council leader easily overrode his friendship with Soaring Eagle. "You are a persuasive person, Spotted Turtle," Walking Squirrel said. "I will vote with you."

The council called Soaring Eagle back into the temple to inform him they would remove him from his position and choose another person from the wolf clan to take his place. Soaring Eagle slammed his hand into one of the pillars supporting the lodge, causing the entire structure to vibrate. "You can't do this without . . . unanimous approval!" he shouted as he glowered at Walking Squirrel.

Walking Squirrel looked away, unable to meet Soaring Eagle's eyes. "The vote *was* unanimous. Your time on the council is over."

Soaring Eagle fumed. "This is not the end for me. I will be back, and you all will regret this decision." Then he stormed out of the temple.

Chapter Fifteen

Great Expectations

Red Willow had been feeling lethargic and sick to her stomach for a few weeks, not well enough to perform her usual tasks with White Owl. Seeking some wise counsel, she visited Eternal Blossom.

"Osiyo, Red Willow," Eternal Blossom said as Red Willow entered the hut. "I haven't been able to spend much time with you since the wedding. It feels like you spend all your time with your new uyehi, and you have forgotten about me."

Red Willow crossed her arms and rubbed one of her biceps. "I have been spending a lot of time with White Owl, but I haven't forgotten you."

"I was just teasing," Eternal Blossom grinned as she looked at her niece. "You should be spending a lot of time with White Owl, but I'm glad you are here now. Tell me about everything. How are you feeling?"

Red Willow squeezed her eyes tight and lowered her eyebrows. "Well, I have been feeling sick to my stomach and exhausted. I'm wondering if I should consult the medicine man."

Eternal Blossom tilted her head to the side and squinted. "Did you have your blood flow during your last moon cycle?"

Red Willow raised an eyebrow, confused as to why her aunt asked her such a question. "No, why?"

"You do need to go to the medicine man . . . to tell him that you are with child."

"How do you know that?"

Eternal Blossom pointed towards her children. "Because I have lived through it—more than once. I know exactly how it works."

Red Willow felt a tingle running through her body as she tried to sort out her feelings. A part of her was overjoyed to realize that she would be bringing a new life into the world, but another part was forlorn to know that her brother and mother would not be there for the experience. Eternal Blossom reached over and hugged her. "I'm so happy that you have received this blessing. I know that the Great Spirit has given you this as a reward for all you have endured."

The two women began to shed tears as they thought back on the loved ones they had lost. Red Willow spent the rest of the day with her aunt, helping her grind the corn from the recent harvest and watching the children play. The sight of the children made Red Willow feel much more exuberant about her pregnancy. She daydreamed about what it would be like to have a child of her own running around, and it warmed her heart.

Red Willow returned to her hut that night to find White Owl waiting for her. "There you are," White Owl said as she walked through the doorway. "I was beginning to wonder if I would ever see you again. Had you been any later, I might've had to move on to the next udalii."

"When you talk like that, I wonder if I should've come back at all," Red Willow retorted as she walked over to her husband and rubbed his shoulders.

White Owl turned and embraced his wife. "Where have you been all day? I thought you weren't feeling well."

"I went to see my agitlogi, and she told me something . . . interesting."

White Owl tilted his head backward and stroked his chest, anxious to hear this exciting piece of news. "And what was that?"

Red Willow turned away, unable to look him in the eye as she shared her secret. "She thinks I am with child."

White Owl rubbed his upper lip with his index finger as he looked quizzically at Red Willow. "And what do *you* think?"

She turned back towards him. "She knows the signs, so I have to trust her."

He stood there silent as a stone, as she waited for some reaction. "Are you not excited?" she asked anxiously.

"I am . . . overwhelmed," he replied as he ran his hands through his hair. "What do we do now?"

Red Willow rubbed her hands together nervously. "My agitlogi says we should go and see the medicine man. He will instruct us of what to do."

White Owl took a deep breath, satisfied they would have a mentor to help them through the process. "We can do this," he nodded. Red Willow smiled a hopeful smile, appreciating his reassurance.

The following day they went together to see the medicine man. "Osiyo Holy One," White Owl said as they entered the doorway of the medicine hut.

The medicine man greeted the young couple enthusiastically, "What brings you here to see me today?"

White Owl rubbed the back of his neck. "My udalii thinks that she is with child. We come to seek your guidance on how to handle this situation."

The medicine man turned a studious gaze on Red Willow. "What makes you think this is the case?"

"I'm not sure what the signs are myself, but my agitlogi thinks I am, based on what I told her," Red Willow replied. "I am often sick to my stomach, and I missed my last moon cycle."

The medicine man nodded his head. "I have seen those same things occur with other women carrying a child. Did your agitlogi tell you anything about what to expect as you go through this process?"

Red Willow's eyes darted back and forth. "No," she said questioningly.

The medicine man smiled. "It will not be easy for you, but it will be a rewarding journey. I will give you some things to ensure that everything will go as smoothly as possible."

The medicine man shuffled over to his shelf of clay pots and pulled out some dried mint leaves. "Take these and make tea with them. It will ease the pains in your stomach. When you finish these, come back to me, and I will give you more. It is also vital that you not eat the flesh of a raccoon or turkey, for it will harm the child. And you must wash your hands and feet in the river every sunrise and sunset to keep yourself pure. Do these things, and the Great Spirit will bless you."

The medicine man fired up a ceremonial pipe to celebrate the incoming child and passed it around to the expectant mother and father. The couple thanked the medicine man for his help and headed back to their hut. They did not realize that there would be so many rules to follow, but they were determined to stick to what the medicine man had told them, wanting their child to come into the world healthy and happy.

Running Wolf was doing his best to fit in with the Catawba tribe. It certainly helped that the tribal council leader, Sitting Deer, liked him. Sitting Deer brought Running Wolf into his household and was instructing him in the ways of their tribe. The pair had become nearly inseparable. They took hunting and fishing trips together, and Sitting Deer even let Running Wolf sit in on tribal council meetings.

Running Wolf's close relationship with Sitting Deer stirred up jealousy amongst some within the Catawba. It was hard to believe an outsider who had been around for such a short time could have gained so much trust from the council leader. They feared he would rise to power and lead the tribe away from its roots, so they hatched a plan to kidnap Running Wolf.

One day, as Running Wolf was out gathering some firewood in the forest, three young men jumped him from behind and tackled him to the ground. He struggled, but their combined strength was too much. They quickly bound his hands and feet, then carried him deep into the woods, planning to kill him and dump the body. Running Wolf could not believe he was being removed from his home again. Hadn't the Great Spirit put him through enough already? This was not how it was supposed to end for him, according to the vision that he had received.

Once the men got him deep into the woods, they forced him to his knees and gathered in a circle around him. One of the young men grabbed him by the hair and pulled his head back to expose his throat.

Another stepped forward with a knife ready to slit Running Wolf's throat, but before the attacker could make his move, a loud bark echoed through the forest. It came from Skye, who had caught Running Wolf's scent and tracked him. Following closely behind Skye were Sitting Deer and three of his warriors.

Skye rushed up and attacked the feet of the man holding Running Wolf. The other two kidnappers quickly took off. The first managed to kick Skye off his leg and begin his retreat, but Skye slowed him down just enough to prevent his total escape. In moments, an arrow from one of Sitting Deer's warriors felled him. Sitting Deer rushed over and removed the bindings from Running Wolf while Skye limped over and licked his friend's face. Running Wolf grabbed his beloved companion and buried his head in the scruff of Skye's neck.

Running Wolf returned to the Catawba camp, deeply shaken. He was now acutely aware that, aside from Sitting Deer, he had no one in the village he could trust. He felt so isolated and was experiencing a tremendous amount of guilt. His actions had been the cause of so many problems in so many people's lives: first his sister, then his mother, and now Sitting Deer. He wished he could just disappear and be swallowed up by the earth so he wouldn't be a burden to anyone ever again.

Sitting Deer took Running Wolf to Rolling Cloud's hut to let him rest and recover. He felt so bad for the boy, knowing how much he had been through in his short life. Sitting Deer thought of himself as a savior for Running Wolf, and those thoughts stirred up memories about the boy that Sitting Deer could not save—his son.

Sitting Deer had many wives and many sons and daughters, but no one could take the place of his precious first-born son. He often thought back to those happier and simpler times when his son was still alive.

Visions of being a carefree young father, taking his son hunting and fishing, filled his head from time to time, but those visions were usually followed by the terrible images of his son's sudden death.

One day when Sitting Deer and his firstborn were out in the woods hunting, his son came down with a terrible pain in his side and began vomiting. Sitting Deer immediately rushed his son back to Rolling Cloud for treatment. Rolling Cloud tried desperately to relieve the boy's condition, but his symptoms worsened over the next few days. He fell into a state of unresponsiveness before his spirit succumbed to the mysterious illness and departed his body.

From that point forward, a grief-stricken Sitting Deer threw himself into the political life of the tribe. He had never before had aspirations of gaining political power, but he needed something to distract himself from the intense sadness he was feeling. Sitting Deer had not grown up in a political family and forged his path onto the political scene. He befriended his clan leader and learned as much as he could about the ins and outs of clan leadership. He assumed the supervisory position when the clan leader passed on, remaining there for several years. Once on the tribal council, he impressed the other council members with his wise and intelligent decision-making, eventually rising to the rank of council chief.

The tribe became prosperous under Sitting Deer's supervision, which was both strong and compassionate. But his immersion in politics was an unhealthy distraction, never giving him the proper amount of time he needed to grieve. He had several failed relationships, and while they had provided him with children, none had given him the fulfillment he desperately craved. He was outwardly successful but remained hollow inside, and he hoped Running Wolf could fill that emptiness.

✖ ✖ ✖

At the Pee Dee tribe, a new wolf clan leader had taken Soaring Eagle's place on the council and Walking Squirrel was now in charge. While Walking Squirrel had indeed betrayed his friend to inherit the position, he quickly discovered that leadership was not in his bloodstream. At heart Walking Squirrel was a man who reveled in following orders rather than giving them. He spent most of his time just wishing that his old friend Soaring Eagle was still on the council instead of this wolf-clan interloper. Fed up with his new responsibilities and with no one to give *him* the orders he so desperately craved, Walking Squirrel went crawling back to see Soaring Eagle at his hut one day.

"What do you want?" Soaring Eagle demanded as Walking Squirrel sauntered up to the open doorway.

Walking Squirrel dropped his head, unable to look his friend in the eye. "You have every right to be angry with me, oginalii. I let you down again, but I want to make it right."

Soaring Eagle scoffed. "Why would I trust you? You change more than the weather. One day blowing this way, one day blowing that way. Your help is no help at all."

"I want you back on the council," Walking Squirrel pleaded, "and I have a plan to make it happen."

Soaring Eagle looked up from his hammock. He still did not entirely trust Walking Squirrel, but the mere suggestion of a return to power overrode the instincts of his distrust. "What plan?"

Walking Squirrel informed Soaring Eagle about his plan to frame the wolf clan leader for theft to get him thrown off the council. Soaring Eagle believed the scheme might work, and he agreed to participate. Under cover of darkness one evening, after most of the tribe had taken their rest for the night, Soaring Eagle and his co-conspirators snuck into the temple and stole the sacred copper falcon. The falcon was an impressive work of art thought to provide power and long life to those who possessed it. The icon was usually kept in a shared location so that its forces could be harnessed in a shared fashion by the entire tribe. Soaring Eagle and his companions took the falcon and hastily buried it behind the hut of the newly chosen wolf clan leader, with a portion of it sticking out of the ground so that someone would notice.

After the year's poor harvest, the last thing the tribe needed was further deterioration of its strength. Therefore, panic quickly spread when someone noticed the falcon's absence the following morning. The tribal council initiated a massive search, and, within a matter of hours, they found the falcon behind the hut of the wolf clan leader. The council returned the falcon to its rightful place in the temple, and order was restored for everybody—except one. The news of the falcon's discovery behind the wolf clan leader's hut sent shockwaves through the village, and a special meeting of the tribal council was called that night to decide the wolf clan leader's fate. Before the meeting, however, Soaring Eagle and Walking Squirrel met in secret to discuss their plans.

Walking Squirrel clasped his hands together in front of his chest as he spoke to Soaring Eagle. "I will do my part to make sure that this thief is removed from his position, but it is up to you to convince your clan to give you back your seat on the council."

"Don't worry," Soaring Eagle replied. "I still have support from the right people within my clan to make that happen."

That night the council brought the wolf clan leader to answer the charges brought against him—theft of the falcon. He stood among the other clan leaders, who had formed a circle around him, next to the ceremonial fire. As head of the council, Walking Squirrel addressed the man first. "The theft of the copper falcon is a grave crime. What do you have to say for yourself?"

The accused stood and addressed the council stoically, "The falcon belongs to all of us. There could be no reason for me to steal it. I am not guilty of this crime."

Spotted Turtle continued the inquiry. "The falcon was found buried outside your hut. Can you explain that?"

"I did not put it there," he responded.

"Perhaps it flew there on its own?" Walking Squirrel interjected.

The wolf clan leader glared at him. "I do not know how it got there."

Spotted Turtle pressed the inquiry. "I must remind you that you are speaking in the presence of the Great Spirit, who sees and knows what is in the hearts of all people."

The wolf clan leader clenched his teeth before he answered this time. "The Great Spirit knows my heart, and He knows that I speak the truth before you."

"That will be enough," Walking Squirrel said, dismissing him.

Once he was gone, the remaining three council members began their deliberation, with Spotted Turtle being the first to speak. "I am convinced he is innocent," he said. "I see no reason to remove him from the council."

Walking Squirrel rebutted, "He must have you under a spell because he is guilty in my eyes. He stole the falcon because he wanted all its power for himself. A man like that, who would put his own needs in front of the needs of the tribe, has no right to be on the council."

Spotted Turtle clenched his fists in disagreement. "You saw what I saw. He said, before the Great Spirit, that he was innocent. He would not risk condemnation by the Great Spirit if he were not telling the truth."

Walking Squirrel again dismissed Spotted Turtle's argument. "That's even further proof that he should not be a part of this council. A man who does not tell the truth in the presence of the Great Spirit should not be a leader. The falcon was stolen and then found behind his hut. Do you have any explanation for that, other than that he is a thief?"

"It is a test for us," Spotted Turtle responded. "We need to use our spiritual wisdom to discern the truth, rather than simply relying on what our eyes tell us. The eyes can be very deceiving sometimes."

"You've been silent," Walking Squirrel said, pointing at Proud Robin. "What do you have to say on the matter?"

"We have no way of knowing the truth," Proud Robin replied plainly, "but we do know the feelings of the tribe. They believe him to be guilty, and they do not trust him. Once that trust is gone, he can no longer be an effective leader. I believe that he should be removed from the council, whether guilty or not."

Spotted Turtle scrunched his face and shot an intensely incredulous look at Proud Robin, as if the man had suggested that Spotted Turtle kill his own mother. "You cannot be serious!" he barked. "You know what that clan could do if we remove this asgaya?" Spotted Turtle gritted his teeth and gestured toward the accused wolf clan leader. "They could send that serpent, Soaring Eagle, back here to sit on this council!"

"They would never do that," Proud Robin scoffed. "They know he is not to be trusted, just as you and I do."

"You give the people too much credit," Spotted Turtle shook his head. "As individuals they might be good decision makers, but when you get them together they behave like a colony of pigeons—easily tricked and manipulated by the cunning hunter."

Proud Robin shrugged. "Neither one of us knows the future. The only thing I know right now is that I vote to remove this man in front of us here today from the council. The rest I leave in the combined hands of the wolf clan and the Great Spirit."

Spotted Turtle sighed loudly then muttered, "You will regret this decision."

And with that, the vote was two to one to remove the wolf clan leader. And it did not take long for the clan to choose their new representative. Much to Proud Robin's surprise and Spotted Turtle's chagrin, Soaring Eagle managed to finagle his way back. Beginning with the tragic events of the Green Corn Ceremony and continuing through the disastrous war party, the tribe was slowly unraveling, like threads on a worn-out skirt. Soaring Eagle's return to power would prove to be the final tug that ripped the cloth into pieces.

Chapter Sixteen
Loose Ends

One chilly and overcast day, snow began to fall at the Catawba village and continued throughout the night, blanketing the ground in a thin layer of pure, soft whiteness. The snow on the ground transported Running Wolf back to the childhood memory of his first snow. It was a magical event for him. He remembered the feeling of the fluffy white powder in his hands and how whimsical it was to throw it up in the air and watch it land back on his face. He remembered chasing his sister through the snow and throwing it back and forth. But he remembered most fondly the smile and the warm cup of tea that his mother had waiting for him when he came in from playing in the cold.

The smiling mother in Running Wolf's memory stood in stark contrast to the corpse that now sat perched in a tree, exposed to the elements. It hurt his heart to think that she might be devoured by scavenging birds or eaten by worms without a proper funeral. He had put in the work to establish his standing within his new tribe, and he felt like he could now spare the time and energy to recover her body.

Running Wolf approached Sitting Deer one evening after dinner. "I have something I need to ask you."

Sitting Deer took a puff of his pipe and looked at Running Wolf. "Ask me anything, young oginalii."

Running Wolf ran his hands through his hair, took a deep breath, and closed his eyes. "There is something I haven't told you yet. When my tribe banished me, they banished my etsi with me. One day, she passed on to the spirit realm during our wandering, and I left her body perched in a tree. I would like to get it and bring it back here for a proper burial."

Sitting Deer pulled his pipe from his mouth and relaxed it on his leg. "I thought we agreed that you would not keep any more secrets from me, but here you are telling me something I have never heard before from you."

Running Wolf's back stiffened, and his voice shifted to a higher register. "I wasn't trying to hide it from you; I just didn't think it was important."

Sitting Deer studied Running Wolf, looking for signs of deceitfulness and not finding any. "I understand your desire to see your etsi properly buried, but I fear for your safety if you undertake this journey now. Besides, what makes you sure you will be able to find her?"

Running Wolf looked off into the distance. "I remember well the place where I left her, and if I go off track, I will have Skye there to guide me. He can follow the scent."

Sitting Deer stroked his forehead and brushed his hair back. "You may go if, *and only if,* you allow me to go with you."

Running Wolf was surprised by Sitting Deer's response. Ordinarily, a man of Sitting Deer's standing would send his subordinates on such a journey. Sitting Deer himself volunteering to go lifted Running Wolf's spirit. "I would be honored," he said, bowing to Sitting Deer.

Sitting Deer offered Running Wolf a share of his tobacco pipe, and the two agreed that they would leave on their expedition at sunrise the following morning. When they had finished smoking, Sitting Deer retrieved a new fox fur coat he had been saving and presented it to Running Wolf. The outpouring of support was almost too much. Running Wolf fought back the tears of gratitude as he placed his hand on Sitting Deer's shoulder, letting it linger there for a few minutes before excusing himself for the night.

Sitting Deer, Running Wolf, and Skye set out on their journey into the woods the following morning. The sun was bright, and the temperature had warmed considerably. The snow was beginning to melt, softening the ground and turning it into a giant brown sponge. Many questions were swirling in Running Wolf's mind as they set off. In what kind of condition would he find his mother's body? How would he react when he saw it? Was all this worth it? After all, the spirit is more important than the body. But he pressed through his anxiety, knowing his mother deserved a proper funeral.

The group walked all day, stopping only for the occasional drink of water. As nightfall approached, they decided to set up camp near a small stream. Sitting Deer made a fire while Running Wolf went down to refill their deerskin water pouches. After everything was settled, the two sat down next to the fire and shared some pemmican while Skye roamed around.

"Tell me more about your etsi," Sitting Deer said, chomping his pemmican.

Running Wolf wiped the pemmican residue from his face. "She was a strong woman, who had to raise my agilvgi and me by herself after my doda died. That hard work took a toll on her and made her sick, but she was strong for me even in her weakness. When I committed my crime, she tried to take my guilt upon herself, and she paid the price for it." He paused and swallowed deeply. "It's my fault that her spirit was taken." He closed his eyes tightly, trying to suppress his tears.

Sitting Deer placed his hand on the boy's shoulder. "I too thought I was responsible for my etsi's death. I never knew her, but my elders told me that her spirit left her body while she was bringing me into the world. I lived most of my life with the burden of believing I was responsible. I have learned to let that go, for it did my spirit no good to hold onto it. I now believe that whatever happened to both of our etsis was the will of the Great Spirit. You and I are nothing more than clay pots, holding only a small amount of water that the Great Spirit pours out as needed. His will is not our will, and I believe that you can be free of your guilt if you can learn to accept that."

Running Wolf rolled his eyes. "People always say that when something bad happens, but I do not believe it. If the Great Spirit willed my etsi to suffer the way she did, then He does not deserve to be called great. I believe that we suffer because people have the freedom to choose, and they choose to do wrong. And the Great Spirit just looks on at the people with shame and disgust, always hoping they will make the right choice and always being disappointed."

Sitting Deer nodded his head, impressed with the young boy's profound insights. "You might be right ... or I might be right. We will never know the real truth on this side of life, for we have such a limited perspective. We are like the seeds trapped inside a squash; we do not see anything outside the rind. But I know from experience that taking on too much responsibility for things that are not your fault can be a big burden."

Running Wolf stroked his forehead. "I just don't like the image of the Great Spirit controlling us from the outside without knowing our inner wounds."

Sitting Deer stared into the crackling flames. "Then change your image of the Great Spirit. Consider your spirit an extension of Himself, and when you suffer, He suffers. It could be that what He gives us in our sufferings is not relief but His comforting presence."

Running Wolf closed his eyes and imagined the Great Spirit suffering alongside his mother as she breathed her last breath, and the two merged their spirits. He felt a great sense of relief, and his chest and shoulders relaxed from lifting his invisible burden. He laid down next to Skye, and his body melted into the ground as he fell fast asleep.

Sitting Deer and Running Wolf woke the following day and continued their trek towards the raised burial site. Around midday, Running Wolf pulled out his mother's gorget and waved it in front of Skye's nose. Skye picked up Gray Dove's scent a little further down the trail and quickly led Running Wolf and Sitting Deer to the tree at the mountain base where Running Wolf had placed her to rest. Running Wolf ran his fingers gently across the markings he had left on the tree trunk, bracing himself for what was to come next. He slowly raised his eyes to peer upon the remains of his mother. The covering had blown off her body, leaving the bottom part of her torso exposed. Her legs were dark and bloated, and scavenging birds had picked at the rotting flesh around her ankles. Running Wolf put his hand on his stomach and lowered his head. Sitting Deer placed his hand on Running Wolf's shoulder and offered to go up into the tree to retrieve the body himself. Running Wolf nodded as tears blurred his eyes.

Sitting Deer climbed into the tree and carried down the body with it slung over his shoulder. He laid the corpse on the ground in front of Running Wolf. Gray Dove's face had remained covered throughout the transport, and Running Wolf was in no mood to remove the covering. He preferred to remember his mother as she was in life instead of how she looked now. Running Wolf said a prayer for his deceased mother, and they wrapped up the cadaver in a bearskin blanket they had brought. They placed it onto the back of the travois and set off towards the setting sun on their return journey.

✖✖✖

Red Willow's belly had begun to expand to the point that it was clear she was with child. Doing everything the medicine man had prescribed, things went smoothly after a rough start. She had resumed many of her activities except for hunting. She spent a lot of time under the mentorship of Eternal Blossom, learning the ins and outs of motherhood.

The family had to be careful this winter about rationing their food. Their food supplies were lower than usual due to the disruptions to the harvest caused by Soaring Eagle's war party. Several of the tribe members were malnourished, and many succumbed to disease as a result. Eternal Blossom tightly controlled the rations her family could have since she knew it would have to last them through the winter. Each person was only allowed a handful of hickory nuts in the morning, a single corn cake during the day, and broth for dinner. It wasn't much, but it would be enough to see them through if they stuck to their regimen. It was a good lesson for Red Willow to learn how to guide a family through tough times.

One day Red Willow and Eternal Blossom were sitting together and grinding some corn as the children played by the fire. "I cannot believe that evil spirit, Soaring Eagle, is back on the tribal council," Red Willow said with evident disgust.

Eternal Blossom continued her work without looking up. "I do not understand it either. He is rotten to his core."

Red Willow took her grinding stone and pressed it vigorously into the corn kernels in her stone trough. "I don't even want to raise my usdi in a village where he is one of the leaders."

Eternal Blossom sighed. "What choice do you have? You and White Owl can't just go out on your own into the woods with a new baby. There is support in the village, even if the leadership is lacking."

Red Willow stopped her grinding. "I can't be the only one who feels that way about Soaring Eagle. There have to be others who want him gone, and if enough of us come together, we can get rid of him."

Eternal Blossom shook her head. "What you are talking about will only weaken the tribe further. I don't like Soaring Eagle any more than you do, but we just have to focus on our own lives and live them so that we will be strong, no matter what bad decisions he makes as a leader. If we do that, then everything else will work out. Focus only on what you can control and be patient."

As Eternal Blossom finished speaking, Fyre approached the women with a dead squirrel in its mouth and laid it down in front of Red Willow. "There is a lesson to be learned from cats," Red Willow said to Eternal Blossom. "They don't take the time to stop and think about taking out their prey. They just do it when they feel like it."

Eternal Blossom rolled her eyes. "You are not a cat. Just be grateful for being what the Great Spirit made you and use the gifts of wisdom and discernment that you have been given."

Fyre jumped onto Red Willow's lap and sat there while the women completed their work. Around nightfall, White Owl returned from his hunt with a few small rabbits. He placed them on the ground next to the women and sat down to rest. Red Willow brought him some broth, and they all sat by the fire, continuing the earlier conversation. White Owl agreed with Eternal Blossom that now was not the time to make a move against Soaring Eagle. He acknowledged that Red Willow was right in her criticisms, but the most important thing for him at the moment was making sure that Red Willow and the baby were safe. The couple returned to their hut for the night, where they made love before falling asleep in each other's arms.

The tribal council met the following morning to discuss the food shortage plaguing the tribe. All of the regular members—Soaring Eagle, Walking Squirrel, Spotted Turtle, and Proud Robin—were in attendance. They began the meeting by presenting the Great Spirit a ceremonial tobacco offering. The men passed around the pipe while they shared their thoughts about the situation the tribe was facing.

Walking Squirrel spoke first. "Our tribe is facing a serious situation. Many in our tribe are running extremely low on food supplies, and several souls have died. We need to solve this food crisis before losing total control. Without some kind of assistance, I fear we will lose many more as the cold season progresses. If anyone has any suggestions, I would like to hear them."

Proud Robin offered up an idea. "Could we require all the eligible men of the tribe to hunt daily and bring back their kill to share in common among the tribe?"

"The problem with that plan is that we lost many of our men in battle," Spotted Turtle replied. "There aren't enough eligible men to hunt for the needs of the entire tribe. Besides that, many of the animals are not active during this season, and the opportunities to hunt them are too few."

Proud Robin came back with a second thought. "What if there is an available food source that we haven't considered yet. We know that the squirrels gather and store their nuts for the cold season. If we track their movements, we can see where they hide their stores, and we could then raid them for ourselves."

"It is a clever idea," Walking Squirrel replied, "but I still don't think it would provide enough to meet the needs of the tribe."

Spotted Turtle was itching to put Soaring Eagle to the test. "Do you have a plan, Soaring Eagle?"

Soaring Eagle stared back at Spotted Turtle with a blank look. "There is nothing we need to do. It is the will of the Great Spirit that the tribe should go hungry and that only the strongest among us should survive."

Spotted Turtle leaned forward and glared at Spotted Turtle. "That is not how we do things in this tribe. We all look out for each other, no matter who is weak or strong." He turned towards Walking Squirrel. "I think our best option would be to seek some outside help. The Catawba are generous people. If we were to reach out to them in our time of need, I know they would help us."

Soaring Eagle raised his arms in protest. "That is a terrible idea. If we let them know we are vulnerable, they will use that knowledge to attack us. We cannot show any weakness."

Walking Squirrel was not yet ready to disregard the counsel of his newly placed right-hand man. "I agree with Soaring Eagle here. We should let this situation be what it is. If we lose many souls, we will just come back stronger once the warm season returns."

Spotted Turtle was livid. He decided then and there he would have to break from the rest of the council and take matters into his own hands. Walking Squirrel adjourned the council, and the men went their separate ways. Spotted Turtle returned to his clan and requested a gathering of the members, where he shared with them the details of the meeting and his next steps.

The plan was simple enough. Spotted Turtle would send someone from the clan to the Catawba tribe to ask for aid under the guise of a hunting trip. He would not be able to make the journey himself because it would arouse suspicion. It would require a volunteer prepared for a difficult trip and not afraid to violate the council's will. White Owl looked at Red Willow and her pregnant belly and knew he would do anything to make their lives better. "I will go," he raised his voice amongst the gathered crowd.

Red Willow looked up at him, eyes wide. *What was he thinking?* Did he not realize that her child would end up fatherless if anything happened to him, just as she was? But she saw the look in his eyes and knew what was in his heart; there was nothing that could stop him. She gripped his arm tightly and rested her head against his shoulder. Spotted Turtle accepted White Owl's offer to serve and thanked him for his willingness. He invited White Owl and Red Willow to his hut for a meal, where they could discuss the plans for the trip in further detail.

Chapter Seventeen
A Time to Rest

Sitting Deer and Running Wolf arrived back at the Catawba village with the body of Gray Dove in tow. Under normal circumstances, they would have begun preparing the body for burial, but Running Wolf did not want to bury his mother in an unfamiliar place. He had heard stories about the so-called "bonepickers" that resided among the Catawba, whose job was to remove the flesh from corpses. Running Wolf asked Sitting Deer if he could have a bonepicker work on his mother's corpse to strip it down to the bones, hopeful that one day he would find his way back to the Pee Dee tribe and be able to bury Gray Dove's bones in her home village. Sitting Deer tenderly obliged his surrogate son's request, summoning Rolling Cloud to arrange the procedure.

Running Wolf took Gray Dove's body to Rolling Cloud's hut, where the bonepicker greeted him. The bonepicker was a heavily tattooed man with fingernails long and sharp as an eagle's talons. Running Wolf laid his mother's body on a platform in front of the bonepicker, who said a prayer to the Great Spirit to bless the task that he was about to undertake. Rolling Cloud lit a small fire, and the bonepicker began. He scraped the flesh from Gray Dove's bones, a little bit at a time, chucking it into the fire as it came off. Running Wolf felt a tiny part of his own heart being torn out with each bit removed. He watched solemnly as his mother's flesh turned to ashes. The stench of the burning sinew was awful, but he tried his best to put it out of his mind so he could be there for his mother.

As the smoke from his mother's ashes began to lift towards the sky, Running Wolf felt the release of his mother's spirit. Overwhelmed, he let out a great cry, unsure if it was joy or sadness, but it did not matter. The release was what mattered, as he and his mother were finally free. A sense of peace enveloped him that he had never felt before.

The bonepicker continued until the bones were scraped clean. Rolling Cloud placed the bones in a specially prepared clay pot and presented them to Running Wolf. Running Wolf dropped his mother's gorget into the pot and closed the lid. Rolling Cloud, the bonepicker, and Running Wolf shared a ceremonial pipe to honor his mother before the Great Spirit. Running Wolf thanked the men for their services and returned with his mother's bones to Sitting Deer's home.

"How did it go?" Sitting Deer asked Running Wolf.

Running Wolf let out a sigh. "I was happy and sad at the same time, but I know now her spirit is free. The only thing left to do is bury her bones back at our home village."

Sitting Deer rubbed his chin, worried to hear that he might be losing his young friend. "I thought you weren't going to be able to return?"

"I hope to return one day . . . when the right people are in power," Running Wolf replied. "I don't expect to go back any time soon, but I believe the Great Spirit has a plan for me to make all my wrongs right, including providing my etsi with the burial she deserves. But until that day comes, I will have her bones here with me, and I have you to thank for that. I am grateful for everything you have done for me, Sitting Deer."

Sitting Deer took a deep breath, happy to hear that Running Wolf would not be leaving soon. "I am glad to be an oginalii to you in your time of need."

Spotted Turtle spread word among the tribe that the men were going on a hunting trip. The time had come for White Owl to undertake his journey. He knew it was too dangerous for him to go alone, so he enlisted two of his fellow bear clan members to join him. The night before they were to leave, White Owl and his companions met to finalize their plans and share a tobacco offering to the Great Spirit. After the meeting, White Owl returned to his hut to spend his last night with Red Willow.

The couple lay down together, and White Owl gently rubbed his wife's belly. "I will miss you and the baby while I am gone."

Red Willow smirked. "I can't speak for the baby, but I know I will miss you too. Promise me you will not do anything foolish to get yourself hurt while you are out there. I want to see you again soon."

"You don't have to worry about me. The Great Spirit will be with me on my journey. He knows how important this is, and He will not let me fail."

"I admire your confidence and willingness to help your tribe," she replied. "I want to give you something special to let you know how wonderful you are."

Red Willow gently rubbed White Owl's chest and nuzzled his neck. His heart raced, body tingling in anticipation of what was to come. Red Willow slowly slipped down White Owl's trousers to reveal his throbbing manhood. She climbed on top of him and inserted him, quivering at the feeling of penetration. She instinctively glided up and down, enjoying the warm and wet sensation of flesh meeting flesh. Their faces began to clench with the exciting build-up until they climaxed simultaneously, releasing all the built-up tension in the most enjoyable way. She got down from on top of him and lay back down next to him.

"I hope that will help you remember me while you are away on your trip," she said through panting breaths.

White Owl grinned from ear to ear and cradled her as they fell asleep. They woke the following day, and he gathered his things in preparation for the journey. She hugged him tightly, not wanting to let go. They lingered for a moment before he set out through the hut door to meet his companions in the village courtyard. She stood in the doorway, watching him until he was out of sight. Wiping a few tears from her eyes, she went back inside.

White Owl met up with his traveling companions, and they set off on their trek, traversing the same area Running Wolf and Gray Dove had traveled many months ago. They took a different approach, however, when they came upon the river that Running Wolf and Gray Dove had struggled to cross. White Owl and his companions set fire to the base of a large tree near the shoreline and waited patiently for the fire to burn a crevice into the trunk. Once they felt the gap was deep enough, they chopped into the burnt trunk with their stone axes until they felled the tree. The falling tree swooped through the air, landing with a thud on the opposite side of the river. The men used the fallen trunk as a natural bridge to cross the river safely.

The journey to the Catawba for White Owl and his companions was a much colder one than Running Wolf and Gray Dove's. They had to stop frequently to stay warm, slowing their travel significantly. After two weeks, they finally made it to the Catawba village—tired and cold but happy they had reached their destination. At the outskirts, they encountered some Catawba men returning from a hunting trip who led them back to the village and quickly informed Running Wolf of their arrival.

Running Wolf felt a swell of emotions upon hearing the news but showed nothing to the Catawba. He knew he should be happy to see his former Pee Dee tribemates, but he was setting down roots and wasn't sure he was ready to be reminded of his past yet. With a strange hesitation, he sauntered through the village to greet the Pee Dee men.

White Owl stopped in his tracks when he saw Running Wolf coming to greet him. Running Wolf greeted him with a pat on the shoulder as White Owl stood motionless, barely able to speak. *Was this a ghost,* he wondered? He hadn't even considered the possibility that Running Wolf could have survived his banishment, yet here he was face-to-face with his sister's husband.

Running Wolf chuckled nervously. "Are you surprised to see me?"

White Owl placed his hand over his heart. "I am more than surprised. I am stunned."

"It is good to see you, White Owl," Running Wolf said, "but what are you doing here?"

"I have much to tell you, Running Wolf," White Owl said as he pointed towards his companions. "But we need to rest and recover for a time before I catch you up. It has been a long and tiring journey."

Running Wolf nodded. "Come with me, and I will make sure you are warmed and fed."

Running Wolf led White Owl and his companions back to the hut that Sitting Deer had given him, where they could rest their weary bodies by a warm fire. As White Owl entered the house, Skye rushed up to give him a long sniff. White Owl rubbed Skye behind the ears, and Skye quickly recognized the scent of Red Willow. He jumped up and down playfully, seeking more affection from White Owl, who gladly obliged. The men sat close to the fire, and Running Wolf served them a hearty portion of stew that had been simmering all day. Running Wolf had so much to ask White Owl; he could not even wait until White Owl had finished eating. "How is Red Willow?"

White Owl continued lapping up his stew. "She is good. We are married now."

Running Wolf leaned his head back and raised his eyebrows in surprise. "So, she finally gave in to your pursuit? Good for you." He gave White Owl a congratulatory slap on the back.

"If you mean to say that she finally made the right choice, then the answer to your question is yes," White Owl smiled before continuing to chow down. "But that's not all, my new udo. Your sister is also with child."

Running Wolf stood up quickly out of his seat, knocking White Owl's bowl of stew onto the ground. Some of the hot liquid spilled onto White Owl's lap, and he jumped up quickly and shook his trousers to diffuse the sting. White Owl gave Running Wolf an angry stare.

"Sorry."

"It's fine," White Owl replied. "It's just . . ." he sighed, ". . . I'm still hungry."

Running Wolf served White Owl more stew and allowed him to eat in peace this time. White Owl finished his meal, and Running Wolf offered the men an after-dinner tobacco pipe. The men relaxed by the fire as they passed the pipe around.

White Owl leaned close to Running Wolf. "I didn't come all the way here just to see you. There is something else more important that we need to discuss. Our tribe is in crisis. We are dangerously low on food because of an ill-timed war effort led by Soaring Eagle. People are getting sick and dying from the lack of sustenance. We need help, and Spotted Turtle sent me here to ask for it."

Running Wolf was deeply distressed to hear of the troubles his tribe was facing. As much as he was enjoying his new life with the Catawba, he felt the Great Spirit calling to him to be the one to help his old tribe. "On my honor, I will ensure you get your help."

White Owl gave a blank stare towards his young relative, skeptical that Running Wolf could honor that kind of promise. "Just get me in front of the tribal chief."

Their conversation continued, with Running Wolf sharing stories of his journey, including Gray Dove's final days. When White Owl learned of his wife's mother's death, his thoughts turned immediately to his wife. He knew that Red Willow would be sad to hear the news, and he preemptively felt her grief. After White Owl and Running Wolf had shared all the stories, White Owl and his companions lay down to rest for the night. Running Wolf was restless and went straight to Sitting Deer to ask him about giving the Pee Dee people aid.

Sitting Deer was relaxing in his hut, enjoying a pipe offering with Rolling Cloud when Running Wolf sauntered in. "I need to talk to you."

Sitting Deer sat up from his peaceful pose. "What is so important that you would disturb me during my meditation time?"

Running Wolf paced the floor excitedly. "I just came from speaking with some of my former tribemates, who have come here on a long journey."

Sitting Deer interrupted Running Wolf. "Why was I not made aware of their presence here?"

Running Wolf stopped and looked at Sitting Deer. "They just got here not long ago and need our help."

Sitting Deer ruminated on the boy's words, taking a few more drags from his pipe. "I cannot help the Pee Dee people right now. I have to focus on my people and make sure they have what they need."

Running Wolf scrunched his face in frustration. "I don't understand. You have been helpful towards me since I have been here with you, yet you won't help my tribe in its time of need?"

Sitting Deer crossed his arms in front of his chest. "Helping you is different than helping an entire tribe. I'm afraid you will have to send your former tribemates back empty-handed."

Running Wolf clenched his fist and shouted, "I cannot believe you would do this! If you don't help them, then I will. I don't know how, but I will find a way."

Sitting Deer stepped directly into Running Wolf's face. "I can't let you do that. It would be an unwise decision for you to try to help your tribe alone. You must stay here with us."

Running Wolf's eyes widened with disbelief. "Am I a prisoner here? You can't control me like that. I will do what I want!"

Sitting Deer grabbed Running Wolf by both arms. "You will not go! This is for your own good."

Sitting Deer summoned his guards, who forced Running Wolf's hands behind his back and whisked him away. They placed him in a secure hut, where they could keep him under constant surveillance. Rolling Cloud watched the entire scene unfold with a sick feeling in his stomach. He knew that Sitting Deer was making a regrettable decision. He left without saying a word, deeply disturbed by what had transpired.

Sitting Deer had White Owl and his companions brought before him the following morning. "I know why you are here, and I know you have come a long way, so I am sorry to tell you that I cannot help your people. My responsibility is to my tribe and my tribe only."

White Owl was discouraged by Sitting Deer's reluctance to help but unwilling to give up so easily. "I understand that you want to look out for your tribe, chief, and we would never ask you to harm them to help us. But there must be something you have in excess to offer our tribe? We would accept any amount of help, no matter how small you think your offer might be. My udalii's udo, Running Wolf, spoke very highly of you yesterday. He said that you were a kind and generous leader, and he promised us that you would be willing to offer assistance."

White Owl's last statement caught Sitting Deer's attention. "You are related to Running Wolf? He never mentioned you when we talked. Do you have a name?"

"My name is White Owl."

Sitting Deer tapped his hand on his thigh and looked out into the distance. "White Owl, you are right to call me generous. And because you were bold enough to speak out, I have changed my mind. I will help your tribe. I will send you three large bundles of pemmican and the dogs to carry them. But if I do this, you must leave this place now and never return."

White Owl thought it was odd that Sitting Deer requested them to leave now and never return, but he was in no position to question Sitting Deer's stance. "I humbly accept your offer. Your supplies will help our tribe greatly, and your name will be honored among the Pee Dee people."

"I will have my men get your things ready for you to leave before the sun reaches its high point," Sitting Deer said. "You are to leave then. Until that time comes, you must go and wait outside the palisade wall."

"May I say goodbye to Running Wolf?" White Owl asked.

Sitting Deer snapped back quickly at White Owl. "He is busy doing a job for me right now, and he will not be finished before you have to leave."

White Owl lowered his head in disappointment. "I'm sorry to hear that. Tell him that his agilvgi misses him greatly and thinks about him every day."

"I will," Sitting Deer replied gruffly. "Now go outside the palisade wall and wait before I change my mind."

Sitting Deer had his men gather the pemmican and set up the dogs with their carrying cart. The pemmican was loaded onto the travois and taken out to the waiting Pee Dee men. The men bowed their heads to thank Sitting Deer for his help and set off on their way. Sitting Deer watched them intently as they crossed over the horizon, standing for a long while to ensure they were far away.

Returning to the tribal council hut, Sitting Deer ordered his guards to release Running Wolf, who rushed into the council hut, burning with fury. "Have you lost your mind?" Running Wolf asked Sitting Deer angrily. "Why did you imprison me? I thought I was your guest, not your prisoner. Where are my tribemates?"

Sitting Deer sat extremely still, not even looking at Running Wolf. "What I did, I did for your good. I sent the Pee Dee men back to their village with the supplies they needed."

Running Wolf pointed his finger angrily in Sitting Deer's face. "What makes you think that imprisoning someone is for their good?"

Sitting Deer looked up at Running Wolf as he tried to explain his actions. "I knew you would try to go back with the Pee Dee men . . . and I knew it would have only been a heartache for you when you were not allowed back into the tribe. I wanted to save you from that."

Running Wolf stomped his foot into the ground. "I cannot believe you would lock me up. You do not get to make MY decisions for me. I have had enough. I am leaving."

"I do not want to lock you up again, but I will if you keep pushing me," Sitting Deer said.

"Then do it," Running Wolf issued the challenge.

Sitting Deer called his guards over, and Running Wolf struggled fiercely with them before they could finally subdue him. The guards led Running Wolf back to the secured hut, where they stood watch.

Chapter Eighteen

Return from the Catawba

Soaring Eagle was beginning to grow suspicious of White Owl's lengthy absence. He confronted Red Willow to see if something more than a hunting trip was happening, visiting her one morning as she was helping Eternal Blossom prepare the day's stew from whatever scraps they could gather. "I have come to speak with Red Willow about White Owl," Soaring Eagle bellowed as he barged in.

Eternal Blossom spit onto the ground in front of Soaring Eagle. "You are not welcome here."

Soaring Eagle glared at her as he stomped his foot into her spit and rubbed it into the dirt. "Even if I am not welcome, it is within my authority to be here as part of the Council. I want to speak with Red Willow . . . and I want to do it alone."

Red Willow came over and placed her hand on Eternal Blossom's shoulder as she stared at Soaring Eagle. "Don't worry, agitlogi. He is nothing I can't handle by myself."

Eternal Blossom begrudgingly left the hut, unable to look Soaring Eagle in the eyes as she passed.

"So, what is it that you have to say?" Red Willow demanded.

Soaring Eagle meandered around the hut, inspecting some items as he went. "I have noticed that White Owl has been gone on his 'hunting trip' for many days. Such a trip should not take this long. Don't you find it strange?"

Red Willow's eyes followed him as he made his way around the hut. "It is the cold season. Animals are scarcer, and travel is slower. I don't find it strange that he's been gone so long. We are desperately short on food, so he is probably trying to hunt as much as possible while he is out there. Unlike some people, he cares about the welfare of the entire tribe."

Soaring Eagle stopped moving and eyed Red Willow carefully. "So, you think that he is only out there hunting and nothing else? Because I have my doubts. If he has been gone this long, I think he is secretly doing something suspicious, or an accident has befallen him and taken his life. In either case, you may find yourself without a uyehi. What will you do then? Where will you turn for help? Surely you will not want to raise a child on your own as your etsi did. I could be that help for you . . . if you will let me."

Red Willow's face scrunched up in disgust. "I'd rather myself and my child starve than take any help from you. So, if that is all you have to talk to me about, you can leave now and let me fix my paltry dinner in peace."

"When things get worse for you—and they will get worse," Soaring Eagle said, shaking his finger, "you know where to find me. I may take pity on you and accept your pleas for help . . . or I may not."

Soaring Eagle left Eternal Blossom's hut with Fyre hissing at him as he walked through the doorway and returned to the village square. Eternal Blossom made her way back and finished helping Red Willow prepare the stew. Once Eternal Blossom completed the cooking, she decided it would be good to light a bundle of cedar sticks to clear the hut of the noxious energy Soaring Eagle had left behind.

A few days later, White Owl and his companions returned to the outskirts of Pee Dee village with their much-needed food. They did not want to be noticed for fear they would violate the council's rule if anyone discovered them with the clandestine supplies. The group waited in the woods patiently until they saw one of the bear clan men come out into the woods searching for firewood. They got the man's attention and sent word through him to Spotted Turtle that they had returned.

Later that night, after most of the tribe was asleep, Spotted Turtle sent out some of his people to sneak White Owl and his supplies safely into the village without being noticed. Spotted Turtle took charge of the pemmican and hid it in a safe place, to be distributed to those in need when the time was right. He thanked White Owl and his companions for their service and bravery and dismissed them back to their homes.

White Owl entered his hut to find Red Willow sleeping soundly, the pregnancy taking its toll on her stamina. Her belly was more prominent than he remembered, a sign of a healthy and growing infant. He stared at his beautiful wife, who was carrying their child, thankful to the Great Spirit that they were both a part of his life. After a few minutes, he decided to wake her. He lay down beside her and nuzzled her neck. Startled at first, she was overjoyed when she saw him. Red Willow hugged her husband tightly, letting him know how happy she was to see him.

White Owl gently pulled away from the embrace and placed his index finger to his nose. "I have some interesting news for you."

Red Willow winced at White Owl. "I'm concerned about what you are about to say."

White Owl moved his hand down to clench his chin. "Your udo is still alive. He resides with the Catawba."

Red Willow sat bolt upright and stared off into the distance. She had always hoped to see her brother and mother again, even though she knew it was improbable. She turned towards White Owl and grabbed him by his shoulders. "Are you serious?!"

"I would never lie to you about something this important," White Owl reassured her. "I saw him with my eyes and heard his voice with my ears."

Red Willow's thoughts quickly turned to her mother. "What about my etsi?"

White Owl slumped his shoulders before responding quietly. "Your udo told me that she died during their time of wandering before they reached the Catawba village."

Red Willow stared blankly into the distance. "She always seemed so strong. I thought she would live forever and one day meet our usdi." Tears welled up in Red Willow's eyes.

White Owl moved close to Red Willow and put his arm around her shoulder. "In my spirit, I imagine they already know each other," White Owl began, "and your etsi loves your usdi as much as she loves you."

Red Willow buried her head in White Owl's chest and began to sob. He held her more tightly, muffling the sounds of her sobs.

Back with the Catawba, Running Wolf remained under house arrest, and Rolling Cloud decided it was time to confront Sitting Deer. He asked for and was granted an audience, and he approached the meeting with cautious confidence, believing he was right to call out Sitting Deer for his insane behavior. "Osda usvi," Sitting Deer said as Rolling Cloud entered the tribal council hut. "Sit down and let us make a smoke offering to the Great Spirit."

Rolling Cloud sat down as Sitting Deer lit up a pipe, took a draw and offered it. The wild shaman took a puff, inhaled deeply, and exhaled slowly. Smoke filled the air around the two men as if the spirits of their ancestors surrounded them. They continued hitting the pipe until all the tobacco was gone, and the men were focused and relaxed enough to begin their conversation.

Sitting Deer was the first to break the silence. "So, what brings you here tonight?"

"Surely you must know why I am here," Rolling Cloud replied, thinking Sitting Deer would realize the insanity of his recent behavior regarding Running Wolf.

"I am afraid that I do not know why." Sitting Deer turned away from Rolling Cloud. "Why don't you enlighten me?"

Rolling Cloud raised his voice to a level he knew would get Sitting Deer's attention. "You have Running Wolf, the atsutsa I foresaw as the key to our tribe's future survival, imprisoned. I believe an evil spirit has possessed you."

Sitting Deer turned quickly and slammed his hand against a post. "He is not a prisoner! I am just preventing him from doing something that could put him in danger. If he is so important to our tribe's future, shouldn't we protect him at all costs?"

Rolling Cloud opened his arms in a questioning gesture. "How can he accomplish what the Great Spirit has planned for him if you prevent him from being in the world?"

Sitting Deer knew Rolling Cloud was right but feared losing his surrogate son. "Now is not the time for him," Sitting Deer replied softly. "He is too young to perform any heroic deeds or be any kind of leader."

Rolling Cloud folded his arms. "That is not for you to decide. The Great Spirit will use the atsutsa when the time is right. And the longer you keep him imprisoned, the more you interfere with that timing. I know you want to keep him safe but doing what you are doing will not bring back your first son. Running Wolf is not a replacement for your son; he is his own person."

"Don't you dare bring up my son!" Sitting Deer thundered. "You know nothing about my grief. And you know nothing about why I do the things that I do. Leave my presence before I do something to you I will regret."

Rolling Cloud recoiled. "I will go . . . I just ask that you search your heart for the right answer. You will find it deep inside of your soul."

Rolling Cloud left Sitting Deer stewing in his anger. He was furious with Rolling Cloud, not for challenging his authority but for pointing out a bitter truth. Admitting Rolling Cloud was right would be admitting his grief for his son was still fresh, still biting. It was a pain he did not want to face. Sitting Deer retired to his hut and fell into a restless sleep.

A few hours later, a dream came upon him: he saw himself sitting alone at the tribal council hut, taking long draws from his pipe. After a few minutes of inhaling the smoke, his feelings of loneliness intensified, forcing him into the village square to find some company. But there was not a soul to be found. The lack of companionship transformed his feelings from melancholy to panic. He ran frantically into the woods, yelling for anyone, but there was only a silence that left him feeling tragically alone. Out of his mind with fear and frustration, he sprinted back to the village, searching through every single hut without finding any signs of life. He was exhausted and finally happened upon the house he had been using to keep Running Wolf under guard. Sitting Deer was thrilled to see his young friend and greeted him enthusiastically but got nothing in return. Running Wolf sat like a stone, unmoving—seeming not even to breathe—as Sitting Deer shouted louder and louder. Alone in the world, with only his unresponsive friend to keep him company, Sitting Deer crumpled onto the hut floor, crying out in pain.

At that very moment, he awoke, terrified by the dream but realizing the Great Spirit had spoken to him through this vision. Sitting Deer had let his obsession with keeping Running Wolf safe overtake his ability to let the boy be the person he was supposed to be. He realized that the tighter he held onto him, the more embittered his young friend would feel towards him. He was, slowly, losing the one relationship that truly mattered because of a misplaced need for control. Sitting Deer summoned his guards to release Running Wolf and bring him to the tribal council hut.

Sitting Deer felt small as Running Wolf charged in. "I am leaving! Immediately!" Running Wolf shouted. "You cannot hold me here any longer. I don't care if I live or die out there because living here under your watch is death."

"You are right to want to leave," Sitting Deer looked down, refusing to meet Running Wolf's angry eyes. "I was wrong to try to keep you under guard here. I am sorry."

"So now you are admitting that you were wrong?" Running Wolf shook his head vigorously. "Where was this wisdom all those many moons ago? You are *crazy* . . . and even if you apologize, I am still leaving."

"I understand. But before you leave, I want to do you a favor," Sitting Deer said quietly. "I want to help your people in any way that I can. Ask me for anything, and I will do it."

Running Wolf arched his back, confused at Sitting Deer's dramatic change of heart. Why would Sitting Deer want to help him after keeping him under guard for so long? He took a moment to clear his head then decided that it didn't matter why. If he had learned one thing, actions were more important than motivations. And in this case, he was focused on the future steps he needed to take. Considering how he could best utilize Sitting Deer's help to rescue his tribe, he thought for another moment before blurting out his response.

"Send your best warriors with me," Running Wolf replied calmly. "I want to remove Soaring Eagle from power by any means necessary."

Sitting Deer nodded. "It will be done."

Chapter Nineteen

The Underhanded One

A week had passed since White Owl had returned from the Catawba. Spotted Turtle was secretly delivering small portions of the pemmican to members of his clan to keep them nourished. Morale improved quickly, and the presence of the food averted a crisis. Spotted Turtle's first inclination was to keep the distribution amongst the bear clan, but he hated watching the rest of the tribe suffer. He reached out first to Proud Robin, knowing he was trustworthy. Proud Robin was thrilled to hear the news and vowed to handle distribution among the deer clan discreetly. The plan worked and would continue to work as long as they could keep it a secret amongst themselves.

Unfortunately for Spotted Turtle, his secret did not evade the notice of the spying eyes of Soaring Eagle. The recent good fortune of the bear clan aroused Soaring Eagle's suspicions and led him to believe they were hiding something from the rest of the tribe. Sensing an opportunity to catch his nemesis engaged in clandestine activities forbidden by the council, Soaring Eagle formulated a plan to ensnare Spotted Turtle.

The plan was simple enough but would require the help of someone he could trust. For that he turned to his former toady, and now chief, Walking Squirrel. Soaring Eagle knew Spotted Turtle had a kind heart and would not be able to resist a plea for help, so he formulated a simple trap: Walking Squirrel would beg for help from Spotted Turtle then report back to Soaring Eagle what kind of help he offered. Walking Squirrel, still guilty about his earlier backstabbing of Soaring Eagle and ever eager to do someone else's bidding, quickly volunteered.

The next day Walking Squirrel approached Spotted Turtle, as instructed. "Osiyo, Spotted Turtle." Walking Squirrel bowed. "How are things with you and your clan?"

"We are doing our best to survive these troubled times," Spotted Turtle began, "just like everyone else."

"Your clan's best seems to be better than all the rest," he replied. "We are all struggling with hunger and disease, yet we have half the strength you all seem to have."

Spotted Turtle looked Walking Squirrel directly in the eyes. "I'm sorry to hear that your people are suffering so much."

He genuinely meant this, but he still did not trust Walking Squirrel enough to share the secret of the pemmican. Sensitive to Spotted Turtle's distrust, Walking Squirrel changed his plan. Leaning over, he whispered in Spotted Turtle's ear, "I think we both know who to blame for all the tribe's struggles."

Spotted Turtle squinted. "What do you mean?"

"I mean that Soaring Eagle is responsible for the famine," Walking Squirrel winked. "If he hadn't taken away so many men when they were needed here at the village during the harvest, we wouldn't have these problems."

Spotted Turtle scratched the side of his face. "I thought you and Soaring Eagle were close. Why would you speak ill of him?"

"I just speak the truth," Walking Squirrel shrugged. "I'm not sure I can be close to him anymore, knowing what a difficult situation he has put us in."

Spotted Turtle was stunned when Walking Squirrel suddenly turned against his close ally. He still didn't fully trust Walking Squirrel, but he knew this might be an opportunity to rally more support. He hesitantly told Walking Squirrel about the pemmican supply and promised to share it with the beaver clan. It was a fatal mistake. After their conversation, Walking Squirrel immediately ran to Soaring Eagle with the news.

"You know this disobedience cannot go unpunished!" Soaring Eagle bellowed as he paced around the interior of his hut.

"What . . . should we do about it then?" Walking Squirrel asked. "You know his clan members will not stand for any kind of public discipline, especially since he is keeping them well fed. And we can't afford to lose the support of that many people.

Soaring Eagle grunted. "You care too much about what other people think and say. This needs to be less about people-pleasing and more about keeping them in line."

"Why don't we just go take Spotted Turtle's pemmican and distribute it ourselves to the *whole* tribe?" Walking Squirrel asked, his palm outstretched. "Then we get to look like heroes."

Soaring Eagle took a deep breath and sighed. "That is not what the council decided to do. Were you not there for that decision?"

"Maybe you are right," Walking Squirrel slumped his shoulders. "But I just can't see how a reprimand is going to be helpful at all."

"That is because you lack vision," Soaring Eagle tersely pointed his finger at Walking Squirrel. "Go meditate on it. Go find the medicine man and get the concoctions that will help you gain insight. Do whatever it takes. Just get a vision for the right way to govern this tribe. In the meantime, I will handle things with Spotted Turtle my way."

Walking Squirrel nodded and turned to head out the door, leaving Soaring Eagle alone with another newly-hatched scheme. Soaring Eagle had an ample supply of sweating-plant, well known among the tribe for its ability to break fevers by inducing intense sweating when ingested. But sweating-plant also had the wicked side effect of producing voluminous amounts of diarrhea if taken in too large a quantity. The combined effect of sweating and diarrhea would be enough to weaken any healthy person. Soaring Eagle intended to use the sweating-plant to contaminate the pemmican that Spotted Turtle was distributing. If he sickened enough people within the bear clan, he could blame the sickness on Spotted Turtle and stir up distrust among the bear clan members. He could then use that distrust to remove Spotted Turtle from his leadership position and replace him with someone more loyal. Soaring Eagle smiled, congratulating himself on his plan's brilliance.

Minutes later, Soaring Eagle went to work preparing a batch of sweating-plant tea. But preparing the tea was only the first step. The tea would be useless if he could not access Spotted Turtle's pemmican supply. Soaring Eagle needed Walking Squirrel to find out where Spotted Turtle was keeping the pemmican. Once Soaring Eagle knew the location, he could sneak in and infuse the pemmican with the poison. The next day Soaring Eagle sent Walking Squirrel back to see Spotted Turtle.

"I have returned for the pemmican you promised to share," Walking Squirrel said to Spotted Turtle.

"I'm glad you returned." Spotted Turtle spoke in hushed tones. "I will meet you back at your hut later today with as much as I can spare for you to distribute among your clan."

"I would like to get some now." Walking Squirrel was rubbing his fingers together as he spoke. "Can you take me to your supply and give me some?"

Walking Squirrel's insistent and anxious behavior aroused Spotted Turtle's suspicion. Walking Squirrel was in no position to make demands on Spotted Turtle about how he handled his supply. Spotted Turtle began to have second thoughts about helping him, so he scaled back the level of support he would offer until he knew that Walking Squirrel could be fully trusted.

"I cannot take you to the supply," Spotted Turtle insisted. "I won't let anyone know the location for fear someone might steal it for themselves. But I will meet you this afternoon at your hut with what I can spare. If this is not good enough for you, you are on your own."

Walking Squirrel was disappointed that he could not pry the location of the pemmican supply out of Spotted Turtle, but he agreed, having no choice but to accept the terms of Spotted Turtle's offer. He hoped that getting his hands on at least some of the pemmican would be enough to satisfy Soaring Eagle. Spotted Turtle brought the pemmican to Walking Squirrel that afternoon, and immediately after Spotted Turtle was out of sight, Walking Squirrel scurried over to Soaring Eagle's hut.

"I have something for you." Walking Squirrel rushed into the hut and laid down the chunk of pemmican that Spotted Turtle had given him.

"Good work, oginalii," Soaring Eagle replied. "Now, where is the larger supply? That is what I asked you to find."

"Well . . ." Walking Squirrel could sense Soaring Eagle's anger rising. "Spotted Turtle refused to give the location of his supply. I only have what you see here."

"This is not what I asked for!" Soaring Eagle bellowed. "This small amount of pemmican does me no good. Why didn't you have someone follow Spotted Turtle to find out where he keeps it?"

"I . . . I didn't think of that," Walking Squirrel felt his face grow hot. "It was the best I could do. I . . . I thought you might be able to make at least some use of it."

"Leave me!" Soaring Eagle pointed to the door. "I'll handle this myself."

With Soaring Eagle's plans disrupted, he decided to shift gears again. If he could not sicken the entire clan of traitors, perhaps he could gravely injure at least one. He took the pemmican Walking Squirrel had given him and began soaking it in the sweating-plant tea that he had made. He planned to create super-infused pemmican that would surely put anyone who ate it at death's door. He soaked the pemmican overnight and plotted a way to get it into the hands of his enemies.

Soaring Eagle knew that there would be no way for him to personally get the poisoned pemmican back into the hands of the bear clan since none of them trusted him any further than they could throw him. He also didn't want to involve Walking Squirrel again because he had lost faith in him to get anything done. Soaring Eagle needed someone on the inside that he could intimidate into taking the pemmican.

The following day Soaring Eagle stalked Eternal Blossom, waiting until the time was right to make his move. Around midday, she went down to the river by herself to wash up. Soaring Eagle saw this as his chance and immediately followed after her. Soaring Eagle crept up stealthily behind Eternal Blossom. "That water is a little cold to be washing in," he said with a spine-chilling tone.

Startled, Eternal Blossom turned quickly to see who was there. When she saw it was Soaring Eagle, she shot him a look of disgust. "What are you doing here?"

Soaring Eagle changed his tone to fake concern. "Why, I'm checking in to see how things are with you and your clan. You all seem to be in good spirits. What is your secret?"

Eternal Blossom felt her anxiety rising as she worried Soaring Eagle might suspect the hidden food supply. "I . . . I don't know what you're talking about. We are all struggling as a tribe together."

"But your clan seems to be struggling . . . less," he rubbed his hands together, "and I think I know why."

"You are talking like an evil spirit has possessed you."

"I know that Spotted Turtle has a pemmican supply, and it did not come from within our tribe." Soaring Eagle walked to the edge of the river and leaned in close. "Since that much is true, you understand he has violated the council's will, and it is only a matter of time before he is punished," he paused, "along with anyone who helped him. I'm assuming that would include some people close to you."

Eternal Blossom's voice quivered. "You have no proof. Only words."

"Hold out your hand, and I will show the proof."

Eternal Blossom looked up from the riverbank and cautiously held out her hand, into which Soaring Eagle forcefully smacked the sweating-plant-infused pemmican. As she took it, stunned silence came across her face.

"Take it." Soaring Eagle got up from his crouched position and began to walk away. "It's yours. I know where it came from, and I have much more to use as evidence against your clan." He turned back menacingly. "And when you go back to your clan, let them know what you heard today . . . and know that their days in this tribe are numbered."

He walked away, leaving Eternal Blossom alone at the riverside to contemplate what he had told her. His knowledge and accompanying threat shook her to her core. She took a moment to compose herself, then returned to the village with the pemmican, immediately heading to Red Willow.

Eternal Blossom barreled frantically into Red Willow's hut and threw the pemmican down onto the mat stretched out on the floor in front of her. "He knows!" Eternal Blossom screamed.

"What are you talking about?"

"Soaring Eagle knows we got the pemmican from the Catawba."

"What makes you think that?" Red Willow asked.

"Soaring Eagle confronted me when I was down at the river," Eternal Blossom answered, breathing heavily. "He told me he knew about everything. I didn't believe him at first, but then," she continued, panting, "he showed me *that* as proof," she said, pointing to the pemmican.

"That pemmican could have come from anywhere." Red Willow shook her head. "That's not proof that he knows anything."

"It wasn't just that." Eternal Blossom was shaking. "I saw the look in his eyes. He *knew* someone was guilty, and he was *excited* at being able to punish someone, like an animal ready to pounce on its kill. We have to take this pemmican to Spotted Turtle to see if it is from his supply. He needs to know about this."

"Fine." Red Willow stood. "Let's go see Spotted Turtle."

Red Willow broke off a small chunk of the pemmican, leaving most of it behind. The women left, and not long after, White Owl returned to the hut to warm himself up after a few hours outside hunting small game. He sat down by the fire and immediately noticed the pemmican. Starving, he broke off a piece and started to eat. He thought it tasted a little strange, but he was so hungry he continued to eat it. Finishing his first portion, he broke off another chunk and scarfed it down, enjoying the feeling of having a full belly.

It did not take long for the sweating-plant symptoms to set in. Soon White Owl felt himself becoming flushed in his upper body. Sweat began dripping from his pores, and his stomach started rumbling. Urgently needing to evacuate his bowels, White Owl stood and started to walk outside, legs shaking. He only made it as far as the door when the rush of explosive diarrhea came upon him, staining his pants and spilling down his legs to his feet. He was distraught and overwhelmingly ashamed. He tried to walk clandestinely down to the river to wash, hoping no one would notice his mess. He stumbled a few times then collapsed on the ground in a thicket, fouling himself once more before finally passing out.

Meanwhile, Eternal Blossom and Red Willow were at Spotted Turtle's hut showing him the pemmican. "Yes, that is from my supply," Spotted Turtle confirmed. "Our secret has been discovered. I knew I was wrong to trust that crooked Walking Squirrel." Spotted Turtle threw the pemmican on the ground in disgust.

"So, what happens now?" Red Willow asked.

"Soaring Eagle will surely try to call me before the council to answer for my disobedience," Spotted Turtle replied. "But I think we are beyond that now. I think it is time for those against Soaring Eagle to rise up."

"But won't that split our tribe in two?" Eternal Blossom asked, a look of concern darkening her face.

"If it does, it does," Spotted Turtle said. "If we let Soaring Eagle continue to be on the council, there won't be any tribe left. He will run it into the ground. I will confer with Proud Robin about what we should do. You should both return to your huts but be prepared if we call on you for help."

Red Willow and Eternal Blossom did as Spotted Turtle instructed, each with different feelings. Red Willow was bursting with excitement about the prospect of getting rid of Soaring Eagle, while her aunt was much more anxious, fearful about what might happen if the tribe turned against itself. Red Willow prepared a light dinner for White Owl, as she was expecting him to arrive before sundown. When it grew dark and he had not returned, her instincts pushed her to go out and search, but she decided against it for the baby's sake and instead went to see Spotted Turtle.

"Have you seen White Owl today?" she asked.

"No, I haven't. Why?"

"He hasn't come home yet, and I am distraught," Red Willow's voice quickened. "This is not like him to be out so late."

"I'm sure that he is fine," Spotted Turtle assured her, "but if it will make you feel better, I will send out some men to search for him."

"Yes, it would," she nodded gratefully. "Wa do. I'll be with Eternal Blossom. If you find him, please let me know."

Spotted Turtle gathered up a search party and sent them out. The men grabbed some torches and began walking, but it was a fruitless endeavor; they could not find him, even though they passed by him multiple times. His body was so deep in the thicket that he remained invisible. After a few hours, they called off the search and returned to the camp. Spotted Turtle visited Red Willow to break the news.

"I'm afraid we cannot find any trace of White Owl," Spotted Turtle said, standing in the entrance of her hut, "but I'm sure he is fine, and he will return soon. He knows how to take care of himself."

Red Willow began to tear up, and Eternal Blossom came over to comfort her. "It will be fine, my ayoli. Spotted Turtle is right. White Owl will be back very soon. He is strong and capable. Why don't we try to get some rest? It is very late."

Eternal Blossom led Red Willow back into her hut. She helped her down into her straw bed and then lay down next to her, holding her tightly as she sniffled her way through more tears. It took a long time, but they finally fell asleep.

During the middle of the night, White Owl awoke to find himself drenched with sweat and covered in dried feces from the waist down. He struggled to his feet and tried to collect his thoughts. Ready to collapse but determined to clean himself, he staggered down to the icy cold waters of the river and waded in waist deep. Dragging himself out, he was instantly shocked by the contrast of the chilly river water with the milder night air. He shivered and lurched back to the village.

Entering his hut, he did not see Red Willow. All he wanted was to fall onto his bed, but he stumbled over to Eternal Blossom's hut and found the two women sleeping there together. He knelt and shook his wife, trying to get her attention. She awoke with a startle to see White Owl, pale and shivering, looking like a ghost. At first, she was delighted, but her joy quickly turned to concern when she saw how ill he looked.

"You are freezing!" a concerned Red Willow said. "We have got to get you warmed up. Take off those cold clothes while I stoke the fire."

Red Willow frantically rekindled the fire while White Owl stripped out of his wet clothes. The commotion woke Eternal Blossom, who was shocked to see White Owl shivering in a state of undress. She quickly threw a deerskin blanket around his body.

After Red Willow had the fire up and going, she beckoned White Owl to come closer to it. She put her arm around him. "Are you alright?"

"I'll be fine," he said through still chattering teeth.

She looked him up and down. "What happened to you? Where have you been?"

His mind was in a fog. "I don't know what happened. One minute I was eating some pemmican, and the next minute I was sweating profusely and shitting myself. I was so embarrassed that I went down to the river to wash myself off, but I passed out in a thicket before making it down there. I woke up a while ago, went down to the river to finish washing off, and then came back here."

The wheels began to turn in Red Willow's head. "Did you say that all of this happened to you after eating some pemmican?"

"Yes."

Her eyes opened wide. "Where did you get this pemmican?"

"At our hut, why?" he replied.

As clear as the spring river water, it dawned on Red Willow what had happened. "That snake!" she cried, clenching her fist. "Let's go," she said to White Owl. "We need to get you to the medicine man now. I'll explain later."

She grabbed White Owl up from beside the fire and escorted him to the medicine man's hut, where she awakened the medicine man from his slumber and tried to explain the situation. Though exhausted, he agreed to help. Red Willow left White Owl in his care and went immediately to see Spotted Turtle. She burst into his hut and pushed him on the shoulder to wake him up.

"He poisoned the pemmican!" Red Willow shouted.

"What is going on?" a groggy Spotted Turtle asked.

"Soaring Eagle poisoned the pemmican." Red Willow paced. "The pemmican I showed you earlier was poisoned. White Owl ate some, and now he is sick."

Spotted Turtle scratched his head. "Are you sure?"

"Yes!" Red Willow exclaimed. "Everything I am saying is true. Soaring Eagle has gone mad, and we need to stop him. NOW!"

Spotted Turtle lifted himself from his bed and ran his hands through his hair as he tried to process what Red Willow was saying. If Soaring Eagle had poisoned the pemmican, he must be held accountable. But the when, where, and how were not clear to him. He placed his hand on Red Willow's shoulder. "I am with you. We must stop Soaring Eagle, but we cannot move too quickly. We want to make sure we do it the right way. Let us meditate on it for at least a moon and see what the Great Spirit would have us do."

Red Willow stormed out of the hut, agitated that Spotted Turtle was not as ready to act as she was. If only she were not with child, she would have gone and slashed Soaring Eagle's throat herself at that very moment. But the new life within her was important above all, and she managed to contain her rage for its sake. She made her way to the medicine man's hut to be by White Owl's side.

Chapter Twenty

The Descent

Running Wolf and about fifty of Sitting Deer's best warriors wound their way through the rolling hills towards the Pee Dee settlement. It was now late winter, an unpredictable time when there could be freezing temperatures and snow one day, followed by mild climate and sunshine the next. Fortunately for Running Wolf and his warriors, the weather had been unseasonably warm over the past few moons, invigorating the men and making for a much less arduous journey. The warm weather even fooled some of the trees into releasing their blooms prematurely.

Some of the Catawba warriors found it strange, being led by such a young brave. They were only taking part in this war party out of a sense of duty to their chief, Sitting Deer. Keeping a suspicious eye on Running Wolf, they waited for him to make even the slightest error in judgment.

If he were to make even a tiny misstep, they were ready to seize on it as an opportunity to call off their mission. Though Running Wolf had not yet done anything to cause them to abandon him, the most difficult parts of the assignment were still yet to come. One night at camp, one of the Catawba warriors approached Running Wolf. Some of the others saw the impending conversation and stopped what they were doing, curious to see how the boy would handle himself.

"How much longer do you think it will take us to reach your home?" the warrior asked.

Running Wolf surveyed his surroundings then looked up at the stars. "I'd say we are no more than a few days away."

"We are very close then," the warrior replied as he looked Running Wolf up and down. He folded his arms, eager to test his young leader. "What is your plan when we get there?"

Running Wolf gazed off into the direction of the Pee Dee village. "I plan to offer aid to the people of the tribe who are suffering,"

Another one of the onlooking warriors chimed in. "And what if the tribe refuses your offer?" A hum of voices echoed the question.

Running Wolf stared intently into the warrior's eyes. "Then I will liberate the tribe from their suffering with force . . . but let us pray that it does not come to that."

"Tough talk for a naive atsutsa," a tall, muscular warrior interjected. "I will pray . . . that you don't have to experience something you aren't ready for." The other men in the group nodded their heads and sniggered.

Running Wolf sensed the ridicule, and though his confidence was shaken, he did not show it. He trembled inwardly and revealed nothing of his concerns. He had his sights set on seeing his family again and putting things straight with his old nemesis. The thought of meeting up with his sister warmed his heart, especially knowing she was carrying the gift of new life. As for Soaring Eagle, he was both confident he could face him down and scared to death of failure. Amid all these whirling thoughts in his head, Running Wolf sought comfort from a familiar source.

He went to the supply travois that the group had brought and got out his mother's bone pot. He held the pot tightly for a minute before placing it on the ground and sitting down cross-legged next to it. Gazing lovingly at his mother's bones, he spoke. "The time is coming etsi. Your uwetsi has done what you asked. I made it to the Catawba safely. Not only that . . . but I am now going back home to protect my family. I know that Doda would be proud. I know that you are now together in the spirit realm. Please send me your wisdom and his strength because I will need both. I love you."

A tear came to his eye, and he placed his hand on top of the pot, soaking in his mother's powerful spiritual energy. After a few minutes, he returned the pot to where he'd found it and headed back to his rolled-out deerskin blanket. Sleeping under the starry sky, basking in the glow of the moonlight as it penetrated through the tree limbs overhead, he had the best sleep he'd had in weeks, knowing his mother's energy was there to comfort him.

�֎ ✖ ✖

It had been a few days since White Owl's poisoning, and his physical situation was not improving. The initial effects from the sweating-plant had subsided but soaking himself in the cold river water had shocked him, leaving his body susceptible to foreign invaders. Feverish and with a cough that intensified by the hour, he needed constant care. Red Willow had been steadfastly by his side, but the medicine man advised her to go home and get some rest for the sake of the baby.

Meanwhile, Soaring Eagle was about to make his move. He had Walking Squirrel call an emergency tribal council meeting to discuss the covert pemmican he now knew Spotted Turtle possessed. Spotted Turtle was hesitant to attend, not wanting to share space with the heinous Soaring Eagle and sensing that something was amiss about the whole situation. In search of some sage advice, he went to see the medicine man.

White Owl was sound asleep, giving the medicine man some much-needed downtime. Spotted Turtle poked his head gently through the medicine man's hut door, careful not to disrupt his work. "Come in," the medicine man motioned.

Spotted Turtle crept slowly into the hut, careful not to disturb White Owl. "I'm sorry to bother you, Holy One, but I need your guidance," he said quietly.

The medicine man stumbled over to his hammock and pulled out a pipe from underneath. "Come, let us sit and talk."

The men sat down and shared a smoke. "What is troubling you unalii?" the medicine man asked.

"You mean besides everything that is going on with the tribe right now?!" Spotted turtle replied, incredulous that the medicine man could even ask such a question.

"Ah yes, that," the medicine man replied flatly. "We live in interesting times."

"Interesting huh? That's the word you want to use?" Spotted Turtle chuckled.

The medicine man turned and pointed at Spotted Turtle. "You must be interested in what is going on, otherwise you wouldn't have come to see me. Am I right?"

Spotted Turtle put his head in his hands and rubbed his face. "You have an answer for everything. And that is why I am here. Soaring Eagle has called a council meeting to level some accusations against me and I am scared."

"Are the accusations true?" the medicine man asked after taking a puff.

"Yes," Spotted Turtle mumbled.

"Then why are you afraid?" the medicine man plainly inquired. "The truth is freedom and not something to fear."

"Not this time," Spotted Turtle responded. "This truth is anything but freeing. I violated the council's will and am potentially facing serious consequences."

The medicine man nodded his head slowly, acknowledging Spotted Turtle's plight. He took another draw on his pipe, even deeper than before, and sat in silence, the pregnant pause filling the atmosphere. "I will say this. There is the will of the council and the will of the Great Spirit. They are two different things. Did you violate both?"

Spotted Turtle tilted his head as he looked at the medicine man. "How would I know?"

"Search your spirit," the medicine man whispered. "Your answer is there."

Now Spotted Turtle sat in silence, his heart pounding to a level almost audible throughout the room. White Owl stirred in his sickbed and let out a moan. "I've got work to do," the medicine man patted

Spotted Turtle on the back. "Peace be with you. No matter where the Great Spirit takes you."

Spotted Turtle stood up and bowed. The comforting words he received helped him make up his mind then and there, deciding that he should appear at the gathering. He had no false notions about being able to sway either Soaring Eagle or Walking Squirrel to his side, but he wanted Soaring Eagle to know that he would not be intimidated.

Spotted Turtle and Proud Robin arrived at the temple side by side in a show of solidarity. Soaring Eagle and Walking Squirrel were waiting for them in their own show of mutual support. Soaring Eagle scowled at Spotted Turtle as he entered, and Spotted Turtle imagined himself rushing over and strangling the life out of Soaring Eagle, but he contained his urge. The atmosphere was heavy, thick with tensions frothing beneath the surface of all the men in attendance. Spotted Turtle and Proud Robin took a seat on the bench opposite Soaring Eagle and Walking Squirrel. A ray of sunlight streamed through the opening at the temple's apex down into the central area that separated the two groups. It was as if the Great Spirit had thrown down an ethereal blockade between the opposing factions.

Soaring Eagle leaned his head forward into the sunlight veil. "Did you think that you could get away with defying the council's will?"

Spotted Turtle also leaned forward and glared at Soaring Eagle, practically spitting through his teeth. "The council is supposed to exist for the good of the entire tribe, not so that its members can make arbitrary decisions. I ignored the council and did what was right for the people, and I would do it again."

Walking Squirrel rose up, anger in his eyes. "You do not understand leadership, Spotted Turtle. Sometimes a chief has to make the hard decisions that are not good for all people in the short term but are good for the tribe in the long term."

Spotted Turtle shot a sarcastic grin at Walking Squirrel. "Do you mean decisions like a failed war party or taking a position that would lead to starvation of half the tribe?"

"Enough!" Soaring Eagle stood and confronted Spotted Turtle. "Your disobedience has gone too far. You must immediately leave your bear clan leadership position, and Walking Squirrel will choose your replacement."

Spotted Turtle lifted himself from his bench and stood face to face with Soaring Eagle. "That is not going to happen. The bear clan is now with me, and I am with them, and neither of us is with you nor Walking Squirrel."

"So, you are all traitors!" Walking Squirrel lifted his foot high and stomped it down hard enough to shake the earth. "Then you can all be expelled. Our tribe will be stronger without you."

A voice rang out from the shadows. "The deer clan is with me, and I am with Spotted Turtle, and none of us is with you two." Proud Robin leaped out of his seat and stood next to Spotted Turtle.

Soaring Eagle could no longer contain his rage. He drew out the sharpened deer bone that he used as a hairpin and stabbed Spotted Turtle in the neck. Spotted Turtle crumpled to the ground in a heap and grasped his neck, trying to stop the blood spurting through his fingers. Soaring Eagle then lunged at Proud Robin with the deer bone pin, but Proud Robin fought him off and wrestled him to the ground. The pair struggled on the floor until Soaring Eagle gained the advantage and found himself on top of Proud Robin. He put his hands around Proud Robin's neck and squeezed until Proud Robin was blue in the face.

Soaring Eagle finished choking Proud Robin and turned towards Walking Squirrel with a dead look in his eyes. A chill moved down Walking Squirrel's spine as he recognized that he was staring into the eyes, not of a man, but a body possessed by evil. He quickly realized that there was no reasoning with an evil spirit and hastily fled the scene in search of some assistance.

Walking Squirrel's feet instinctively took him to the medicine man's hut. If anyone knew how to handle a man under the spell of evil, it would be him. Bursting in, he found the medicine man attending to White Owl. "I need your help," he panted. "Soaring Eagle is under the grip of an evil spirit. I saw him murder two clan leaders, and I do not know what he will do next."

The medicine man was still for a moment, then removed his headdress and slowly stroked his silver hair. "I cannot leave this man here alone. He is very sick."

"But you must do something!" Walking Squirrel paced anxiously.

The medicine man got up from White Owl's bedside. He walked to the corner of the hut and retrieved the blowgun he had crafted from river cane many moons ago. Shuffling over to his shelf, he picked up a small wooden dart with a sharp-pointed tip and a feather attached to the back. Then he dipped the dart's tip into a sludgy residue and coated it with the thick, sticky substance. Being careful to hold the dart by the end with the feather, he handed it and the blowgun to Walking Squirrel.

"Shoot him with this," the medicine man said. "It will be enough to tame his evil spirits. Once you subdue him, bind him and do what you will with him."

Walking Squirrel furrowed his brow, confused about what could be potent enough to take down a man with a single shot. "What is on this dart?"

"Do not touch the tip." The medicine man slapped Walking Squirrel on the wrist before he was able to run his finger down the dart. "It is evaporated wysoccan residue—very potent, and not for being handled by the unwise. Go and use it on Soaring Eagle before you hurt yourself with it."

Walking Squirrel gently loaded the dart into the blowgun and set off back towards the temple. To his surprise, Soaring Eagle was still there, standing in the middle of the sunlit opening, arms outstretched, soaking every ray of light into his deranged spirit. Walking Squirrel stood and stared before Soaring Eagle was alerted to his presence.

"I knew that you would come back, my oginalii." Soaring Eagle sauntered out of the sun and into the temple's shadows. "There is only one thing left for me to do before I have all of the council's power."

"I have been with you from the beginning," Walking Squirrel said, tightening his grip on the blowgun he held behind his back, "and you would turn on me now?"

"I do not want to hurt you, oginalii," Soaring Eagle started strolling towards Walking Squirrel, focused on his eyes and oblivious to the weapon he was hiding, "but your position as the only living clan leader prevents me from having ultimate power. You must understand my situation?"

Walking Squirrel brought his blowgun forward, bent his knees, and anchored his feet to the floor. "I understand that you are under the control of evil spirits."

"If it were only that simple," Soaring Eagle said, intently walking towards Walking Squirrel.

"Do you see that hawk?" Walking Squirrel asked, as he drew the blowgun to his mouth and inhaled sharply. As Soaring Eagle looked up towards the sky, Walking Squirrel sent the dart flying with a quick puff of air, and the projectile pierced Soaring Eagle in the neck, stopping him momentarily in his tracks. More stunned than incapacitated, Soaring Eagle recouped quickly, pulled the dart from his neck, and flung it to the ground. He continued his advance for a few more steps but soon lost his balance. Stumbling to his knees, he tried to catch himself on the corner of a bench. Soon he found himself unable to control his breathing, which grew rapid and shallow. He pressed on his chest, trying to slow his breathing down, but he lost and regained consciousness moment to moment until his entire world faded to black.

✖ ✖ ✖

Soaring Eagle was in the void for what felt like an eternity. It was a terrifying abyss, a world without visual or auditory stimulation. Escape from the darkness finally came in the form of a pinpoint of light that increased gradually, ultimately enveloping Soaring Eagle's consciousness. The light revealed a vast and desolate wilderness that was only slightly less frightening than the dark void. A forest of tall, black trees that were barren of leaves surrounded him. The ground was a deep red semi-solid surface. Trudging through the red mud, his feet alternating from being sucked into the sludge and pulled out forcefully, he began the slowest trek he could ever remember taking.

He slogged through the shady forest until he reached the edge, where there was a large clearing that sloped down into a deep valley.

In the low part, staring at him with blank looks on their faces were all the Pee Dee men killed during his vanity terror campaign against the Tuscarora. The men were as pale as ghosts and had dead black eyes but were otherwise in the form they'd been in life. Spotted Turtle and Proud Robin stood out prominently in the group's front line; their faces were expressionless. Seeing all these men who died under his watch in one place made Soaring Eagle realize the full extent of his destructive behavior. He turned away from the souls, unable to look at them without a deep sense of regret. A cold hand touched his shoulder. Turning his head slowly to the side, he saw his dead father, in the same form as those souls in the valley. Soaring Eagle's anger towards his father spilled out. "Are you here to shame me for what I have done?" Soaring Eagle yelled.

"You did this," Soaring Eagle's father put his hand on his son's shoulder, "but you did not do this alone. You did it with my help, although you were unaware of it. I hurt you and you, in turn, hurt others. I'm sorry that I did not do more for you in life to keep you off this path."

Soaring Eagle's heart sank into his chest. Deep inside, he knew that his father was right, that he had not done all this alone. He had lived his whole life wanting an apology from his father, but now that it had come, the apology did not satisfy him as he had thought it would. Looking back at the valley of souls, he let out a deep sigh. "It is too late for me," he hung his head low. "I did what I did, and I suffer the consequences."

"It is never too late," Soaring Eagle's father admonished him. "I have repented, and you can too."

"How can I repent to everyone?" Soaring Eagle looked out at the immense crowd of spirits. "There are so many of them."

"Repent to their source, the One," Soaring Eagle's father looked up at the sky, "and then we can all return to Him together in peace."

"Return to the source?" Soaring Eagle's eyes widened. "I have to go back to the tribe and fix what I have broken."

"There is no going back for you." Soaring Eagle's father looked away from his son and stared out into the distance. "All that is left is your repentance."

Soaring Eagle reflected on everything that had happened in his life as he fought back the tears. Suddenly the weight of all the hurt he had inflicted on the people he had tormented constricted his spirit with an agonizing grip. Unable to stand it anymore, he sincerely apologized to the Great Spirit for all the damage he had done. Immediately, a flash of lightning ripped open the sky, and, one by one, the souls were lifted into the brightness. Soaring Eagle watched, gaining a measure of peace from each soul that joined the collection. When the valley was emptied, Soaring Eagle and his father embraced and took their place together with the others in the unity of light.

Walking Squirrel watched in shock as Soaring Eagle collapsed to the floor. The medicine man had said this blowgun dart was supposed to subdue Soaring Eagle, not kill him. He walked over to Soaring Eagle and checked for signs of life. Soaring Eagle was lying still, his chest motionless, not oscillating up and down. Walking Squirrel leaned down and placed his ear gently next to Soaring Eagle's mouth and nostrils. Not sensing any breath, he realized Soaring Eagle's spirit had departed from his body.

Walking Squirrel stood up and surveyed the scene in the temple. The corpses of all three of the other clan leaders surrounded him. He could not have imagined that this day would have ever come. How would the Pee Dee tribe ever be able to pick up the pieces after this unthinkable disaster? How could they continue together as a tribe after suffering such a series of setbacks, each one progressively worse than the previous? Walking Squirrel sat down and put his head between his knees in despair, unable to fathom the future.

Chapter Twenty-One

The Offender Returns

Just a few short days later, Running Wolf and the Catawba warriors appeared on the outskirts of the Pee Dee village, unaware of the chaos unfolding within. The weather pattern had shifted dramatically, as it often does during the time of year when seasons collide. The winds were howling through the trees that separated the men on one side from the Town Creek ceremonial center on the opposite side, and the temperature had dropped precipitously.

Running Wolf stood there, deeply breathing in and out, inhaling the old atmosphere for several minutes. It had been many moons since he had laid eyes on this place, and he was a different person from the boy who had been banished. He reflected on who that boy was, an aimless and reckless youth, and all the pain and pleasure he had experienced in this setting.

One of the warriors ambled up. "So, we are here," the warrior grunted. "What now?"

Running Wolf shook his head, trying to bring himself back to the moment. If he was honest with himself, he was still unsure how to proceed. His options were to either sneak in alone and garner support from his allies or come in with his warriors as a sign of strength and hope their presence would encourage his tribal supporters. Since this was his mission, he ultimately decided that he should be the one to take the first risk.

"Wait with the other warriors here while I try to make contact with my oginaliis." Running Wolf stared into the distance at the palisade wall surrounding the temple. "If I am not back by nightfall, make your return to the Catawba village."

The warrior shrugged in tacit agreement, more than happy that he and his fellow tribesmen would not be placing themselves in imminent danger. Running Wolf went to his supply travois and retrieved an entire wolf skin, including the head, that he had with him for just this situation. He draped himself with the skin, got on his hands and knees, and began crawling through the trees towards the village. Eternal Blossom's hut was the closest structure, and he set out directly towards it.

Running Wolf was unsure about seeing his aunt, given how things had unfolded before his banishment. As he drew closer and closer, he began to feel that something was not quite right. There were no children outside playing, no fires were burning outside in the common area that the clan shared, and there was no one surveilling the area. In short, there was a strange lack of any human activity. He cautiously removed his wolfskin cloak and strode over to his aunt's hut, looking back over his shoulder and wondering what was afoot.

As he reached the doorway of the hut, his heart began to race. His mind urged him forward, but his spirit held him back. He stood there for a moment, paralyzed by his internal struggle. His young nephew spotted him and rushed to hug him on the leg. The commotion stirred Eternal Blossom, who was cleaning a clay pot with her back turned. She turned towards the doorway, pot in hand, and spotted Running Wolf. She struggled to comprehend the image as it appeared to her. Did she see a ghost? In her famished state was she hallucinating?

"Osiyo, agitlogi." Running Wolf greeted her with his head hung low, rubbing his forearm sheepishly.

His words proved to his aunt that he was no apparition but her real nephew standing in her doorway. A temporary rage overcame her, and she threw the clay pot at his feet, shattering it to pieces. Then she rushed over and shoved him in the chest repeatedly without budging him an inch—as if she were trying to move a stone cliff face. It was not long before she found herself exhausted, hands on her knees, trying to catch her breath.

Running Wolf reached gently into his leggings and retrieved his mother's gorget, gingerly stretching it forward. She clasped her hand across her mouth in shock at the sight of her masterpiece, holding back tears. She realized that her anger towards him was misplaced, as he cared as much about Gray Dove as she did. She let her tears flow and reached up to put her arms around her nephew. He let out a big sigh, and they shared a long embrace.

After the hug, Running Wolf's curiosity about the barren village demanded answers. "What is going on here?" he asked. "It is so quiet. It feels . . . wrong."

"The people are in a state of mourning and repentance." Eternal Blossom grasped her nephew tightly. "Tragedy has befallen the tribe. Soaring Eagle murdered two clan leaders before being murdered himself. There is no leadership, and the tribe is terrified of what will happen next."

Running Wolf pulled away. "Did you say that Soaring Eagle is dead?"

"Yes!"

Immediately his fears of facing Soaring Eagle faded, but he now found himself in a conundrum. He had spent all his energy preparing for a confrontation that would not happen, and he was unsure what his next move would be. "What can I do to help if I don't need to confront him?" he asked his aunt, genuinely confused.

"I don't know," she sighed. "We need a miracle."

A burst of inspiration ran through Running Wolf as if it were a flash of lightning directly to his mind. There was not a lot he could offer on his own, but he was not alone. He had the support of his warriors and the chief of the Catawba tribe. His connections gave him the ability to save the Pee Dee from dissolution and disaster. For the first time in his life, Running Wolf saw himself as someone who solved problems instead of someone who caused them. A feeling of pride surged in his chest, such that he had never felt before.

"Go tell Red Willow I am back and here to help," he said. "I will get my Catawba warriors, and I will return."

He eagerly made his way back to the warriors, full of excitement at the prospect of rescuing his suffering tribe. But on returning to the camp, his enthusiasm took a hit, finding most of them napping lazily or milling about in the woods out of boredom. *These* were his tribe's liberators? Running Wolf shouted at the men to get up and gather around. The warriors were none too pleased about being disrupted by the overeager young brave, but they slowly and gruffly complied. He informed the men of the situation back at the village and led them back down the same way he had come.

Eternal Blossom had summoned Red Willow, and they were both waiting for Running Wolf to make his reappearance. Red Willow saw her little brother approaching in the distance, followed by the warriors, and she could not believe her eyes. She pulled her hair back out of her face for an uninterrupted view. Running Wolf noticed his sister and, even as far away as he was, he could see her swollen belly. His heart was beating like a drum, excited at the prospect of seeing his sister again. He made his way down until they stood face to face. A long moment of silence passed between them, but so much was said without the need for words.

Red Willow finally spoke, "Never forget," Red Willow looked at Running Wolf and then back behind him at his group of warriors, "I will always be stronger than you, no matter how many warriors you command."

Running Wolf let out a chuckle as she reached out to embrace him. It was an awkward hug, with her stomach protruding so far, but it was worth every second.

"Where is White Owl?" Running Wolf asked as they released their embrace. "I thought he would be here with you."

Red Willow hung her head low and caressed her belly. "He is in the care of the medicine man. He is very sick."

From his sister's somber tone, Running Wolf knew that White Owl was in rough shape, but he felt he could solve everyone's problems with his newfound optimism. "Don't worry, agilvgi; I am here to help."

Red Willow appreciated her brother's naive hope. "I know you are udo, but what is your plan?"

"I am here to offer new life to the entire tribe," he responded. "Anyone who wants to come back with me to the Catawba is welcome to come and be integrated with the tribe there."

Red Willow was intrigued by what her brother was saying but skeptical that he had the authority to do it. "How are you able to make this offer?"

"I am close with the Catawba chief, Sitting Deer," Running Wolf replied. "He will do what I ask."

Red Willow's mouth was agape. Who was this man-child standing here in front of her? "Even if you can make an offer like that, do you think anyone here will listen to you?" Red Willow asked. "The last time these people saw you, you were being led away by armed guards because you were accused of murder."

Running Wolf realized his sister had a point. In his enthusiasm to be a hero, he had lost sight of how the tribe would perceive him upon his return. He had pictured himself striding into the temple courtyard, triumphantly lauded as a savior on the same site where the villagers had decried him an object of scorn many moons ago. As hard as it would be to set those dreams aside, he knew it would add more chaos to the tribe's already chaotic situation if he were to be in charge.

Running Wolf shrugged. "I guess you're right. They might not listen to me . . . but they will listen to you. Take my warriors with you, gather the villagers, and let them know the Great Spirit has answered their prayers. Convince them to go to the Catawba village."

"I will go, but I will not go alone." Red Willow looked over at Eternal Blossom. "Eternal Blossom will go with me, and we will complete your mission together."

Eternal Blossom nodded in agreement. Running Wolf split his warriors into two groups. Red Willow and her contingent of warriors met with Walking Squirrel. At the same time, Eternal Blossom went with her contingent throughout the remainder of the Pee Dee village to gather everyone into the temple courtyard. Running Wolf set off back towards the Catawba supply cart with a new mission on his mind.

Red Willow created quite a scene as she strode into the beaver clan enclave with the Catawba warriors trailing behind her. For the first time since the murder of the clan leaders, the people, who had been mourning and fasting, emerged from their huts to lay eyes on what was unfolding. The sight of a pregnant woman leading this impressive group of warriors was astonishing, and they took it as a sign from the Great Spirit that things were about to change. Unfazed by the onlookers, Red Willow made her way straight to Walking Squirrel's hut. She barged in and was horrified by what she found.

Walking Squirrel's limp body was seated against the wall and blood covered his chest from a gaping wound in his neck. The knife he had used to slit his throat was still there in his cold, dead hand. She covered her mouth with her hand in horror and made her way back out through the doorway. Putting her head in her hands, she tried to collect herself. She wanted to let it all out with a scream and a flood of tears, but she knew the villagers were watching, and she had to be strong.

Noticing her distress, one of the warriors came over to check on her. "Is everything alright?"

Red Willow took a deep breath and collected her thoughts. "I will be fine. Have your men round up all these villagers and follow me into the courtyard."

The men went from hut to hut and gathered all the deer clan members who were not already part of the onlooking crowd. A thin layer of fog was rolling into the courtyard as Red Willow led the group of villagers into the square in front of the temple mound, the warriors following close behind. Running Wolf was there waiting, cradling Gray Dove's bone pot close to his chest. The outline of his silhouette through the mist made him look like a ghost. Red Willow made her way over to her brother, a strong sense of intuition telling her what was in the pot he was holding. She came face to face with him. "Is that what I think it is?"

He nodded solemnly. "May I see?" she asked. He took the lid off the pot, revealing Gray Dove's bones. Red Willow peered down as tears welled up in her eyes. She gently pulled out one of the femurs and cradled it softly in her arms. The young life in her belly immediately sprang into action, kicking and stirring. Her sadness turned into tears of joy as she realized that her mother and her child had made an instant spiritual connection. She held tightly to the bone for a few more minutes, soaking in all the warm feelings. Taking one last deep breath, she let go of the bone, placing it back in the pot. "So, what comes next?" she asked.

"I've had a lot of time to meditate on that question. The answer that keeps coming back to me is to honor her by burying her where she thought she would leave this life." He turned his gaze towards the top of the temple mound. "The place where she was going to sacrifice it all for the sake of her family."

Red Willow followed Running Wolf's lead and looked towards the top of the temple mound. "I think she would like that."

At that moment, Eternal Blossom and her warriors entered the courtyard with all the remaining members of the Pee Dee tribe. A mass of broken souls crowded into the temple plaza. Their faces were gaunt, their bodies thin from their malnourishment, and they all carried a look of exhaustion and fear. The sight of all those weary visages hit Running Wolf like an arrow to the chest. The same people who had scorned and derided him as they banished him from the tribe were now objects of his compassion. Eternal Blossom made her way through the throng to where Red Willow and Running Wolf were standing. "Everyone is here; what now?" she asked.

Running Wolf looked into the eyes of his sister and aunt. "It is time for us to offer our tribe a new way of life."

Running Wolf picked up his mother's bone pot and beckoned Red Willow and Eternal Blossom to follow him. "Where are we going?" Eternal Blossom asked as they were about to set off.

"To the top of the temple mound, so we can make our proclamation," he answered, without turning back.

Eternal Blossom stopped dead in her tracks. "I cannot go there. If you go there, you go without me."

Running Wolf stopped and turned to face her. "That is also where we will bury our etsi's bones," he said as he lifted his mother's bone pot in the air. "Don't you want to be there with us?"

Eternal Blossom placed her hand over her mouth, and she started to tremble. "You have your etsi's remains? When were you going to tell me?"

Running Wolf walked closer. "I wasn't trying to hide it from you. I . . . I just haven't had time to tell you yet."

Eternal Blossom stroked the bone pot gently with her fingers. Running Wolf stood silently for a moment, allowing her some time to grieve before he spoke again. "Do you want to come with us to the temple mound now?"

Eternal Blossom took a deep breath before answering, "I still cannot go . . . but it is good enough for me to know that she will rest forever in her home."

Running Wolf bowed to her and resumed his walk towards the base of the temple mound with Red Willow. When they reached the foot of the mound, he was unsure if he should continue up the steep steps with his mother's remains or place them aside to help his pregnant sister with the climb. Before he could make up his mind, Red Willow had already begun her ascent. "She doesn't need any help," he thought to himself as he started his awkward trek up the foggy incline with the bone pot in hand.

Brother and sister climbed together, through and above the fog, to the top of the temple mound. Running Wolf sat his mother's bones down next to the same stone bench that Soaring Eagle's guards had placed her on many moons ago as a sacrifice. He did not know whether to cry or laugh, so he let out a tearful chuckle as he stood, staring down. It was a surreal moment for him that they both were now back at this place where their journey began.

The villagers were starting to gather at the base of the temple. Running Wolf walked over and stood next to his sister as she peered down through the thick, misty air at the crowd. Their haggard visages made them appear even more ghoulish than Running Wolf's ghostlike presence. It indeed was a sea of lost souls. Running Wolf stiffened his chest and began to address the multitude, forgetting he had vowed not to be the leader of this group. But before he could get even a syllable out of his mouth, Red Willow grabbed his arm and stopped him. "I said you should let me handle this."

"They are dead," Red Willow shouted through the fog. "All of them. Spotted Turtle, Proud Robin, Soaring Eagle, and even Walking Squirrel . . . your clan leaders, are all dead. And you are all hungry, tired, and scared. It is plain for anyone to see that the Great Spirit has cursed this ground, but He has not forgotten us as a people. He has sent my brother, Running Wolf, back to us with a plan to make us whole again. Together, we can leave this cursed place and make a new home amongst the Catawba people. I know such upheaval is a frightening thought, and I share that fear with you, but sometimes great turmoil is followed by great joy when you take a risk to change your life. Those who wish to go live with the Catawba, go back to your huts, put out your fires, and gather your belongings. We leave at first light. Those of you who wish to stay, may you regain the blessings of the Great Spirit in this place."

Rumblings and murmurs ran through the crowd before they finally disbursed, each returning to their huts. Red Willow sat down on the bench, exhausted from the climb and the tension of addressing the entire tribe. Running Wolf sat next to her without saying a word. He put his arm around her shoulder, and she leaned her head into his chest. They sat and stared at the mass of souls disappearing through the fog. "Do you think they'll go?" he asked.

"What choice do they have? There is nothing good for them here."

Running Wolf tapped his heel against the stone bench. "I just feel like sometimes people hold tightly to what they know, even if what they know is hurtful to them."

She nodded. "That is often true. We just have to hope that the Great Spirit can open the hearts of those people who need to have them opened."

They sat in a few more minutes of silence before Running Wolf removed his arm. "It is time to bury Etsi."

Red Willow lay down on the bench and folded her arms across her chest. "I cannot help you now. I am too tired."

Running Wolf rubbed his face and ran his hands through his hair as he got up. He had only a small stone ax for digging, insufficient for the job, so he had to improvise. Digging out a wide circular trench, he placed Gray Dove's bones in the center. He removed the lid from the clay pot and turned it upside down, covering the bones, then backfilled the trench around the pot with dirt to hold it in place. For the final step, he gathered the rocks used to encircle the central firepit of the temple and stacked them around the top of the pot. It was a rather impressive accomplishment for a makeshift burial plot— a fitting tribute to the woman who always made the best out of terrible circumstances in her broken life.

When he was finished with the burial, he walked over and offered his hand to Red Willow. She reached out to clasp it, and he pulled her quickly up off the bench. As she rose, an intense wave of pressure gripped her abdomen. Her face clenched from the pain, and she quickly bent over and put her hands on her knees. "I didn't pick you up that hard," Running Wolf joked to his sister.

The pressure quickly subsided. "No, you are not strong enough to hurt me like that. It was something else. I am going to the medicine man to check on White Owl; I'll talk to him about it while I am there. Go back to your warriors and tell them what we plan to do."

Running Wolf helped her back down from the temple mound, and they went their separate ways. Red Willow strode gingerly towards the medicine man's hut, finding it unoccupied upon her arrival. She searched the interior and the perimeter of the dwelling without seeing any signs of life. Her heartbeat quickened as she feared the worst about her husband. Was he dead and the medicine man now delivering the body to her hut? She leaned against the support post of the house, head in her hands. Just then, she heard a voice echo behind her.

"I am glad you are here." It was the medicine man, returning from one of his plant foraging trips with a handful of medicinal leaves. "I have some news for you." She turned and faced the medicine man with a fearful look in her eye. "White Owl's fever dropped suddenly last night, and he regained enough of his strength that he no longer needed my care. The Great Spirit placed his blessings upon him, and he returned to your hut earlier this morning."

She instantly let out a heavy sigh before another gripping pain enveloped her. She grasped her stomach, her face clenched tightly. The medicine man couldn't help but notice, and he nodded understandingly. "I have seen this pain before. Your time is coming. I have something for you." He walked over to his shelf and retrieved some blue cohosh root. "Make a tea from this root and drink it daily until your day arrives."

As her pain subsided, she reached out to take the roots. "I have to tell you that the tribe will be moving on from this place and making a home with the Catawba. Will you be joining us?"

"Are all of the villagers leaving?" The medicine man looked around at the shelves on the walls with jars full of his carefully curated plant medicines. He closed his eyes and communed with the energy radiating from the leaves and roots and stems that filled the hut. It was a lifetime of work, something that he would have difficulty leaving behind if it came to that.

"We won't know until the next sunrise," she replied.

"Then that is when I will decide. If everyone goes, then I will go. But if even one person stays, I will stay. I must make sure that *all* are allowed to be healed, and I will not forsake my duty towards anyone in the tribe."

"I understand. Wa do, Holy One." Red Willow bowed as she left the medicine man to return to her hut, while he began to gather together the herbs he considered essential for a potential journey.

Back at her hut, Red Willow found White Owl sitting on the floor, stroking Fyre's fur as she sat on his lap. "I'm so glad you are well again," she said as she knelt next to him and surrounded him with her arms.

White Owl was still physically weak and confused, but he was overjoyed to see his wife again. "Can you tell me what is happening to our tribe? I go to see the medicine man for a few moons, and I return to a tribe full of Catawba warriors and people telling me strange stories about leaving this place. I don't understand any of this."

She took a deep breath and exhaled. "I don't even know where to begin. All of the clan leaders are dead, and Running Wolf has returned to take us away from this cursed place and lead us to a new home with the Catawba."

White Owl rubbed his still glassy eyes, struggling to process what she was telling him. "I can't make any sense of this right now. I'm just going to trust you. You say that we are leaving?"

"Yes, at first sunlight."

"I will be ready when the time comes," White Owl replied. "But until then, I need to rest."

Fyre jumped off his lap as he resituated himself into the fetal position for a nap. Red Willow brewed up her cohosh root tea. When it was finished, she poured it into a small clay cup. She sat and sipped the tea as she peered out the hut's doorway, wondering what the next few moons might have in store for her and the rest of the tribe.

Chapter Twenty-Two

Time to Move On

The sun slowly peaked its head above the horizon the following morning, burning the dew off the ground as it rose. Red Willow threw a pitcher of water over the central fire of their hut, dousing it for the final time. Fyre came scurrying up, eager to return home after a night on the prowl. She rubbed the bobcat's neck and went to rouse White Owl from his exhausted slumber. "Osda sunalei, my love. It is time to get moving."

White Owl rubbed his eyes and sat up with his hands on his knees. "I could sleep for days," he said, still worn out from his illness and recovery.

"There will be time for sleep later," Red Willow replied. "Now is the time to go."

White Owl stood up and stretched his arms high above his head. He strolled to the doorway to get a breath of fresh air and was startled by what he saw. The response to Running Wolf's invitation was more significant than anyone could have anticipated. The bear clan campsite was abuzz with activity. Each of the families was dousing their fires and preparing their supplies for the journey to the Catawba.

Red Willow handed her husband a chunk of pemmican, but the mere sight it was enough to tie his stomach in knots. "I can't eat this," he said, a look of disgust on his face.

"I understand, but that is all we have right now, and you need to regain your strength."

He closed his eyes and slowly choked down the pemmican, followed it with a long drink of water to cleanse his palette, then wiped his face clean with his hand. She beckoned him over to help her prepare the supplies for the trip. She draped a long leather bag around White Owl's shoulders and began filling it with the items they would need—boiling stones, antler tongs, a knife, a water pouch, the blue cohosh root, and more pemmican. The last thing to go into the bag was the most important, the rabbit stick from her father. She gripped the shaft tightly and held it close to her chest as visions of her father filled her mind before tossing it in.

Red Willow patted White Owl on the back, indicating to him that she had finished. Another sharp pain radiated through her abdomen as she had turned away to pick up Fyre. "Are you alright?" White Owl asked, noticing her pained expression.

She placed her hands on her stomach, trying to calm the pain. "I'll be fine. These pains come, and they go. Why don't you go ahead to the temple courtyard? I will meet you there soon."

He cocked his head to the side and squinted his eyes. "Are you sure I should leave?"

She motioned yes, and he hesitantly made his way out. As her pain subsided, she found herself alone in her family hut one last time. Scanning the room, her mind filled with images: the hammock, the bearskin rug, and the new clay jug that her mother had fashioned before her death. Her eyes moistened as she pondered all the memories. She gently wiped away her tears with her forearm and picked up Fyre. Then she took one last long look around before making her way to the plaza to meet with the rest of the tribe.

The sun shone brightly that morning as Red Willow strode into the courtyard. A sea of souls awaited her, and all eyes turned as she made her entrance. Considering herself the unlikeliest of leaders, especially in her current condition, she made her way to the front of the crowd, where she joined Running Wolf. "Is the whole tribe here?" she asked, a look of surprise on her face.

"I had my warriors search all the clan sites, and there was not a single person to be found at any of the huts. Everyone is here and ready to go."

Red Willow looked out at the throng. Their faces were still worn and haggard, but for the first time in many moons, an aura of hopefulness tinged their expressions. It was palpable, something Red Willow could drink into her spirit and soak into her bones. It was a strengthening feeling for her to think that things might work out for the best.

"They will want you to say something before we leave," Running Wolf said, leaning over towards his sister.

She sighed. "They don't want empty words. They just want better lives for themselves and their families . . . and that is what we are going to give them."

"Don't tell me that." He pointed to the crowd. "Tell *them* that."

She nodded and made her way over towards the base of the temple mound. This time she climbed up only a few stairs, just enough to be slightly higher than the assembled masses. "I can tell that you are all ready for a change, a chance to find something better than your current circumstances," she began. "Today is the first day of your new lives—lives that will be much different from those to which you have grown accustomed. We will make our way to the Catawba and live among them. It will not be easy, but I believe that it will be rewarding and lead us all into a new era of prosperity. May the Great Spirit bless us as we undertake this journey."

"May the Great Spirit bless us," they chanted.

Red Willow climbed down the stairs, wincing as another cramp seized her abdomen. White Owl offered his arm, and together, they joined Running Wolf and the Catawba warriors at the head of the crowd, then led the procession of Pee Dee people out of the Town Creek village. The medicine man was the final villager to make his way through the gates of the palisade wall. He stood and watched as a small patch of clouds rolled in and blocked out the sun's rays, casting a dark shadow over the now eerily vacant settlement.

The large collective traversed the newly well-worn pathway between the Pee Dee and Catawba villages. The group moved at a glacial pace due to the inclusion of children and the elderly, but they remained organized and cohesive. They shared the pemmican supply that had been in Spotted Turtle's care for their sustenance and took small hunting excursions to supplement their dietary needs. The overarching mood of the tribe remained one of cautious optimism, fueled by a desire to leave behind their presumably cursed homeland. Red Willow's abdominal pains increased in frequency and intensity, and she experienced some bleeding from her pelvis Eternal Blossom knew that Red Willow's time was soon to come; her only question was whether it would be before or after they reached their destination.

Eternal Blossom's query was answered when the tribe was only a day's journey from the Catawba. Red Willow awoke that morning after a restless night, feeling a weird and wet sensation on her legs. "Did I wet myself in the night?" she wondered. At that moment, the muscles in her abdomen cramped and squeezed in a way she had never experienced, as if her physical form was being ground down like the corn she had helped mill. She cried out in pain, waking White Owl and Eternal Blossom.

White Owl sat up and rubbed his eyes. "What is it?"

Red Willow was unable to answer. "Her time is here," Eternal Blossom said, putting her arm around Red Willow to comfort her.

White Owl rubbed his chest nervously as he looked down at his laboring wife. "What do we do now?"

Eternal Blossom quickly took control. "Go and tell Running Wolf that his sister is bringing your usdi into the world. I will stay here and be her guide on this journey."

Eternal Blossom grasped Red Willow's hand and reassured her that everything would be fine, while White Owl made his way to Running Wolf. Grabbing him by the shoulders, looking him directly in the eyes, he shouted, "It's happening! Your agilvgi is bringing our usdi into the world as we speak."

Running Wolf quickly ran his hand through his hair. He was equally anxious and excited because he knew both the dangers of childbirth and the joy a new family member would bring. "I'm happy for you, White

Owl," he said, before turning his thoughts to the tribe. "We are almost there."

"Well, what are you going to do now?" White Owl asked him.

"Do you remember the way to the Catawba from here?" Running Wolf questioned in return.

"I do."

Running Wolf began to pace. "Does Red Willow have another agehya there to help her make it through the birth?"

"Yes. Eternal Blossom is there with her." White Owl squinted, unsure why Running Wolf was asking all these questions.

Running Wolf stopped pacing and stood face to face with him. "Go back and stay with her while I lead the rest of the tribe forward towards the Catawba. When it is finished, and she and the usdi are safe, lead them to meet up with us at the Catawba."

White Owl's pulse raced. Running Wolf wanted to split up the tribe and leave his sister with as little help as possible during her time of need? "I don't think that is a wise idea."

Running Wolf rubbed his chin with his palms. "I understand your fear, but these people are desperate for something good." He gestured to the huddled Pee Dee group. "I can't keep them waiting any longer. You have to trust Eternal Blossom and the Great Spirit to bring Red Willow through."

White Owl reluctantly nodded and turned to head back. Then Running Wolf shouted, "Wait!" White Owl spun back around. "One more thing . . . make sure you give her my love." White Owl smiled and hurried away.

White Owl could hear Red Willow moaning in the distance as he approached. The bellowing sounds reverberated through his head, and his heartbeat quickened. He picked up the pace and rushed to see what was happening. Eternal Blossom was fanning Red Willow with a leafy branch and encouraging her to breathe through her pain. "Running Wolf is taking the tribe ahead while we stay here to help Red Willow through her labor," White Owl said, wincing at his wife's distress.

A determined look crossed Eternal Blossom's face. "Stay here with her and try to keep her comfortable while I get a birthing cord."

Eternal Blossom headed back towards the tribal encampment to retrieve her supplies, leaving White Owl and Red Willow alone. He sat down and rubbed her back gently. "I'm scared," she said, between deep breaths.

White Owl felt a large lump developing in his throat, and he swallowed deeply, trying to choke it down. He was almost as scared as she was, but he could not show it. "You know you are the strongest agehya in this tribe . . . and if the rest of them can give birth, you can do it ten times over."

She tried to let the words of encouragement sink in, but the radiating pains, which kept intensifying, were her only focus. Eternal Blossom returned with her birthing cord and dismissed White Owl since it was customary for the tribe to only let women be present during childbirth. Searching the nearby trees for one with a low-hanging and sturdy branch, her mind settled on a suitable one. She piled up fallen leaves around the base and tossed the cord over the branch so that both ends were dangling down.

"Over here," Eternal Blossom said, directing Red Willow to her prepared spot.

Red Willow gingerly walked over. "What is all this?" she asked through a clenched jaw.

"This is where your usdi will get their first look at the world!"

Red Willow surveyed her surroundings, and it nearly crushed her spirit. She did not want to bring her firstborn into the world as a homeless traveler, but there was no choice. She resigned herself and awaited further instructions as the intense pain shot down into her lower back. Eternal Blossom could sense her increasing discomfort and knew that she needed to find a distraction.

"Let us prepare the area for the arrival of your blessing with a special song and dance," Eternal Blossom said. "Follow me and do as I do."

Eternal Blossom began to shuffle around the leafy pile in a wide circle, chanting a loud, staccato rhythm. Red Willow grimaced, unable to understand why her aunt thought it would be a good idea to sing and dance right now. Despite her misgivings, Red Willow joined in the chanting and dancing, trusting that Eternal Blossom might know something she did not. They continued their circling rhythms for what seemed like an eternity as her pelvic floor stretched and engorged throughout the activity.

Red Willow finally had enough. "The usdi is here!" she screamed, as an overwhelming desire to push the baby out enveloped her.

Eternal Blossom realized the baby was unwilling to wait any longer. She directed Red Willow to stand over the pile of leaves underneath the tree branch, where the birthing cord was dangling overhead. "When you feel the need to push, grab the ends of this cord and pull down as hard as you can."

Red Willow nodded wildly, through salty tears and sweat dripping down her face. She grabbed the ends of the cord with each of her hands and waited to push. When the impulse came, she pulled down with all her strength and pushed out from her pelvis, letting out an agonizing scream. Eternal Blossom simultaneously shouted at her stomach to try to scare the baby out of her uterus, as was customary within the tribe. It was a raucous but ultimately unfruitful effort. Red Willow took a deep breath, readying herself for the next onslaught before her body compelled her to push once again. On her third push, the torment reached a new level, as she felt her vagina tear open ever so slightly while the baby's head began to make its way out. It was almost too much, and she sensed passing out was a real possibility. Eternal Blossom steadied her, and, with one last valiant effort, she pushed out her baby boy onto the waiting leaf cushion.

Red Willow threw herself against the base of the tree trunk and took several deep breaths, unaware that the process of childbirth was still not complete. She gazed at the infant lying there in the pile of leaves, still attached to her via the umbilical cord, and desperately wished to reach out and cradle him. But more contractions swept across her abdomen. "How is this still not over?" she thought to herself. With a few more small pushes, she released her placenta, concluding her life-giving journey and beginning her foray into motherhood.

Eternal Blossom made her way over to the baby boy as he wailed and cried in the leaves. Crouching down over the little one, she drew out her deer antler knife to slice the umbilical cord away from the placenta. Then she picked up the noisy infant and delicately carried him over to his exhausted mother. Eternal Blossom stood and observed, tears welling in her eyes, as her niece cradled the newborn in her arms. The sacredness of the mother-child bonding moment was palpable, and it was her wish to remain a part of this tender scene for eternity, but she knew that her work was not yet complete. "I'll be right back," she said tenderly to her niece, before excusing herself to locate the new father.

Eternal Blossom ambled through the woods to find White Owl crouched down next to a small brook, anxiously tossing pebbles into the babbling flow. She sidled up to him and placed her hand gently on his shoulder. "It is finished," she patted him gingerly.

White Owl looked up at her and sighed deeply. "Can I see them now?"

Eternal Blossom smiled softly and nodded. "Follow me."

The pair made their back to mother and baby, with White Owl nervously pacing behind Eternal Blossom the entire way. As soon as White Owl saw his new family in the distance, he could no longer contain himself. His pace quickened step-by-step until his feet were flying in a full-fledged sprint. When he reached his wife and son, he knelt down and cradled his hand behind Red Willow's neck, pulling their heads together in a dynamic embrace. They both shed tears of joy as the baby sat cradled in his mother's arms and let out a few muffled cries.

Eternal Blossom turned to the rituals of childbirth. It was customary for the tribe to bury the newly delivered placenta in the corner of the village to bind the child's spirit to the spirits of the tribal ancestors who had come before, and that task fell to her. But what was she to do with this placenta in a completely foreign territory? She knew that she could not just leave it there for some wild animal to devour, but burying it on unfamiliar land seemed strange. Would such a burial condemn the boy as a wandering spirit, without a forever home? She stood over the mass of bloody tissue, meditating on what to do, when a strong breeze blew across the forest and covered the afterbirth with abundant leaves. Eternal Blossom looked down at the buried tissue and considered it a sign from the Great Spirit. She searched the area for some soft ground and, with great effort, used her knife to carve out a shallow hole in the ground. She gently placed the placenta into the hole, said a prayer for peace and blessings in the boy's life, and covered it with a layer of dirt.

Chapter Twenty-Three

Commingling

A lone Catawba woman paced along the forest floor a few miles outside her village, searching for the most delicious hickory nuts to feed her family. It was a clear and temperate spring day, seemingly like any other. The woman was intently focused on her work when, without warning, a large flock of birds took off violently from a tree branch overhead, startling her and causing her to drop her basket of nuts. She took a second to compose herself, during which time she happened to glance out towards a clearing in the distance. There, appearing out of the woods, were a cadre of Catawba warriors leading a parade of unfamiliar men, women, and children. She stood and watched in amazement as the group grew progressively larger. "I must be dreaming," she thought to herself as she struggled to process what she was witnessing. As the group grew closer and closer, she realized that this was not a dream. She left the toppled basket of nuts and scrambled back towards the village to tell the others what she had seen.

Sprinting into the village square, she looked for anyone with any kind of authority. Rolling Cloud was roaming the courtyard and took notice. "What seems to be troubling you, agehya?"

"I . . . " she panted, "I saw many strangers headed towards our village, and I do not know what it means."

Rolling Cloud rested against his walking staff and continued his inquiry. "Were they warriors or common people?"

The woman closed her eyes, trying to recapture the scene. "Warriors, but they appeared to be Catawba. The strangers were just common people of all types—men, women, and children."

As he stared off into the distance, a sly smile crossed Rolling Cloud's face. He remembered the Great Spirit's vision about Running Wolf uniting the people, and he realized that its fulfillment was at hand. Smiling at the woman, he spoke quietly, "You do not need to fear. This is the work of the Great Spirit. Go in peace."

The woman bowed her head and departed to share the news with her husband. Rolling Cloud felt hopeful about the imminent arrival of Running Wolf and his compatriots, believing it would portend a sublime future for the combined tribes. Before sharing the woman's report with Sitting Deer, he stood for a moment and pondered the possibilities that the Great Spirit might have in store, soaking them into his soul.

At Sitting Deer's hut, Rolling Cloud found the chief engrossed in a game of taludza. Taludza was the tribal game of chance, played by rolling two-toned dried beans in a basket in an attempt to land all of the beans with the same color facing up. Players would take turns rolling the beans and were awarded a dried corn kernel from a central pot for each successful roll. Play continued until one person collected all the corn kernels from the central pot and from the other players and was declared the winner. Sitting Deer had been playing an unusual amount of taludza since Running Wolf had been gone to keep his mind off the boy's fate and was particularly absorbed in this day's contest.

Rolling Cloud stood silently in the doorway, imbued with a feeling of self-importance, waiting for the distracted Sitting Deer to acknowledge his presence. After a few more turns, Sitting Deer finally addressed him. "Do you need something?" he asked curtly before resuming his game.

Frustrated by Sitting Deer's dismissive attitude, Rolling Cloud fixed him with a steely gaze then stubbornly dug his heels in to wait for a proper greeting. Sitting Deer continued his game, increasingly annoyed. "What is so important that it cannot wait?" he blurted.

Rolling Cloud crossed his arms in front of his chest. "The atsutsa has returned," he said gruffly then left.

Rolling Cloud's words crackled like lightning in Sitting Deer's ears, snapping him out of his diversion. He stopped his game and rushed out to corral Rolling Cloud before he could walk away. Catching up, Sitting Deer grabbed him by the arm and twisted him around. "How do you know?"

Rolling Cloud jerked his arm away. "Do not put your hands on me again!"

Sitting Deer hung his head, acknowledging his transgression. "Forgive me," he said, "I have lately been under the charge of many disturbed spirits. But if what you say is true, it will lift those spirits off me."

Rolling Cloud composed himself. "I had a report from an agehya that she saw Running Wolf making his way towards the village earlier . . . and he was not alone."

A slight smile curled the corners of Sitting Deer's mouth. "I know he's not alone. I sent my warriors with him."

"There are more souls than that," Rolling Cloud replied with a chuckle that revealed his prophetic amusement.

Sitting Deer squinted. "What do you mean?"

Standing shoulder to shoulder with Sitting Deer, Rolling Cloud whispered, "You will see," before closing his eyes and dashing away.

Sitting Deer was thrilled to hear that his surrogate son was returning. Still, he did not understand what Rolling Cloud meant by "others." Anxious to find out for himself what was transpiring, he rushed out of the village in the direction of Running Wolf. He ran harder and faster than he had run in a long while, stopping dead in his tracks when he beheld Running Wolf and the entire Pee Dee tribe in the deep distance.

As he bent to catch his breath, a sinking feeling developed in the pit of his stomach. In contrast to Rolling Cloud's hopefulness for the tribal union, all that Sitting Deer could imagine were the potential pitfalls. How would he feed and house an entire extra tribe? How would his villagers react to a large influx of foreigners? He was convinced that Running Wolf was making a grave mistake, and he could not wait to let him know how he felt.

After Sitting Deer had collected his thoughts, he continued towards the mass of people. He stopped a few yards short of Running Wolf, and the two stood face-to-face. Sitting Deer rubbed his hands rapidly, trying to resolve his inner conflict. Part of him wanted to lovingly embrace his stand-in son, while the other wanted to scold his naive fosterling for bringing him this potential burden. He spoke up plainly, "Why did you bring these people here?"

Running Wolf's eyes darted, disappointed by Sitting Deer's less-than-welcoming reception. "I thought you said you wanted to help?"

Sitting Deer pursed his lips, trying to contain his frustration. "I did help, in case you failed to notice, but what you are asking now is beyond what I can give."

Running Wolf looked back at his weary Pee Dee tribemates. "All that we ask for is a chance—a chance to prove to you and your tribe that we can all coexist in peace and harmony."

Sitting Deer shrugged. "Even if I were to help you, I don't know if I have enough provisions."

"These people are used to living with limited means," Running Wolf pointed towards the huddled mass. "They will not ask for much, and they will work hard to build up their supplies if you just give them some help."

Sitting Deer relaxed and started stroking his chin. "I must bring something as important as this to the tribal council for us to decide. You and my warriors can come with me, but the rest of these people must stay here, far outside the village, for now."

Running Wolf lowered his head. His people were so close to having a new home they could almost taste it, but that dream would have to wait. He nodded reluctantly, agreeing to Sitting Deer's conditions, and returned to the Pee Dee crowd to share the disappointing news. Most of the tribe took the word of delayed entry in stride, as they figured it would only be a few days before the Catawba people would decide, and what was a few extra days relative to the misery of the preceding weeks?

After departing from his people, Running Wolf made his way swiftly towards the Catawba village, slowing only as he reached the gate in the palisade wall. He stopped there and took a moment to reflect on how different it felt to be standing in this spot now instead of the first time he had been here. He had come initially as a timid and helpless young boy, and now he was making his return as a bold and confident young man. After the moment's reflection, he entered through the gate, and the tribe welcomed him with open arms instead of the suspicious stares and mocking laughter he had encountered the first time. Skye, who had been staying with Sitting Deer while Running Wolf was away, rushed in and jumped up to place his meaty paws on Running Wolf's chest. Running Wolf smiled at his companion, massaging him behind the ears.

Unbeknownst to Running Wolf, Sitting Deer had planned to delay the tribal council vote until the next full moon, more than two weeks away. The longer he could put it off, the more time he would have to himself with his friend, Running Wolf. Running Wolf enjoyed the hospitality of the Catawba people, while the remainder of the Pee Dee contingent camped out on the distant outskirts of the village. They were a people in limbo, uncertain what their future might hold. Word of their arrival had spread throughout the village, creating an enormous volume of gossip. Some were fearful of the presence of the strangers, some were angry, but most were simply curious about what their coming foreshadowed.

Even though Sitting Deer had forbidden the entrance of the Pee Dee people into his village, he was not without mercy towards them. The following day he sent a group of emissaries out to greet them and offer some supplies. The Catawba envoys approached with caution and were met at the front of the encampment by the interim Pee Dee chief. The two sides exchanged wary gazes, each trying to size the other up. The Pee Dee chief squinted and raised his eyebrows at the sight of the triangular heads of the Catawba, having never laid eyes on such a strange phenomenon. The Catawba men gazed at the pitiable herd of ragtag Pee Dee villagers with looks of disdain.

The silent stares continued until one of the Catawba consuls broke the silence. "We come in peace to offer you these provisions to help ease your stay here," he said, pointing to two baskets of dried fruit and deer jerky and three giant jugs of drinking water.

The provisional chieftain bowed his head in gratitude to the Catawba contingent and called forth some of his men to retrieve the supplies and bring them back into the encampment. Feeling ashamed that he had nothing to offer in return, the man called for his wife to be brought out and presented as a gift exchange. The Catawba group examined the situation before trading knowing looks amongst themselves. Understanding the will of the group, their leader spoke out. "We appreciate your proposition, but we cannot accept it. These gifts that we give to you are freely given so that you may know the Catawba are a generous people."

The Catawba cohort respectfully bowed their heads to the Pee Dee leader and headed back to their village. Once they were clearly out of sight, the wife of the Pee Dee leader scowled at her husband in a manner befitting the fiercest wildcat in the forest. She shoved him in the shoulder with the thrust of a gale-force wind before walking away in a huff. The bogus chieftain hung his head in shame, overwhelmed by the challenges he and the rest of the tribe had faced in the preceding moon cycles. He shuffled off slowly to rejoin the rest of his worn-out companions.

It was a week or so before Red Willow, White Owl, Eternal Blossom, and the new baby boy caught up to the rest of the Pee Dee tribe. Red Willow had morphed into a highly responsible adult seemingly overnight. Her milk had by now fully come, and, with much guidance from Eternal Blossom, she had consistently gotten her baby to nurse. As for White Owl, he was doing his best to perform the, at this time, nearly superfluous role of father. It was his job to ensure that his burgeoning family arrived safely at their destination.

Their fatigued fellow tribemates greeted the group with enthusiasm, but none of those salutations mattered to Red Willow. There was only one person she desired to see: Running Wolf. Searching through the crowd and finding no sign of him, she finally stopped and asked one of the people his whereabouts. "He went into the Catawba village a few nights ago, and we haven't seen him since," the woman responded.

Red Willow peered inquisitively towards the distant village, with her baby boy strapped into a cradleboard attached to her back. A glimpse of smoke rose from behind the tree line. Questions came tumbling through her brain: "What is Running Wolf doing in there? Why is the tribe being denied entry? What does this all mean for our future and, most importantly, my son's future?" She had no patience to wait for answers to these questions; she needed to know now.

Making her way back through the horde, she came face to face with White Owl. "We have to talk. Running Wolf left the tribe to go to the Catawba village a few nights ago and has not returned. I need you to go and find out what is happening."

White Owl gazed wearily at his wife. "I promise you we will figure things out at the next rising of the sun. But for tonight, it is best for us to rest and recover. We have been through so much."

He gently stroked her arm while the baby fussed slightly in its cradleboard. As the baby began crying, White Owl grabbed him and handed him to his mother, gently lifting his wobbly little head to her engorged breast. She agreed they could all use some rest. The new family rejoined the rest of the tribe just as they were all sitting down to share their modest meal of deer jerky and dried fruit. White Owl was relieved to see that they were not serving pemmican as the sight of it made him shudder. Everyone partook of the meal together before retiring for the evening.

The following morning's dawn illuminated the sky with a dazzling array of pinkish hues. Red Willow was awake to bask in its glory as she nursed her helpless little man. She could feel her mother's presence radiating throughout the colorful energies dancing into the campsite. Moved to tears, she could not tell whether they were tears of joy for the new day and new life or sadness for the loss of Gray Dove. The eventual rising of the sun brightened the campsite enough to wake White Owl from the depths of his slumber. He lifted himself off the ground and made his way over to his wife and the baby.

"Do you remember your promise to me?" she asked as he knelt and nuzzled her neck with his nose.

He immediately stopped nuzzling. "Yes," he replied matter-of-factly before reaching out his finger to rub the nose of the little one. "I will go to the village once I have nourished my body."

Red Willow nodded her head in satisfaction. "Wa do, my love," she said, expressing her gratitude.

White Owl made his way to the campsite where they stored the provisions. He took a deep drink of water and munched on a piece of deer jerky, mulling over his strategy for dealing with the Catawba people he would encounter. When he was finished eating and drinking, he skulked behind the trunk of a tall oak tree to relieve himself before heading out on his mission. Then he trudged through the dewy grass for a solid thirty minutes, thoroughly soaking his leather moccasins.

A few of the Catawba men noticed White Owl's approach and went to meet him about a hundred yards outside of the palisade wall. "Can we help you with something?" one of the men asked curtly.

White Owl bowed his head in deference. "Forgive me if I am too forward. I am from the Pee Dee tribe and have come to speak to my tribemate Running Wolf. He came into your village a few nights ago, and the rest of our tribe is wondering what has happened to him."

One of the men looked curiously at White Owl. "I know who you are. You have visited our tribe before."

"Yes," he replied. "I came during the cold season to ask for help."

The other Catawba man grunted. "So, you came during the cold season, and we helped you . . . and that was not enough? Now you come back asking for more, and we are supposed to bail you out again? You all must be so weak. We don't have any use for that here. You and your tribe need to leave this place and find your own way!"

White Owl clenched his fist as he listened to the man's rant, seething at the aspersions cast against his tribe. Only his weariness prevented him from raising his clenched fist to punch the man in the face. He took a few deep breaths before responding. "We will leave when your chief tells us we have to leave . . . and not before. For now, I would like to see my tribemate in your village."

White Owl began to walk around the men, but the agitated one slid in front of him to block his movement. "Prove to me that you are not weak. You have to go through me if you want to get into the village," the man sneered.

White Owl was coiled into an attack position, but he was interrupted by a loud cracking sound before he could make a move. Rolling Cloud, who had been watching the entire incident from a distance, approached and smacked the perturbed man upside the head with his staff. The man crumpled to the ground in a heap, cursing Rolling Cloud as he lay there.

Calmly stepping over the fallen man, Rolling Cloud pulled White Owl to the side. "The council will hold a vote at the next full moon to decide what to do with your tribe. Do not fret over the outcome of the vote, for it will be in your favor. The Great Spirit wills it to be that way. For now, go back to your tribe and tell them to maintain their patience for their time is coming."

White Owl looked over Rolling Cloud's shoulder towards the village. "I want to speak with Running Wolf."

Rolling Cloud placed his hand on White Owl's shoulder to regain his attention. "If Running Wolf felt he needed to talk to your tribe, he could. He is not being held captive. He is free to come and go as he pleases."

White Owl tilted his head to the side, pondering Rolling Cloud's words. "Can I trust what this strange man is saying? It sounds reasonable and good, but what are his true motives? And why is he preventing me from seeing Running Wolf?" he asked himself. Ultimately, he could not bring himself to place his complete confidence in this strange priest, but his new-father fatigue left him unwilling to press the issue any further that day.

"I will go," White Owl said as he looked into Rolling Cloud's eyes, "but if we do not receive word from Running Wolf during the full moon, I will be returning . . . and I will not be alone."

White Owl went back to the Pee Dee camp with the news of the delayed Catawba tribal council. Frustration began to mount within a contingent of the group as they realized the full moon was still days away. They were tired, hungry, and thirsty, and they just wanted a decision, no matter the outcome. Running Wolf's absence and Red Willow's total engagement with her newborn son had created a leadership vacuum, and cracks were starting to appear in the group's cohesiveness. The impatient faction was like a cornered black bear, ready to lash out in defiant anger or climb a tree to escape and live another day.

Chapter Twenty-Four
Merger

The lustrous moon hovered over the horizon one fateful evening, cascading its beams from behind the Pee Dee camp outwards in the direction of the Catawba village. It was ever so close to being full, save for a tiny sliver of darkness shading out one edge. Everyone in the tribe knew that this penultimate moon waxing was a harbinger of the pending vote to decide their fate. The supplies the Catawba had provided were dwindling, and the people's angst was rising like the white circle in the sky above.

Up to this point, there had been no reckless actions taken by the agitated faction of the Pee Dee. Now, driven by a misplaced desire to ensure a successful outcome for the tribe, a few men concocted a deranged plot to kidnap the Catawba chief. Only they could say why they thought this would be effective. But the potential efficacy of the scheme was less a consideration than their craving to do something bold to shake things up.

When the moon was at its apex, and both tribal populations quiet and still, three Pee Dee men left camp and stealthily made their way into the Catawba village. The men managed to creep from hut to hut undetected. Finally reaching the most elaborate of the dwellings, which they presumed was the chief's residence, they stood there for a few minutes, trying to work up their courage.

One of the men clenched his fists and pounded his chest, sending a rush of adrenaline into his veins. He stepped past the other two and through the open doorway while they remained frozen on the exterior wall. Unbeknownst to the men, Running Wolf was at that very moment making his way to Sitting Deer's hut. He had been unable to sleep and was coming to confer with Sitting Deer once more before the vote.

Running Wolf noticed the two men standing outside the hut and immediately recognized them as fellow tribe members. Raising his hands in frustration, he screamed, "What are you doing here?"

His shout startled the men into motion and they scattered into the distance. Sensing the commotion, the inside man panicked and lunged suddenly towards the sleeping Sitting Deer. Running Wolf rushed into the hut just as the man pulled Sitting Deer out of his hammock. Pouncing on top of the man, Running Wolf tried to pry him off the chief.

Sitting Deer awoke in shock and confusion, a strange man lying on top of him grasping at his throat. He struggled to free himself, but the man pressed down with the whole weight of his body, and he could not move. Sitting Deer fought to catch his breath, his heart pounding mightily in his chest, speeding out of control like an overeager drummer.

His left arm throbbed with intense pressure, as if being crushed between two stones. Panic quickly turned to terror.

Sitting Deer broke free long enough to cast a glance over the shoulder of the attacker. There he saw the face of his young friend, Running Wolf. Under ordinary circumstances, the sight would have been comforting, but under such acute stress he convinced himself that Running Wolf, the boy he loved like his son, was behind a plot to kill him. The pressure from his arm radiated into his chest, and his pounding heart broke from sorrow. His throat began to burn like the flame of the Green Corn Ceremony. Images flashed into and out of his consciousness as the room spun. The last thing he saw was an image of his long-dead son. The beloved boy appeared to his father and stretched out both hands to welcome him for an infinite embrace. The sight of his cherished progeny provided Sitting Deer one last burst of strength to free his arms from his assailant and reach upward. He gasped deeply for one final breath before his spirit departed from his body.

The maniacal Pee Dee man pulled back when he realized Sitting Deer had expired. Running Wolf and the man collapsed together in a heap, exhausted. They soon found themselves staring up at the sharp ends of several spearheads, as the noise had drawn the attention of the tribal authorities. The presence of Running Wolf and the Pee Dee intruder together, adjacent to Sitting Deer's corpse, quickly aroused suspicions of foul play. The men were taken into custody, with Running Wolf vociferously and persistently shouting his proclamations of innocence. Stung by the loss of their leader, there was no possibility of the tribal council holding their scheduled vote at the following night's full moon.

White Owl awoke from a fitful sleep the morning after the full moon's appearance. There had been no word from Running Wolf and no signal from the Catawba camp that any vote had occurred. He wondered if the Catawba people were stringing him and the rest of the tribe along. His heart sank at the thought they were being cast aside without any consideration like an imperfect mussel shell. He knew his tribe deserved better, but how would they get what they deserved?

"It's not happening," White Owl said to Red Willow, who was sitting and nursing the baby next to Eternal Blossom.

Red Willow understood the cold, hard truth of what her husband was saying. "So, what now?" She cradled the tiny infant tighter to her bosom.

"We can't go back, especially without your brother," White Owl replied. "We need answers, and if the only way to get them is through force, we will use force."

She scoffed at his suggestion. "Have you seen your people lately? They are in no shape to fight. If you go with force, you will all die with force."

"Then what do we do?" he asked, stretching out his arms in frustration. "I will not raise our usdi as a wanderer without a home."

Red Willow stroked her baby boy's face gently. "I will go and get the answers we seek."

White Owl spun around frantically and grasped at his necklace. "You don't want me and a group of warriors to go, but you expect me to let my udalii go alone? An evil spirit possesses you!"

"I won't go alone," Red Willow replied calmly. "I will take the usdi with me."

White Owl stomped his feet several times in anger. "I will not let you put all of my new family in harm's way!"

Red Willow walked over to him, baby in her arms, and placed her hand on his shoulder. "I am not afraid, and you don't have to be either. Where I go, the Great Spirit goes to guide my feet and keep me safe."

Tears welled up in his eyes. "I want to believe that, but I can't. My eyes have seen too much pain and heartache."

She wiped the tears from her husband's face. "I know the pain and heartache you know, and even more. But I believe that the Great Spirit moves me into a deeper strength. And with that strength, I can do what needs to be done, including facing whatever awaits in the Catawba village. I'm not asking you to believe, but I'm asking you to trust."

White Owl nodded in quiet agreement.

There was strange energy floating through the air that morning as Red Willow left to make her way to the Catawba village. The weather pattern had shifted rapidly overnight, from unseasonably warm to oddly cool. Dark clouds were rolling in on the horizon, and there was a palpable instability in the atmosphere.

With her beloved infant in the cradleboard on her back, Red Willow trudged over the same ground between the two camps that her brother and husband had previously traversed. Winds swirled around her, slowing her pace. Determined to push forward, she braved the rough weather, finally stopping about a hundred yards outside the palisade wall. From there she surveyed the scene. There was no soul in sight, as everyone had sought shelter from the oncoming storm.

The cries of the baby on her back reverberated through her ears. Gently, she moved the little one and his cradleboard from her back to her bosom. Her confidence in her mission had not wavered— until now. The crying baby and howling winds had frayed her nerves to the breaking point. Her heart was fluttering like a hummingbird's wings and her face flushed, warm as the embers of her family fire. Without warning, she felt the weight of an unfamiliar hand across her shoulder.

Jumping back with a shudder, she found herself confronting Rolling Cloud, the only man either brave or crazy enough to be outside. He looked her up and down, waiting for the Great Spirit to lead him into engagement. After a few tense moments, he proclaimed the message given to him.

"Your brother will unite us," he uttered in a dreamlike voice, "but only with your help."

Red Willow tensed her eyelids and furrowed her brow. How did this man know who she was? But her confusion lasted only a moment, interrupted by the strange image that she spotted out of the corner of her eye. To the west of the village, a few hundred yards away, a large and dark rope-like structure was ascending from the ground to one of the nearby dark clouds. It was as if the finger of the Great Spirit had forced its way out of the earth and into the sky.

The winds swirling around Red Willow and Rolling Cloud had noticeably diminished in a way that felt ominously unsettling. Red Willow watched the tobacco pipe-shaped tube move along the ground, making its way straight at the village. As the spout moved closer, the winds once again churned around her. She looked on in horror, eyes as wide open as the full moon, as the pulsating cylinder crashed into the corner of the palisade wall. Pickets were ripped from their bases and tossed into the air. Terrified villagers spilled out of their hiding places with a clamor as the funnel tore its way into the village.

Suddenly all Red Willow's self-preservation instincts vanished, and she began walking towards the violently spinning vortex against her conscious will. Other villagers scrambling past cast incredulous glances as they retreated, while she continued to push forward, ignoring her safety and her baby's. As she drew closer to the raging whirlwind, the whirling force gripped her body tightly. Perilously close to the point of no return, she sensed the tug of the maelstrom down to her core, feeling her spirit slowly being torn, piece by piece, away from her body.

At the very moment of her spiritual dissolution, the sky opened in a torrential downpour, disentangling the spinning whirlwind into a series of far less intense breezes. The rain lasted roughly ten minutes before the entire tumultuous weather system made its withdrawal from the village. Red Willow stood amidst the storm's debris in a state of shock. The wailing cries of her terrified infant slowly penetrated her daze, and she did her best to comfort the boy. When she finally regained clarity, a startling revelation came: she had placed her precious newborn son in an unsafe situation, even if that wasn't her intent. Her heart sank like a stone in her chest, and tears welled up in her eyes at the thought of what might have happened to her vulnerable little one.

The crowd was astonished. By all their reckoning, this woman should have died. "Who was she, and by what power did she make this devastating cloud pass away?" they all wondered. Red Willow could sense them fixing their gaze upon her. She tensed her body, uncomfortable with the thought of so much attention. In her mind, what she did was not a demonstration of power but rather something she was foolishly compelled to do by some unseen force.

Running Wolf emerged unscathed from the rear of the village, where he had been kept under guard. The land spout had left the back half of the town untouched, but its proximity was enough to frighten the guards from their post. His heart quickened when he saw his sister standing amid the cluttered debris scattered about in the storm's aftermath. He rushed to her side to check on her.

"Are you alright?" he asked, placing his hand gently on her shoulder.

Still in shock, the best she could give him was a half-hearted nod. The gathered Catawba villagers continued to gawk at the mangled village and the strange woman who had seemingly stalled the destructive finger of the Great Spirit. Running Wolf placed his arm firmly around his sister and returned the crowd's gaze as if to protect her from whatever strange plan was brewing.

The bizarre stare down continued until Rolling Cloud stepped between the two parties. He did not address either side but rather stared off into the distance. "The time has come to unite our two tribes. There can be no more stalling. The Great Spirit's demands were made clear today."

One of the more arrogant and defiant Catawba villagers worked up the nerve to object, "You are not the chief. We don't have to do as you say!"

Rolling Cloud walked slowly and purposely towards the dissenter until his bushy mane cast a shadow over the man's forehead. He began to speak forcefully, his hot breath blowing directly into the man's eyes, "Since you seem to be such a dull spirit, let me say this another way, a way that even the simplest can understand," Rolling Cloud began. "Do you see that large hole in that wall?" he asked the man as he pointed back towards the wrecked village. "That needs to be repaired, along with many dwellings that the storm just destroyed. Do you think it would be easier to build back with only a few hands or with a great multitude?"

He let the question hang in the air.

"A multitude," the man begrudgingly mumbled.

Rolling Cloud intertwined his hands behind his back and began to pace. "Are there any other objections?" he called out.

The only sound heard was the gentle whistling of a leftover breeze. Satisfied, Rolling Cloud ambled over to Red Willow and Running Wolf. "Go to your people and tell them to come to the village. Tonight we will celebrate the union of our two tribes with a burial ceremony for Sitting Deer; out with the old and in with the new."

Sister and brother looked intently at each other. Both still mentally shaken from their recent individual traumas, they garnered enough strength to make their way back to the Pee Dee camp and share the happy news. Rolling Cloud's nonchalant assertion that the tribes could so easily merge was surprising, but it was an offer neither would refuse. The dazed Catawba villagers slowly filed back into their badly damaged settlement to begin picking up the pieces.

Rolling Cloud took charge of preparing Sitting Deer's body for the impromptu funeral. He strolled over to the now-demolished hut of his deceased friend and searched through the rubble. After removing a few layers of debris, he uncovered the rigored corpse. The pale countenance of the face and the foul scent of the body was enough to send shivers down the usually unperturbable priest's spine. He dragged the carcass away from the wreckage and said a silent prayer for his companion.

Ordinarily, the burial process would include painting the body with red dye to give the lifeless remains an appearance of rebirth. Rolling Cloud had no red dye, but he did have access to an abundance of wet red clay from the brief torrential rain. He scooped up a handful of the sludgy mixture and began to cake it onto Sitting Deer's face, scooping, slapping, and rubbing the gooey red earth onto the body, all the way down to the waist. Electricity surged through his soul as he could almost feel his dead friend and chief reanimating out of the soil. "This must be what it feels like for the Great Spirit to create life out of the dirt," he thought. But alas, Rolling Cloud had no true powers of revivification. When he'd finished, Sitting Deer was still a corpse, albeit a much muddier one than when he started.

While the red dirt took care of Sitting Deer's paleness, there was still the odor emanating from the body. With no extract of boiled willow root to use as a purifying body wash, Rolling Cloud walked to the village's wooded area and pulled several stems off a mint plant. He returned and placed the stems into the thick mud across Sitting Deer's chest. Then he folded the chief's arms across the mint stems to hold them in place. For the finishing touch, he retrieved a large deerskin blanket and wrapped the corpse tightly, leaving only the face exposed. Rolling Cloud was proud of his work.

As dusk approached, the entire Pee Dee tribe marched raggedly up to the wrecked Catawba village. It was now a meeting of two broken tribes, but perhaps the two halves would be able to make one whole. Rolling Cloud went out to welcome the strangers with a small contingent of Catawba villagers. Most of the Catawba people remained behind, sorting through their belongings. The Pee Dee people were shocked to see the village in such disarray and wondered what kind of situation they were entering. At the behest of Rolling Cloud, the assemblage of Pee Dee villagers streamed into the heart of the town, passing the busy Catawba townspeople as they went. The two factions exchanged curious glances, both unsure of the coming union.

Night descended, and Rolling Cloud gathered both groups in the village courtyard. Sitting Deer's body was laid out on a raised platform surrounded by four long upright torches with flames leaping up and gently licking the night sky. The tribes gathered around the platform in two crescent moon-shaped configurations, the Pee Dee members on one side and the Catawba on the other. An eerie silence pervaded the large assembly, only interrupted by the occasional crackle and pop from the flaming torches. One side was silenced by their mournful respectfulness, the other by their uncertain hesitancy.

Rolling Cloud strode to the tribal council lodge overlooking the burial platform to address the crowd. "We are gathered here together tonight to say both donadagohvi and osiyo. To our beloved leader, Sitting Deer, we say donadagohvi, wishing him a successful journey into the next world. The Great Spirit shows us in creation that out of death springs new life. We have to look no further than the sacred corn, where one dying plant gives off enough seed to create many new plants in its place. So, as we say donadagohvi to Sitting Deer, we say osiyo to our new Pee Dee brothers and sisters. They have traveled many steps to get to this place, searching for a fresh start and some help. We thought at first that we might be the ones to help them, but thanks to the judgment of the Great Spirit, we might be the ones in need of their help. Either way, this tribal union is our collective destiny. It was foretold to me in a vision by the Great Spirit, and I believe it to be the start of something great and powerful. If you have fears and doubts, now is the time to cast them out. Lay them upon our great chief and let him carry them away with him to the Great Beyond."

Rolling Cloud signaled down to a drummer, who began to pound a steady beat behind the Catawba townspeople. A second percussionist positioned himself behind the Pee Dee people and echoed the first drumbeat, creating a reverberating pulse across the divided tribes. The stereophonic vibrations resounded deep in the people's souls, stirring collective emotional turbulence minutes away from frothing to the surface.

Running Wolf had situated himself on the frontline of the Pee Dee faction, directly across from the body of his deceased mentor. The push of the drumbeat led him unconsciously forward to the edge of the funeral bier. He reached out and placed his hand on Sitting Deer's cold, lifeless shoulder. A feeling of guilt washed over him, but he remembered the words Sitting Deer had spoken to him many moons ago: "Guilt is a burden that you should not have to bear. This death is the will of the Great Spirit," he said to himself.

Running Wolf's gesture was an inspiration to some of the Catawba people, who thought he was responding to Rolling Cloud's call to release fears and doubts, and several of them stepped forward to mimic the act. The sight of the first few townspeople marching up to the burial platform opened the floodgates to the remaining Catawba, and soon the entire tribe was crowded together next to their deceased chief. Only a few were able to lay their hands on the body, but the rest linked themselves together hand-to-shoulder in a great chain of being. The Pee Dee people followed their counterparts' lead and made their way forward. Both groups now stood huddled around Sitting Deer's bier as the drumbeats echoed through the night sky.

Rolling Cloud let the moment of unification linger, basking in its glow. Then, at the properly felt time, he gave his drummers the signal to stop pounding. The abrupt halt startled the people, who had slipped into an almost-hypnotic state. Rolling Cloud strode down from the tribal council lodge towards the burial platform, and the crowd parted, allowing him access to the body. He removed a bag of cedar ashes from his pants and smudged two fingers' worth across each of the chief's eyelids, signifying the forever sleep upon Sitting Deer. When he had finished, he addressed the crowd.

"There is only one thing left to do," Rolling Cloud bellowed. "We must take Sitting Deer to his final resting place. I need two asgayas from this side," he said, motioning towards the Pee Dee, "and two asgayas from this side," he said, turning to the Catawba. "Together, you will take the chief to his burial platform in the forest, binding our tribes as we move from past to future."

Running Wolf and White Owl stepped forward from the Pee Dee group, and they were soon joined by two of the remaining high-ranking officials from the Catawba. Rolling Cloud directed each of the men to grab a small handle sticking out from each of the platform's four sides. The men grabbed the handles and lifted them to rest on their shoulders. Together they processed slowly out of the village, led by Rolling Cloud and his torch. Once the funeral procession was out of sight, the groups found themselves awkwardly standing across from each other. The two sides looked at the departing parade gradually receding into the darkness. Many Catawba people were exhausted from the strenuous day and retreated to what was left of their huts.

The Catawba that remained had one thing on their mind, "Who was the agehya that confronted the storm?" The murmuring and staring at Red Willow grew more intense until one of the townspeople finally got up the nerve to approach her. "How did you do it?" the villager asked.

Red Willow looked past the townsman into the distance. "I . . . I don't know what you are talking about," she said.

"You stopped the storm," the man pointed his finger at her. "Where did you get that power?"

She shook her head vigorously. "I did not stop the storm," she protested.

"My eyes did not deceive me," the man returned. "I saw a violent storm. I saw you approach the violent storm, and I saw the violent storm disappear. You can say what you want, but I know the truth. You are an agehya of extraordinary strength, and many of us believe you will do great things for the new tribe. We want you to know that you have earned our loyalty and support today."

The man bowed his head to Red Willow and then turned to retreat to his dwelling with the rest of his kin. Her brain buzzed as she tried to process the day's events and how they had shaped these peoples' perceptions of her. Did they think she was some sort of higher spirit? If only they were right, if only she did have some kind of supernatural power, she would have made sure that her life had turned out differently. A sharp wail from her starving infant quickly jolted her back to reality. She grabbed the boy from his cradleboard and nuzzled him against her engorged breast. As she sat there nursing her tender baby boy, she felt different from the previous times she had fed him. Doubts crept into her mind about her fitness to be a mother to this innocent young soul, doubts that were nearly impossible to shake.

The burial cadre reached its destination, the final resting place of Sitting Deer. There stood a beautiful oak tree that was beginning to bud, with hundreds of tiny pink sprouts sparkling as they reflected the light of Rolling Cloud's torch. The tree had many sturdy branches that forked out in different directions. It was the perfect spot to give Sitting Deer's body over to nature. The branches were high enough to keep it out of reach of wild animals, and the leaves would soon provide a shady cover. Running Wolf and White Owl climbed into the tree to receive the burial platform, while the two Catawba men lifted it high above their heads. After Running Wolf and White Owl secured the platform between the forks of the branches, they made their way back down. Running Wolf gazed up at the remains wedged into the tree branches and was instantly reminded of his mother's lifeless body looking much the same way. He felt a large knot tighten his stomach, and he doubled over, trying to breathe through the pain.

White Owl rushed over to check on Running Wolf. "Are you alright?"

"I'm fine," Running Wolf exclaimed as he lifted his head from between his knees and tried to compose himself.

Rolling Cloud looked on at the young man's actions, confident he would make a fine leader. He understood that a good leader's strengths could often be perceived as weaknesses. The group lingered for another long moment to fully honor the departed chieftain before heading back to what was left of the village.

Chapter Twenty-Five
A New Chief

A week had passed since the merger of the two tribes. Things were progressing slowly, as expected, after the devastating sequence of events leading up to the union. To try to smooth the transition, Rolling Cloud had paired up individual Pee Dee family units with individual Catawba family units, creating a subset of mixed groups within the larger conglomeration. These clusters of families were learning each other's ways and customs during their rebuilding.

Informal conversations about what the new tribe's leadership structure might look like were taking place among the higher-ranking members of the old Catawba tribe. Some wanted to consolidate all the power within their faction, believing the disheveled Pee Dee offered nothing of value. Others were more charitable in assessing the Pee Dee and were willing to welcome their entry into positions of authority.

This latter set was particularly enamored with one member of the Pee Dee group, whom they wanted to see placed in the highest-ranking position.

The former Catawba clan leaders approached Rolling Cloud one evening at dusk as he returned from his woodland wandering. Suspecting there was more to their presence than a simple welcome home, Rolling Cloud strolled up cautiously. He stopped directly in front of the group and rested his hands on his walking stick. "Osiyo, my unaliis," Rolling Cloud said, with clear sarcasm. "Wa do for welcoming me back from my roaming."

One of the men stepped up and addressed the old priest. "We are here to seek your spiritual guidance, Holy One."

Rolling Cloud let out a small grunt and shook his head. "And here I thought you fine young asgayas were simply here to welcome me home." The men exchanged perplexed looks and mumbled to themselves. "Anyway, what can I do for you?" Rolling Cloud chuckled.

The clan leader cleared his throat. "Our tribe has a divided mind. Some of us want to shut the Pee Dee people out of power completely, while others want to include them in a new tribal council and even go so far as to think that one of them should be named chief. We cannot come to harmony in this situation, and we seek your guidance from the spiritual realm."

Rolling Cloud stared off into the distance, pretending he was deep in meditation, but he already knew what his advice would be, thanks to his initial spiritual vision of Running Wolf becoming the leader of a new nation. He carefully crafted a response to the clan leaders, not wanting it to appear that he was manipulating them into the decision the Great Spirit had already made.

"I have a question for those who would like to keep the Pee Dee out of power," Rolling Cloud began. "Are you prepared for the violence that will unfold if you do so?"

Confused looks crossed the men's faces. Rolling Cloud continued, "The Pee Dee people are like a wild dog with a broken leg. If you approach them to trap them, they will lash out with a wild fury, further injuring themselves and you. But, if you approach them cautiously with an outstretched arm of help, you can tame them to create a lifelong companion."

The Catawba man at the front let out an intense "Ohhhh." His fellow leaders nodded, almost in unison. "I believe we understand what you are saying, wise one," one said, slowly stroking his chin. "It is not in our interests to exclude the Pee Dee from the new council."

"You all are wiser than your appearances would suggest," Rolling Cloud deadpanned. "And what else has been suggested to you by your clans?" he asked, eager to hear that they wanted Running Wolf to be named chief and fulfill the prophecy.

"Many of our numbers want to see the storm whisperer rise to lead us," one of the clan leaders answered.

Rolling Cloud froze, his mouth agape. He had been given the vision of Running Wolf as the leader by the Great Spirit, and now these people want to interfere. Was this all a big deception by the One he so trusted?

The men looked on as Rolling Cloud stood rigidly silent. "Are you alright, Holy One?" one piped up.

He maintained his expressionless countenance, unresponsive to the man's query, offering no words as he drifted back into the shadowy forest.

Red Willow was still reeling from her intense encounter with the storm. Her post-traumatic stress response had disrupted some of the earlier bonds she had developed with her son. One afternoon, as she was sitting with Eternal Blossom and struggling to nurse her baby boy, she could no longer contain her emotions. "I feel like I am drowning," she exclaimed. "The Great Spirit gave me this precious usdi, and I fail to take care of him the way he deserves. He's not getting enough food, and I can't even keep him out of harm's way! I am a disgraceful etsi."

Eternal Blossom's heart ached for her niece. She knew the emotional and physical difficulties of caring for and raising an infant. "You are traveling a well-worn path. Many, if not all, etsis struggle when they first receive their tiny blessings."

Red Willow shook her head disapprovingly. "You are wrong, agitlogi. No one has walked the path I am on. My spirit is exhausted. My soul screams at me to run away, but how can I do that when I am responsible for this precious young life?"

Eternal Blossom now saw Red Willow's feelings as more than ordinary post-newborn sadness. Something deeper was happening within her niece's spirit, something she needed to acknowledge. "Your soul is right," Eternal Blossom intoned. "You need to go and be with yourself until your spirit feels complete again. When was the last time you were able to do this?"

Red Willow's jaw opened wide, stunned at the suggestion she leave her baby. "I can't do that. I can't just abandon my atsutsa. That's what makes these feelings so difficult to handle. I want to run, but I can't."

Eternal Blossom leaned in close. "Leave the usdi here with me and go. I can care for him. I still nurse my youngest and my milk will be as sustaining as yours would be."

"Are you serious?"

"Everything I am telling you is genuine," Eternal Blossom answered. "I trust you to make the best decision for yourself, which will be the best for the little one in the long run. And if anyone can survive on their own, it is you. I know you are the strongest agehya, and your doda taught you well."

Red Willow leaned back. She looked down at her little one, fussing and kicking in her arms after a less than satisfying meal. Her rational brain wondered if a break might be good for both of them, but her instinctual mother brain fought these thoughts at every turn. She could not make a decision.

"Take a few nights to ponder what I am offering you," Eternal Blossom said, placing her hand on Red Willow's shoulder. "When you are ready, bring the usdi to me and begin your journey."

Red Willow nodded and wiped away her trickling tears. She put the baby in the cradleboard, strapped him onto her back, and returned to her makeshift dwelling. White Owl was there, busily constructing a new shelter for his family with the help of his adopted Catawba brethren. He noticed her approaching with his newborn son and stopped his work to greet them.

"Osiyo udalii," White Owl said before quickly turning his attention to his beloved offspring. He reached his finger out, and the baby quickly grasped it and held it tight. White Owl smiled, greatly amused.

Red Willow interrupted the playful father-son bonding moment. "I need to talk to you."

White Owl snapped quickly to attention, sensing something wasn't right. "What is it?"

"Just come with me," she said, leading him to a quiet spot away from the rest of the tribe.

White Owl's pulse raced with anxiety. "So, what is it you think we need to talk about?" he asked.

Red Willow bristled. "I'm afraid I can't do this right now."

"You're afraid you can't do what?"

"Any of it," Red Willow said, her voice shaking. "I'm afraid I can't be a good etsi. I'm afraid I can't meet these new people's expectations of me. I'm afraid I can't do everything I am required to do. It is all so overwhelming."

White Owl rested his hand reassuringly on her shoulders. "You are a capable agehya. If you were not, I would not have married you. I understand you have doubts, but they are nothing we can't overcome together."

"It's more than that, though," Red Willow replied. "During Soaring Eagle's destructive reign, I thought it would be easy to leave my home, the place of my ancestors. But the birth of our atsutsa has conjured images in my spirit of everything we have left behind. My spirit cries for me to leave, to find a place to deal with the burdens that have been placed on it."

White Owl began to pace. "Leave?" he cried out, his voice now high-pitched. "How could I ever raise an usdi on my own? I can't believe what I am hearing!"

His increasing agitation surprisingly calmed Red Willow, as if the Great Spirit was trying to balance out their emotions. "I would never burden you with caring for the usdi by yourself," Red Willow said, her voice even, almost soothing. "If I decide I need to go, my agitlogi has promised she will care for the little one."

White Owl stopped his pacing and looked his wife directly in the eyes. "And what about me? I thought you loved me."

She placed her hand gently on his cheek. "I do love you. But I could love you better if I freed my spirit of the weights dragging it down."

White Owl exhaled deeply. "I cannot make you stay here if your spirit tells you to go. I will watch over our atsutsa while you are gone, and I will prepare our new home for when you return."

Red Willow leaned in and hugged White Owl tightly. He reciprocated, passionately nuzzling in a nearly timeless exchange. The loving embrace watered the garden of their souls deeply, enough to withstand the upcoming drought.

A few days passed before the Catawba tribal council officially made their intentions clear. The council would hold a ceremony to install Red Willow as the new chief at the next full moon, less than a week away. They informed Rolling Cloud of their decision and asked him to share the news with Red Willow. Still confused by the contradiction between the unfolding events and the dream the Great Spirit had given him, Rolling Cloud reluctantly agreed to meet with her.

Red Willow and Running Wolf were sitting together one morning, sharing a corn cake for breakfast when Rolling Cloud made his appearance. Strolling up to the pair, he rested his arms on his walking stick. "Osda sunalei, Holy One," Running Wolf greeted him. "What brings you here?"

Rolling Cloud gazed down fondly at the young man he believed should be the tribe's leader, then turned his eyes to Red Willow. "I am here to inform your agilvgi that she has been chosen to lead our new tribe . . . that is, if she accepts."

Red Willow had sensed this moment might be coming, but the news caught Running Wolf entirely off guard. He sat in stunned silence awaiting his sister's response. While she did not wish to lead, she also did not wish to decline and seem weak. She had another plan in mind.

Leaning forward, Red Willow informed Rolling Cloud she would accept, much to his chagrin. He nodded. "I will inform the council of your decision," he sighed before turning and walking away.

Running Wolf's blood raced through his body, heating him like fire as his cheeks burned red. "Congratulations," he stammered to his sister before he stormed away from camp.

Ordinarily, his reaction would have caused Red Willow to chase him down and call him out, but she was too exhausted to care. Besides, he would not be jealous if he knew what she had planned. She decided to chastise him differently by not sharing her scheme with him and letting him wallow for a while in his envy. She sat cuddling her cherished baby, immersing herself in his soulful radiance.

Late in the evening, the night before her installation ceremony, Red Willow paid a visit to Eternal Blossom. The time had come for her to say a temporary goodbye to the most important being in her life. It was an agonizing walk as her spirit filled with pain. She reached the doorway of Eternal Blossom's hut and called out to her aunt to join her. Eternal Blossom went out to greet her niece.

"I heard the news," Eternal Blossom said, "and I think I know why you are here."

Tears of sadness welled up in Red Willow's eyes. "I'm not going to do it," she said, her voice breaking. "They think I will be their leader, but I am not. They want to take from me, but they don't know I have nothing to give. It is time for me to take care of myself, so I will be able to take care of my atsutsa when the time is right."

"I am so proud of you," Eternal Blossom said, embracing her niece. "It is not easy to do what is best for you under the burden of being responsible for so many other things. Go and heal your spirit. The usdi will be as healthy as he was the day you left when you come back. You do not need to worry."

Red Willow wiped her tears and pulled the little one from his cradleboard. She stared into his wandering eyes as he drooled and cooed. Her mind told her it was time to hand him over, but her body was uncooperative. Eventually Eternal Blossom reached out and pried the baby from her hands, urging Red Willow to leave before the separation anxiety became unbearable. Red Willow walked slowly and painfully backward, her eyes never leaving the baby until Eternal Blossom and the infant disappeared into the hut, leaving her alone in the dark. As she trudged joylessly back to her dwelling, suddenly this all felt so selfish. What if she would be a good leader after all? What if, for some reason, she were never to lay eyes on her baby boy again? The conflict twisted her spirit into knots.

She returned to find White Owl waiting. "How did it go?" he asked.

"It is done," Red Willow replied, "but now I don't know if I want it to be. My spirit is coiled like a snake, and I cannot straighten it."

White Owl looked at his wife with empathy. "This is why you are making this choice," he said as he took her by the hand, "to give yourself some relief from the burdens you are bearing. The only thing staying here now will do is drown your spirit even further. Take this time to go and cleanse your soul."

She collapsed into his arms, and he caught her and held her tightly. Gently lifting her off her feet, he carried her to the pile of straw that they now called their bed. He placed her down tenderly and proceeded to lie down next to her. They gazed out of their temporary home at the thousands of tiny dots lighting up the next sky, and as White Owl admired his beautiful wife, they fell fast asleep.

Red Willow awoke before dawn to the sound of crickets piercing the air with their high-pitched chirping. The cacophonous racket ordinarily would have annoyed her, but this morning she had no emotional response. She had shut herself off, knowing she needed to put her head down and just make it through the day. Her spiritual journey would provide time to sort out her complicated feelings.

Red Willow got up and began to collect what she would need in her time away: her boiling stones, water pouch, and a small chunk of pemmican her adoptive Catawba family had graciously given her. Lastly, she retrieved her rabbit stick, staring down at it and remembering her father. She was finding it impossible to squelch her emotions. She pulled the stick close into her heart for a brief moment before placing it gently down on the pile of her things.

The sun began its ascent over the horizon, waking White Owl. He slowly stood and greeted Red Willow. "Osda sunalei," he said, wrapping his skinny arms around her shoulders from behind.

His loving embrace was not helping her contain her emotions, but she tried her best to keep a level head. "I will need to leave soon to prepare for tonight's ceremony. I need something from you."

"Anything you ask for, udalii," White Owl replied.

"I have put together the things I will need for my journey," she pointed to her piled-up items. "Bring them to the ceremony tonight and have them ready for me when I leave the village courtyard."

It was a stark reminder to White Owl that he would soon be without his wife for an indefinite time. He looked at the traveling kit and sighed deeply. "I will do that for you."

"I know you want something from my body as a reminder of me while we are apart," Red Willow said, sensing his forlornness, "but my spirit and body are not ready for that right now. I promise you I will come back from my journey with a renewed passion for the desires of the flesh."

He nodded. She stroked his cheek tenderly as they peered lovingly into each other's eyes. They shared a few handfuls of hickory nuts before Red Willow left to prepare for the ceremony.

Nightfall descended on the Catawba-Pee Dee village, and with it came the attendant ascension of the brightly gleaming full moon. The newly united tribe members gathered in the courtyard facing the elevated tribal council lodge. A large bonfire crackled and popped behind the assembled throng, breaking the awkward and solemn silence as they awaited the rite of installation. Running Wolf was at the front, looking up at the lodge much as he had looked up at the Pee Dee temple on that fateful night so many moons ago. His jealousy still lingered, but he knew his mother would have disapproved if he had let that keep him away from his sister's big ceremony.

Within minutes, a group of dancers emerging from the council lodge broke the silence. They were dressed in beautifully dyed deerskin dresses, splashed with purple, red, and green hues, and they wore circular necklaces adorned with white, red, and black plumage. Rattling their bean-filled gourd shakers to provide an accompanying rhythm for their dance, they stomped and shook their way down from the lodge platform and encircled the gathered crowd.

A pair of drummers appeared from the recesses of the lodge interior. They marched out, beating a deep melodic tempo, and moved to opposite ends of the balcony, extending outward from the shelter. The dancers howled ecstatically, buoyed by the sweeping melodies. The crowd followed their lead and the combined voices echoed deep into the well-lit night, raising the huddled group into a mass frenzy.

Without warning, the drummers and dancers went quiet. The whooping crowd continued their chants, falling off little by little, until Rolling Cloud stepped onto the porch and waited patiently for the multitude to completely cease their clamoring.

"A new age begins tonight," he said in a less than enthusiastic tone, his pride still stinging from the thought that his spiritual vision was mistaken. "Our two tribes will officially become one. What has come before separately will now go forward collectively. The people's will has chosen a leader for our combined nation, and we now offer her up to be blessed by the Great Spirit."

Red Willow strode out in a long and flowing hickory bark cloth robe dyed pure white with limestone to signify the purity of heart of the wearer. She had painted her face with alternating red and white stripes, red symbolizing war and white representing peace. The two colors were present in equal proportions to signify the need for balance—always prepared for war, yet always hopeful for peace.

A dull murmur arose at the sight of their supposed soon-to-be leader. The former Pee Dee members were proud to see one of their own ascending to such a position of prestige. For them, it marked the end of their steep downward spiral and the beginning of a new upward trajectory.

Red Willow struggled to contain her anxiety. The slight smiles on the faces of her fellow tribemates convinced her they were all counting on her to make them proud, and the pressure gnawed away at her soul, like a cluster of beavers making their way around the base of a tree. She began to second guess her plans for leaving. "How could she let all these good people down after all they have had to endure?" she thought.

Rolling Cloud initiated the ceremony by snatching up a jug of water and hoisting it above his head. "A leader must be pure in spirit. The outpouring of the sacred water will cleanse away all the remaining impurities in the chosen one."

Rolling Cloud turned towards Red Willow and tilted the jug, raining its contents down on her. She shivered as the cold water chilled her to the bone. Scanning the crowd, she saw White Owl standing on the edge, holding the pouch that contained her supplies, a distant and sad look on his face. She felt her guilt ratcheting up further, twisting her stomach into knots as tight as her neatly braided hair.

Rolling Cloud continued the ceremony by retrieving a large eagle feather and raising it high into the sky. "A leader must have a clear mind. The waving of the feather will sweep away any confused thoughts in the chosen one."

Red Willow stood awkwardly as Rolling Cloud waved the feather across her forehead with a flourish, waiting for the supposed effect. When nothing changed within her mind, she closed her eyes and leaned her head back. Opening her eyes, she looked down at Running Wolf, his envy plainly visible. "This atsutsa is much too immature to lead this tribe," she thought to herself, her initial plan of turning over leadership and taking time for herself quickly fading.

The final phase of the ceremony involved crowning the newly installed chief with the prior chief's headdress. Rolling Cloud sauntered over to the lodge wall, where Sitting Deer's headdress hung from a peg.

Inspecting it thoroughly, he lingered, loath to place it on Red Willow's head and confirm that his dreams had been mistaken. Eventually he walked over and stood behind Red Willow, headdress in hand.

"Unaliis, I present to you your new chief," Rolling Cloud said, gracefully lowering the headpiece.

The headdress was at least two sizes too big, forcing Red Willow to lift it awkwardly away from her face. Her heart pounded in her chest as she gazed out over the multitude. With drummers once again thumping and dancers gyrating, an uproar echoed as the crowd celebrated their new leader. It was decision time for Red Willow, and she was now on the fence about what path she would take.

Among the crowd she spotted her aunt holding her baby, standing away from the raucous gathering. Turning to get a better look, she was stunned. It was not her aunt but her *mother*! "My spirit is playing tricks on me," she thought as she closed her eyes tightly, then opened them, expecting to see her aunt. But the vision of Gray Dove holding her baby persisted. As her mother looked down at the boy with a glowing smile, for the first time in a long time, the little one seemed utterly serene and content.

The radiant Gray Dove looked up at her daughter. "Take time for yourself and do your healing work," she seemed to say, without a single movement from her lips. "Everything here will be just fine." Misty-eyed, Red Willow was now certain of her path.

The crowd grew silent, waiting for an address from their new chief. Red Willow's eyes darted as she struggled to find the right words. Finally, she sputtered, "Udaliis, I promise you that you will have a leader you can be proud of," her voice trembling. "You will have a leader on whom you can count. You will have a leader who will bring you glory as you have never seen before. And that leader is . . . my udo, Running Wolf," she exclaimed, lowering her right arm in Running Wolf's direction.

The confused villagers stood in stunned silence as the crackling and popping of the bonfire took center stage once again. After the initial shock wore off, they quickly turned their collective attention to the boy in the front row. Sensing all eyes turning to him, Running Wolf's face turned beet red.

"What are you doing?!" Running Wolf roared up to his sister through clenched teeth.

Red Willow motioned for him to join her on the lodge platform. A raft of murmurs emanated from the crowd with a few shouts of derision sprinkled in. Running Wolf tried to avoid going up, but he was pushed from behind, and he begrudgingly trudged up the steps to the elevated platform.

Rolling Cloud looked on as the boy ascended, grinning like a satiated wildcat. His vision was true; the Great Spirit was not playing tricks on him! When Running Wolf reached the balcony, Rolling Cloud greeted him with a joyfully long hug. Baffled, Running Wolf received the embrace limply, shooting a confused look in the direction of his sister. Rolling Cloud finally released him, and Running Wolf turned to stand next to his sister, now facing the crowd.

"Unaliis," Red Willow bellowed, feeling more confident with her brother standing beside her, "my first act as chief is to relinquish my leadership role and bestow it on Running Wolf."

She beckoned Rolling Cloud to perform the rituals on Running Wolf, and he gladly obliged, bringing over his feather and water jug. By this time, an immense upheaval was storming through the crowd, and several former Catawba villagers who had supported Red Willow were fuming at this unforeseen disruption and yearning to make their fury known.

One of the agitators made his way to the front and shouted at Rolling Cloud. "The agehya cannot do this on her own! This needs to be approved by the council!"

Rolling Cloud stared down at the rabble-rouser and guffawed. "Call your council. Do whatever your spirit leads you to do. I will do the will of the Great Spirit!"

Lifting the water jug, Rolling Cloud anointed Running Wolf in the rite of purification. As he turned to pick up his feather, the troublemaking rebel climbed the steps and tackled the old priest from behind. The pair briefly struggled, with the agitator finally gaining the upper hand and pinning Rolling Cloud. He scowled down at Rolling Cloud with a menacing look, bits of spit spilling out with each angry breath. It appeared Rolling Cloud would be losing the fight, until he reared his puffy-haired head back and thrust it violently forward at the face of his attacker. The man wailed in agony, a large gash on the bridge of his nose spilling blood. As the attacker rolled away from the aged cleric, Rolling Cloud gingerly raised himself to his feet and exclaimed, "I said I will do the will of the Great Spirit," before completing the mind-clearing ritual on Running Wolf.

There was only one thing left to do to complete the ceremony. Red Willow clumsily lifted the oversized headdress from her skull and gingerly laid it on Running Wolf's crown. The siblings shared a moment of pregnant silence as they gazed into each other's eyes. A flood of shared memories entered their silent dialogue in a deep spiritual mind-meld. The combined joys and sadnesses, tragedies and triumphs pulsed through their collective soul and swelled their hearts with abundant emotions.

Red Willow lifted her hand and placed it onto her brother's shoulder. She pulled him close and whispered, "Never forget that I will always be your big agilvgi. Make Doda proud."

Running Wolf chuckled at his sister's verbal jab and wiped a tear from his eyes. Then Red Willow descended from the platform and made her way through the crowd. The people bombarded her with jeers and taunts, but they did not faze her, as her mind was entirely focused on her spiritual healing journey. She strutted directly towards White Owl, waiting for her with her supply kit.

White Owl reached out to offer Red Willow the pouch with a gloomy look on his face. "You can carry it," Red Willow said as she continued striding past him.

"What are you saying?" White Owl called out to her as she continued out of the village.

Red Willow turned to her husband and waved her hand. "Let's go! We are wasting time."

White Owl's spirits quickly lifted, and he rushed to catch up with his wife. The pair disappeared together into the dense and dark forest. The brightly glowing moon was now high in the nighttime sky, casting its radiant beams down onto the treetop canopy. Only a tiny handful of the shimmering rays pierced the canopy to reach ground level. It was the perfect atmosphere for dozing, and that is all that Red Willow had on her mind once they were far enough into the forest. She exhaustedly collapsed onto the forest floor, and White Owl quickly followed.

The pair lay on their backs next to each other and Red Willow sighed a sigh so deep it felt as if she was going to inhale the moon out of the sky and into her lungs. Her eyelids were as heavy as the copper falcon and her body as limp as a dead fish, but her restless spirit would not allow her to get the sleep she desperately needed. "Did we do the right thing?" she asked as she turned to face White Owl.

"Right or wrong … here we are," he replied, shrugging his shoulders.

This was not the reaction she needed or expected. She had hoped to be reassured by her normally confident husband that they were on the right path, both literally and figuratively. But it did not take her long to realize that her husband was a changed man—and how could he not be after all they had been through? She gazed at White Owl with a profound sense of empathy born out of the knowledge of their shared tribulations.

"At least we are here together," Red Willow said as she reached out to caress White Owl's hand.

A look of contentment spread across his face as he realized the value of being truly loved. "You are my strength and shelter," he said with an easy nod, "and I want you to know that I am yours as well."

Red Willow smiled a soft smile. They faced each other, on the ground, alternating deep breaths until they both passed into a deep sleep. Red Willow slept the sleep of a hibernating bear, only briefly awakened by the distant rustling of an animal in the leaves. When she realized there was no danger, she rolled over and closed her eyes, but this sleep was not peaceful as the dream-maker began projecting his images into her drowsy spirit.

It began with the rustling of leaves again, but this time the noise was confined to Red Willow's isolated consciousness. Her father, Hunting Bear, strode into view. He gently pressed his index finger against his lips to ensure her silence and beckoned her to follow him toward a dense stand of chokeberry bushes. The bushes were aglow with sparkling white flowers shimmering like a full moon and berries as red as the blood that poured from the animal carcasses that were essential to her survival.

As Hunting Bear pushed aside a few of the branches to create an opening, Red Willow moved in to take a look. There sat her mother, Gray Dove, watching a child at play. Red Willow's newfound motherly instincts could sense that her own mother was at peace—a peace she herself could not ever recall her having. A rush of warmth radiated through her body. "It is good to be in this place," she thought to herself. Then Hunting Bear placed his arm gently on his daughter's shoulder, prompting her to turn and face him. He pulled her in close and swaddled her tightly in a long embrace before making his way through the bushes to be with his wife and son. As Red Willow watched, she found herself suspended between two worlds: that of her past and that of her future. A part of her longed to stay in this past, hoping to experience the familial happiness she'd been robbed of so many times, but the greater part of her knew this was not meant to be. Whatever notions she entertained, the Great Spirit had plans of His own for her—plans that would close this chapter of her life story and open another.

Glossary of Cherokee Words

agehya (woman)

agidutsi (uncle)

agilvgi (sister)

agitlogi (aunt)

asgaya (man)

atsutsa (boy)

ayoli (infant)

chunkey (native American game played by rolling stones and tossing spears)

doda (dad)

donadagohvi (goodbye)

eduda (old man)

etsi (mom)

oginalii (my friend)

osda sunalei (good morning)

osda usvi (good evening)

osiyo (hello)

sidanela (family)

taludza (tribal game of chance)

udalii (wife)

udo (brother)

utana (adult)

uwetsi (son)

uyehi (husband)

uyo ayeldvi (I'm sorry)

usdi (little one)

wysoccan (Jimson Weed)

wa do (thank you)

www.ingramcontent.com/pod-product-compliance
Lightning Source LLC
Chambersburg PA
CBHW072032190726

48293CB00012B/1873